Ladies In Waiting

Ladies In Waiting

Second Edition – October, 2015
Copyright © 2015, Linda Rettstatt

3rd Act Books

ISBN-13: 978-1518771552
ISBN-10: 1518771556

Editing – Amie Denman

Cover Art by Calliope-Designs.com

Warning: All rights reserved. The unauthorized reproduction or distribution of this copyrighted work, in whole or part, in any form by any electronic, mechanical, or other means, is illegal and forbidden without the written permission of the author/publisher.

This is a work of fiction. Characters, settings, names, and occurrences are a product of the author's imagination and bear no resemblance to any actual person, living or dead, places or settings, and/or occurrences. Any incidences of resemblance are purely coincidental.

DEDICATION

To the women who have gone before me in this life journey and shared their wisdom and their fears. To the women in the midst of change, you *Ladies In Waiting*, for whom the path may still be shrouded in doubt, but who step ahead with courage and grace. This is our story.

Chapter One

You've Arrived

Liv slowed as she approached the slate blue Victorian topped by a widow's walk. Two cars, a newer model Toyota and an older, faded tan Volvo, sat parked to one side. She peered up at the carved Celtic knot above the entry way and the sign that read *Síocháin*.

"Shee-ock-awn," she pronounced. It translated to peace. She could only hope.

She took in a deep breath as fearful questions tumbled over one another in her brain. What if the other women recognized her? What if she had come all this way to delve into her own psyche and found no one home? What if the Lexapro stopped working and she had a meltdown and couldn't get out of bed? Would they call local EMTs and have her committed? Would she be locked away just like…? Her palms dampened. Her heart quickened, and her stomach did a somersault. She felt as if her joints were held together by chewing gum.

A woman stood on the porch and waved. Liv parked her Lexus, the only thing of value she had left from her former life, and turned off the ignition. She gathered up her purse and the pillow she carried when traveling.

"Bree isn't here yet. We're waiting here on the porch in the shade."

The woman approached wearing a long pale green gauzy skirt and retro peasant style blouse that billowed at the shoulders. Her smile spread into her clear blue eyes. She had a sturdy figure and wore her long dark hair loose around her shoulders. Liv had always thought the style too young for a woman near her own age, but it worked for this woman. She reminded Liv of a gypsy.

"I'm Markova, but my friends call me Markie. Can I give you a hand with anything?"

"I'm Liv Zach…McKenna. McKenna," she repeated for emphasis. "I just have one bag. Thanks." Liv tucked the pillow under her arm and popped open the trunk to remove her suitcase. "Was I confused? I thought we were supposed to be here at four."

"We are. Bree must have gotten held up somewhere." Markie waited for Liv, then fell into step beside her. "This is a wonderful spot for a retreat. Don't you love the smell of the ocean?"

"Mmm. Yes." Truthfully, she could smell the ocean at home on Long Island. She had told herself the reason for this retreat was to have time to regroup and this was the most affordable way to do it. But if she were to be completely honest, she had just run away from home to hide for eight days.

Markie touched her arm. "Did you have a long drive?"

"About six hours." And Liv felt the last four in her muscles. It wasn't the drive that made her tense. It was life these days. Her body was in fight-or-flight mode most of the time. Probably, she assumed, even in sleep, if her restless nights and groggy mornings were any evidence. Even Markie's light touch caused her to startle.

"You must be tired." Markie held back to let Liv ascend the steps ahead of her. Another woman, rocking in a wicker chair, fanned herself with a magazine. "This is Andi Ryan," Markie said.

Andi offered a hand, which Liv accepted. "Liv

McKenna."

"Hi. Have we met before?" Andi asked, studying Liv's face.

Liv pulled her hand away. "I don't think so." She smoothed her recently darkened and shortened hair.

Andi shrugged. "You look familiar."

"I get that a lot." Liv heard the tremor in her voice and cleared her throat.

Unlike Markie, Andi was trim and petite, with short dark brown hair and hazel eyes. She wore form-fitting jeans and a snug T-shirt bearing an embroidered butterfly across the front. The outfit seemed a bit young for a woman over fifty. Liv ran a palm down her wrinkled khakis and plain white cotton blouse, feeling drab. Drab could be good, though. People didn't notice drab. It was like walking around in beige all of the time, able to become a part of the background, blend into the fabric. Disappear.

Markie sat in one of the high-backed wooden rockers and Liv took the other. "So Andi and I were just getting acquainted. Andi teaches school in Toms River, and I'm an artist. I live in Doylestown, Pennsylvania. What about you?"

"I work in a medical practice on Long Island."

"Doctor or nurse?" Markie asked.

"Neither, I'm afraid. I'm a receptionist. It must be wonderful to be an artist." In recent months, Liv had honed her skill of seamlessly changing the subject to steer the focus away from herself.

Markie shrugged. "It's all I know how to do."

Liv nodded. "What grade do you teach, Andi?"

"Sixth. I get them just before they turn." Andi tugged at the neckline of the t-shirt and blew down onto her chest.

"Turn?"

"Into the alien forms we call teenagers." Andi flagged the magazine in front of her. "Damned hot flashes. Where the devil is Bree? It has to be cooler inside the house."

Liv pulled the brochure about the retreat house from her purse. "I don't think so. According to this, there is no air conditioning. Just fans."

"What?" Andi bolted upright and reached over to snatch the brochure from Liv's fingers with such force, Liv blinked. "You have got to be kidding me. Oh, hell no. How did I miss that?" She fanned furiously with both the magazine and the brochure. "I'm going to die here."

"I know what you mean about hot flashes. I used to wake up in the middle of the night absolutely drenched. Get up and change my nightgown and the sheets. Sometimes twice. Have you tried phytoestrogens?" Markie asked.

"Phyto…what?" Andi wrinkled her forehead.

"Herbs. Natural estrogens. They really helped me. Soy, for example."

"You mean like in tofu? Blech. I can't swallow that stuff. It tastes like…well, there is no taste. Just texture. I could gag just thinking about it."

"You might try sage, then."

"Are you a homeopath?"

"Sort of. I prefer natural medicine, when possible. But you have to do what you think is best for you."

Liv sank back in her chair, letting herself fade from the conversation. She had developed a knack for becoming invisible while sitting right there in front of other people. A chameleon. If she were of a different culture, that could be her totem.

Andi glanced at her watch. "What are we going to do if this Bree doesn't show up? Maybe we should see if there are any vacancies at one of the motels in town. One with air conditioning."

Markie shrugged, seemingly unruffled. "I'm sure there's an explanation."

Liv stretched her legs and breathed in the ocean air. "I could sit right here all evening."

A plume of dust followed a sage green van up the driveway. The vehicle turned and lurched to a stop. A younger woman, probably early thirties, emerged. A soccer ball rolled out as she slid open the side door to retrieve a small suitcase. She set down her bag and chased the ball as it rolled down the sloping drive. After tossing the object back into the van, she shielded her eyes and gazed up at the house.

"Think that's Bree?" Andi asked.

The woman hesitated, then shoved her keys into a large purse and trekked up the drive to the porch, dragging the suitcase. She stopped at the bottom of the steps, curly red hair standing out in a wild halo, and with tiny hand-print smudges on her tan shorts and decorating her white tank top. "Hi." She breathed the greeting more than spoke it as if she had been holding her breath for a while.

"Hi," Markie said.

"Is this the women's retreat?"

"It's the New Beginnings retreat for women over fifty. I think you must be in the wrong place," Markie said.

The woman sighed. "No, I'm in the right place. I'm Cee Cee Carter." Her oversized canvas purse whomped against each step on an off-beat from the suitcase as she climbed up to join them.

"Have a seat. No one's here to open up yet." Andi motioned to the chair between herself and Markie.

Cee Cee dropped her purse onto the wooden floor with a clunk.

"What do you have in there?" Andi asked. "A Glock?"

"My kids like to hide stuff in my purse for me to find later. God only knows what's in there now." She bent and opened the canvas bag, removing a small metal Tonka dump truck—the source of the thunk—a tattered pink stuffed bunny, a half eaten banana, and a baggie of Cheerios.

"At least they packed you a lunch." Andi got up and paced, pulling the fabric of her shirt away from her body.

Cee Cee spit on a tissue and wiped furiously at a sticky-looking hand print on her left breast. "I gave the kids waffles for lunch. Now I feel like one of those fly strips."

"I remember those days." Liv smiled. "Fingerprints everywhere for years." She retreated into her memories, a luxury she didn't often afford herself. Sadness knifed her chest. She gave herself this one brief moment with Aaron when he was a baby. He loved to wear his food like body paint and would raise his little spattered arms when he had finished eating and shout, "Mama. Done."

Liv would wash him off before picking him up. Now she wished he would come to her covered in muck from head to toe, and she could walk into his open arms. She shook herself back to the present before she sank too far into the memory and the tears started.

"You don't look old enough to attend an over-fifty retreat," Markie said to the younger woman.

Cee Cee hesitated and then murmured, "I'm thirty-two."

Andi leaned forward. "Thirty-two? What are you doing here?"

"I…uh…" Cee Cee bit her lip. "My mother was

registered. She couldn't make it, and since it was already paid for, I came. Ben—that's my husband—Ben and I have four kids. Sean is nine, Benji is almost four, and the twin girls, Katie and Beth are eighteen months." She blew at a strand of hair on her cheek. "I needed a break."

"It's good you came, then," Markie said in a honey-smooth voice and with a kind smile.

Cee Cee looked up. "Really? You think I'll be allowed to stay? I mean, I'm not fifty. I don't want to disrupt the retreat for any of you."

"Oh, please, disrupt," Andi said. "Anything to take my mind off these damn heat surges. Hell will be a piece of cake after menopause. Are you sure there's no air conditioning in there?" she asked, turning to Liv.

Liv nodded. "According to the brochure." Liv was grateful for the distraction of Andi's hot flashes and Cee Cee showing up. At least no one asked more questions of her. She willed herself to relax, rolling her shoulders to release the tension.

"Here's comes another car," Andi said.

They all watched as a shiny black Acura parked in the open space opposite the other four vehicles.

The driver climbed out and straightened her crisp white blouse that was neatly tucked into a pair of grey linen slacks. She was tall, maybe five-foot-ten, and wore her blond hair pulled back in a chignon, oozing class. She peered over the top of her sunglasses at the four of them, then straightened her shoulders and walked briskly up the drive. "Which of you is Bree Gilmore?"

"None of us," Andi said. "We're waiting for her."

The new arrival glanced at her watch. "I was told to be here at four, and it's four-forty-two now. I got delayed in traffic. Where is she?"

"We don't know. You might want to have a seat." Andi nodded toward the empty porch swing. "I'm Andi

Ryan, by the way."

"Julia Lane." Julia stared at the swing and then at the women seated in the only chairs. Cee Cee jumped up. "I'll take the swing, if you'd like to sit here."

"Thank you." Julia looped the strap of her purse over the arm of the vacated chair and sat, straight and stiff. "How long have you all been waiting?"

"I've been here since two-thirty." Markie rearranged her skirt. "I came early to meditate on the beach and to commune with Gaia. I wanted to create a spiritual balance."

Andi lifted her eyebrows and grinned. "I didn't have anyone with whom to commune and, since I'm already balanced, I arrived at three-forty-five. And Liv got here shortly after I did. Then Cee Cee pulled in," she said, nodding toward the younger woman. "We're really not sure what happened to Bree."

Julia pursed her lips. "Lovely. Are we just supposed to sit here and wait?"

"Seems that way." Andi resumed fanning her blazing face with the magazine.

Markie removed a purple velvet pouch from a pocket in her skirt. "While we're waiting, let me give you all a gift for the retreat. I took the opportunity on the beach to charge these crystals." She offered each of the women a translucent pink shard of stone.

Andi turned the crystal over in her hand. "What is this?"

"Rose quartz. It promotes self-love and healing."

Andi snorted. "I haven't had to rely on self-love for a while, if you get my drift."

"Oh, not that kind of self-love. Inner love and acceptance. Peace." Markie smiled blissfully.

"Voodoo," Julia said, handing the stone back to Markie.

Markie stared at the quartz in her palm, then shrugged and dropped it back into the pouch.

"Thanks." Cee Cee glanced at her purse and then tucked the stone into her pocket. "If I drop it in that abyss, I'll never see it again. The thing's like a black hole."

Liv clutched the cool stone, enjoying the way its angular edges pressed into her palm. "Thank you," she said to Markie. She found the other women to be warm, but Julia made the hairs on her arms prickle. She was rude and abrasive and, Liv thought, exuded an over-inflated sense of self-importance. Liv judged Julia as someone quick to judge. And she immediately felt remorse for having judged Julia at all, given what she herself had been through these past months.

"Does anyone have Bree's cell phone number? We could call her," Cee Cee suggested.

"I only have the office number," Liv said. She glanced toward the front door. "Which will probably ring in there."

Markie pushed up to her feet and descended the steps. "I'm going to look around. I'll bet there's a key hidden out here. Everyone hides a key in case of emergency."

"You're going to break in?" Julia stared down at her like a hawk eyeing prey.

"It's not breaking in if you have a key." Markie lifted rocks and planters to search beneath them.

Cee Cee joined her in the hunt. "We have a ceramic frog by the front steps where we hide a spare key."

"I'm sure everyone's fooled by that," Julia muttered.

"Oh, lighten up," Andi snapped. "It's not like we've hatched a plan for murder. Yet."

Julia blanched and stopped talking, but still managed to express an opinion with her sour expression. Liv watched the exchange with relief. Maybe Julia would be unlikable enough to keep the heat off of Liv. It had been bad enough being the pariah in her own social circles. Spending eight days in a house with four strangers and being the odd person out would be unbearable.

Cee Cee pushed on a large boulder. "Could someone give me a hand with this?"

Andi laughed. "If you can't move it, I doubt anyone would hide a key under there."

"Oh. Right. Good point." Cee Cee returned to the porch and stared at the frame above the front door. "Some people put a spare key up above the door. Who's the tallest?" She glanced around. "Julia?"

Julia glared as if Cee Cee had asked her to donate a kidney to a total stranger. "I am not participating in a break in. It's against the law."

"Oh, for Pete's sake." Andi dragged a chair behind her and then climbed up on the seat. She had chosen the wicker rocker. It tilted precariously as she mounted it and stretched to reach the top of the ledge. "Bingo." She held up a key. The chair rocked, and Andi grasped at air to keep from falling. Cee Cee steadied the chair while Liv reached to steady Andi.

"Thanks. All I need is to fall and break something," Andi said. "Let's see if this key works."

"Stop." The word wasn't a request, it was a command.

They all turned to face Julia. Liv wondered if Julia may have been a prison warden at one time.

"What if there is an intrusion alarm?" Julia asked. "Have you even considered that possibility?"

Markie looked around. "I don't think so. There

are no signs in the windows or on the lawn. I say we go for it." She climbed the steps.

Andi directed the key into the lock. "Don't worry, Jules. We'll tell the police you were an innocent bystander."

"The name is Julia."

"Sorry, Ju-li-a." Andi turned the key and swung the door open. "We're in, ladies. Oh, God. It's stifling in here." She led the procession into the house, turning on ceiling fans and opening windows as she went.

"Wow, look at this place." Cee Cee stopped in the foyer and Liv nearly ran into her. "How beautiful, and it smells like cinnamon. What do think the name means? Syo-chain."

"Shee-ock-awn," Liv said. "It means 'peace'."

Cee Cee tilted her face toward Liv. "How did you know that?"

"I looked it up." Liv settled her suitcase at the foot of the stairs. Liv was always Googling on the computer. Adam used to tease her that most women spent their time shopping online, and then said his checkbook should be grateful she only thirsted for knowledge. *His checkbook.* A familiar tiredness sucked the air out of her and her knees became weak. She wanted to lie down. Sleep had been her salvation much of the past year. "Do you think there's a list of room assignments, or do we just find a room to settle in?"

"Let's look around," Andi said. "We can add snooping to our list of felonies." She looked pointedly at Julia who ignored her.

They all startled when the phone rang.

"Maybe we should answer. It could be Bree."

"Why would she call this phone when no one's here?" Cee Cee asked.

"We're here," Andi said.

The answering machine kicked on. "Hello? Oh, I hope you ladies found the key and let yourselves in. This is Bree Gilmore. Hello?"

Markie picked up the phone. "Hi, Bree. This is Markova." Pause. "Yes, we were wondering." Pause. "Oh, my. I hope he'll be okay." Pause. "Yes, we will. Don't worry about us. We'll be fine." Pause. "Okay, we'll see you tomorrow."

Markie set down the phone. "Bree's brother was in a car accident last night in Baltimore. She's still at the hospital waiting to see if he has to have surgery. She said there is plenty of food and that we should make ourselves at home for tonight. She hopes to be back by lunch tomorrow."

"Is there a wine supply? Did she say?" Andi asked. "I need a drink."

"Alcohol. Now there's a solution for hot flashes," Julia muttered.

Andi ignored the comment, her gaze directed on Markie.

"She didn't say, but I'm sure if there is, we'll find it. If there isn't, we can go into town and pick up something," Markie said. "Bree said she was glad we had the ingenuity to search for a key. She left in a hurry and didn't have any of our cell numbers with her. She was about to call a neighbor and have him come and let us in. There are envelopes for each of us on her desk in the office next to the kitchen."

The women trooped behind Markie. Five large manila envelopes were spread across the top of the oak desk, each bearing the name of a woman. Markie set hers aside and distributed the others. "Andi, here's yours. Liv. Jules. Sorry, Jul-i-a. And…Ruth?" She gazed at Cee Cee. "I guess this is yours."

"Ruth is my mom." Cee Cee pressed the envelope

to her chest as if it were a prize. "Thank you."

As each woman opened her envelope to remove a key and a sheet of paper, Liv began to laugh. All she could think of was the old TV show, *Mission Impossible*. The other women stared at her. It had been so long since Liv had allowed herself to just laugh—the gut-deep, laugh-until-you-cry laughter that clears the bits of worry and emotion one stores inside. Tears blurred her vision. She had no doubt it was anxiety rolling out of her, but it felt good all the same.

"Want to share the joke with the rest of us?" Andi asked.

"I'm sorry. I was thinking about *Mission Impossible*." She lowered her voice. "Your mission, should you accept it...."

"I loved that show," Markie said. "Hey, do you think these instructions will self-destruct in ten seconds?"

"I hope not. I need to know where to find the alcohol." Andi turned the page over and then back again. "It's not here."

"Invisible ink," Markie said. And she and Liv both laughed and snorted.

Julia shook her head and sighed with a tone of disgust.

Cee-Cee blinked in confusion.

Liv liked Markie. She was pleasant, soft-spoken, and earthy—the result of the hippie era colliding with new age philosophies. Andi was okay, too. A bit irritable, but that was understandable. She probably wasn't getting much sleep. Liv liked the fact that Andi was outspoken—no hidden agenda there. Cee Cee tugged at Liv's heart. She reminded her of Lauren, her own daughter, who had married and moved to London two months earlier. Liv missed her terribly. Cee Cee, still youthful and of child-bearing age, would be a breath of fresh air in this group.

Then there was Julia. Liv drew in a breath and exhaled, releasing bad karma. If she were still a practicing Catholic, she would have made the sign of the cross.

"Here's a room list." Julia picked up a paper from the desk. "I'm in the Rose Room. God, I hope it's not pink." She handed the list to Andi and strode back toward the foyer.

"Maybe the room was named for a black rose," Andi said, and they all chuckled. "Okay, I'm going to find the Lavender Room, and then I'll see about dinner."

"I love to cook. I'll help," Cee Cee offered.

Each woman set off with her room assignment and luggage in hand.

Liv found the Jasmine Room on the eastern end of the house on the third floor. The window afforded a view of the water. Pale yellow walls and a white ceiling welcomed her like one of those cartoon smiley faces. A spread on the bed bore a matching white and yellow floral design. Everything about the cheery room stood in sharp contrast to Liv's insides. The medication her doctor had prescribed helped, but she still had moments of anxiety that took her feet out from under her.

The laughing jag earlier had felt good, but she knew it was prompted by stress and was nothing more than a release bordering on hysteria. Still, it was better than sobbing or throwing things. A week ago, she had come to the realization that she and Adam had both received prison sentences. He was serving his behind bars in a white collar facility in upstate New York, which may actually be easier than her sentence served in public. At least in jail, the inmates were on equal ground. Liv had learned how quickly friends could become enemies or, even worse, indifferent strangers. Her world had crumbled so fast, she had barely had time to duck for cover.

Ladies In Waiting

She opened the window and stood gazing out at the calm green waters of the Atlantic Ocean. She breathed in and exhaled, repeating the process a few times—a technique taught by her therapist and intended to help her relax. It was working. That and the Lexapro. And maybe this place. She shoved her fingers into her pocket and withdrew the pale pink crystal. She had been raised with strict religious teaching, but right now she would take all the help the universe could offer. After holding the glass up to the light, she placed the quartz on the windowsill with the hope it would dispel the self-loathing that gnawed at her.

With her divorce final, her maiden name restored, and a new haircut and color, Liv was starting to find a new identity. That's what had drawn her to this retreat—*Embracing the New You: Reinventing Yourself After Fifty*.

She picked up the booklet that lay on the nightstand beside the bed. The cover of the brochure bore the image of a Celtic knot and the word *Síocháin*. A yellow sticky note read: *Welcome, Liv! You've arrived!*

Chapter Two

Andi

Andi unpacked her bag and stood the empty suitcase inside the closet. The Lavender Room was situated on the front corner of the house on the second floor and offered two windows. Andi opened both and turned the ceiling fan on high, waiting for the flow of air around her. Her gynecologist had suggested estrogen therapy for the hot flashes, but Andi resisted. She told herself it was because of the potential cancer risks she had read about. But who was she kidding? She resisted because of her denial she was in menopause.

She wasn't ready for menopause and all it brought—weight gain, mood swings, memory loss, hot flashes. And worse, what it signified—aging. The end. The end of life, looming too near. She thought of Michael. Dear, sweet Michael. Dear, sweet, *younger* Michael. At fifty-three, Andi was mystified that Michael DiGiorno wanted her. He was thirty-eight, nearer to her daughter's age than to hers—as Katrina loved to remind her. Katrina had been close to her father and probably would never accept any new man in Andi's life. But Kat found it particularly scandalous that Andi had taken up with a man fifteen years her junior. "He could be my brother. It's like you're sleeping with your own son. Eeewww." Andi had burned with shame at realizing Kat knew she and Michael were sleeping together.

It was scandalous, and it explained why Andi fought to keep the relationship hidden. Her own dirty little secret. The one issue that reared up and flared between Michael and herself on a regular basis. He interpreted her insistence they keep a low profile as embarrassment at being seen with him. She argued that, as a teacher, other narrow-minded people could make life difficult for her, put her job at risk.

Andi laughed at his interpretation. There wasn't a living, breathing woman who would be embarrassed to be seen with Michael DiGiorno. He was tall, dark, muscled, tanned, with classic Italian good looks. And he loved her. At least, he said he did. Between Katrina's accusations that Michael only wanted Andi for her money and all the tongue-in-cheek jokes about 'cougars,' Andi remained unconvinced.

She pulled her cell phone from her purse and flipped it open, hitting Michael's number on speed dial.

He answered on the second ring, "DiGiorno Construction."

She frowned, realizing he hadn't assigned her a special ring tone. When he called her, Springsteen's *I'm On Fire* blared from her phone. "Hi, it's me."

"Hey, how's my girl?"

Girl. He always called her his *girl.* She smiled. "I'm fine. Just wanted to let you know I got here okay."

"I miss you already."

"I miss you, too."

"Tell me again why you have to spend eight days in Cape May to find the new you? I thought I'd already found her," he teased.

Oh, he had found the new Andi, all right. He knew exactly where to look and how to search. She shivered, despite the heat, thinking of his touch, his lips on her neck and moving down, his hands deftly exploring her body.

"Andi?"

She moved to stand directly under the fan. "I'm sorry." She thought a woman's sex drive waned with menopause. But it was as if she was supercharged all the time, ever since she had met Michael. She swallowed and drew in air.

"You sound out of breath. You okay?"

"I just ran up the stairs," she lied. "I needed to hear your voice. I'll try to call you again tomorrow evening. I've gotta go."

"Okay, babe. Love you."

"Love you, too." She snapped the phone shut and returned it to her purse. She did love him, and that realization scared the daylights out of her. The sex was phenomenal. She had discovered a newfound freedom, a depth of passion she had never known existed.

"Jesus, Andi, get a grip. You'll be responsible for burning down the house." With that thought, she headed to the kitchen.

Cee Cee stood examining the menu that had been posted on the fridge.

"What have we got?" Andi walked up beside her.

"It says tonight's dinner is baked chicken, sautéed asparagus, fresh corn on the cob, and a salad. I found a gas grill in the back yard. We could cook the chicken faster on that and cut down on the heat in here."

"I like the way you think," Andi said. "You want to do the grilling? I'll take care of the salad and asparagus. Maybe we can find someone to shuck the corn and get it on to boil."

Julia appeared in the doorway.

"Oh, good. A volunteer," Andi said.

"I beg your pardon." Julia arched an elegant eyebrow.

"Maybe you could help us with dinner?" Andi nodded at the ears of corn Cee Cee had set out on the center island.

Julia stared at the pile of green. "I don't eat corn on the cob."

Andi removed lettuce and tomatoes from the fridge and carried them to the sink. "Well, the rest of us do. And, in case you hadn't noticed, you're not the only one here."

Julia pulled up a stool to the counter. "Oh, I've noticed."

"Great." Andi set the trash can beside the counter. "You can put the leaves and silk in here."

"I know how to shuck corn." Julia paused and examined her nails, as if considering the collateral damage that might occur.

Cee Cee removed a thawed package of chicken breasts from the fridge, rinsed each breast and placed it on a plate. She covered the meat with plastic wrap, carried the plate outside, and returned for seasonings. "The grill's heating up. It shouldn't take long for the chicken to cook. Let me know when the water is boiling."

When Markie and Liv entered the kitchen, Andi assigned them the task of setting the table. Spending her days in a classroom with eleven-year-olds, Andi was used to taking charge. Not that these women were children. Well, except for maybe Julia, who was behaving like a sullen teenager.

"Julia, where are you from?" Andi asked, hoping to ease the tension between them.

"Philadelphia," Julia replied. Then she asked warily, "Why?"

"You look familiar. But I doubt we've ever met. I live in Toms River, New Jersey."

"No, we've never met." Julia lowered her head and ripped the covering from an ear of corn with a vengeance.

She seemed angry, but not with Andi. With the world. There was something about Julia that piqued Andi's curiosity. The woman didn't seem to want to be there, yet had freely chosen to come to the retreat. And that anger that sometimes masqueraded as arrogance…Oh, there was something there.

Julia looked up. "What? Am I doing this incorrectly?"

"No. You're doing fine."

Julia deflated just a little. "I don't have time to cook very often. I generally order out."

Andi nodded and continued chopping carrots and slicing a cucumber for the salad. "What do you do in Philadelphia?" she asked.

"Do?" Julia's expression changed to one of panic.

"Your job?"

Julia hesitated. "I work at the courthouse. I provide legal aide."

"So you're a lawyer."

Julia pressed her lips together, then said. "Yes."

"You married?"

Shaking her head, Julia said, "No. You?"

Andi hesitated. "I'm widowed. Three years."

Julia glanced up. "He must have been young."

"Paul was fifty-two. He had a massive coronary." It still shook her to say the words, though she felt she had grieved the loss of her husband. Obviously, since she was in a new relationship with Michael. But it still seemed surreal that Paul could be dead at fifty-two years of age. He had been healthy, athletic, filled with life one minute, and gone the next. She sighed.

"It's none of my business," Julia said.

"It's okay. Just strikes me as unbelievable at times. Were you ever married?"

"Once, for a short while. It was a long time ago."

"Children?"

Julia shook her head. "No. We weren't together long enough."

Andi scraped the chopped vegetables into the bowl and tossed them with romaine lettuce. Then she washed the asparagus spears and arranged them in a basket for steaming. The forced small talk was draining her, so she gave up.

Julia cleaned the final ear of corn and carried the bowl to the sink. She picked up the vegetable brush and scrubbed the leftover silk from each ear before dropping them, one by one, into the boiling water on the stove.

"I'll let Cee Cee know she can start the chicken." Andi returned and watched as Julia measured out a quarter cup of sugar and poured it into the pot.

"My mother taught me to do that, too," Andi commented.

"What—the sugar? Yes, I remember that from my childhood. Supposedly it sweetens the corn."

Markie came back to the kitchen and removed a box of tofu from the fridge. "I don't eat meat, so I'm going to prepare this. Anyone else want to try it? There's plenty."

Andi pursed her lips together and shook her head. "No, thank you."

"None for me, thanks." Julia wiped her hands on a towel and asked, "Anything else I can do?"

"Maybe get drink orders? There's ice in the freezer, and I noticed a pitcher of lemonade in the fridge," Andi said.

"Lemonade? I was thinking more along the lines of Margaritas," Julia said. "I'll see if the makings are on hand."

Andi grinned. *Just when you think you have someone pegged, they surprise you.*

Twenty minutes later, the women sat around the dining room table, sipping on and complimenting Julia's Margaritas and one another's culinary efforts.

"This is a delicious meal. Thank you," Markie said. "How did you prepare this asparagus?"

"I steamed it a little, then sautéed it in olive oil, garlic, and just a hint of lemon juice," Andi said. "How's the tofu?"

"You want to try it?" Markie asked. "It could help with the hot flashes."

Andi stared at Markie's plate. "I think I'll stick with the hot flashes. Thanks."

When the meal was over, Liv suggested they clean up the kitchen and have dessert on the porch.

"Great idea. Bree left a pan of brownies, and there's ice cream in the fridge." Markie stood and began to collect plates. "I found Bree's agenda on the desk. Tonight was supposed to be dinner and get acquainted time. We can share more about ourselves over dessert."

"Oh, goody," Julia mumbled.

"And just for that, you get to go first, Jules." Markie grinned and headed to the kitchen.

Andi stifled a laugh and could not make eye contact with any of the others. Poor Julia. She was going to have a rough time here if she didn't soon loosen up and extract that stick from her ass. Then Andi thought about the sharing. Would she tell them about Michael and her fears because of the age difference? She considered what little she already knew about each of these women. Markie would probably be accepting and supportive. Cee Cee might be shocked because Michael was close to her age. She wasn't sure about Liv, but she was fairly certain Julia—the legal eagle—would issue some judgment.

Andi thought perhaps she would just mention that she was widowed and now dating again.

She picked up a plate holding a brownie and a scoop of ice cream. "Which wine goes with this? If I'm sharing any deep, dark secrets, I'll need a drink."

Chapter Three

Markie

Markie grinned at Andi. "A cougar in our midst."

"Oh, please. I hate that term. I promised myself I wouldn't tell the whole truth. I almost left out the age difference because I never know how people will react. Maybe it's more my problem than anyone else's."

Shrugging, Markie said, "Problem? I think it's a compliment to have a younger man attracted to you."

"Maybe." Andi drained her wineglass. "What's your story? Come here to delve deeper into your artistic side?"

Markie smiled wanly. "Something like that. I've been an artist all my life. Natural talent, I've been told. And a good thing, because I dropped out of high school in the eleventh grade and lived with other artists in a commune in California." She glanced at the others. "Go ahead and say it. I know you've thought it. I'm an aging hippie. A leftover from the sixties. Well, since I was born in the mid-fifties, I guess you'd be right. I was once a groupie for *The Grateful Dead*."

"The who?" Cee Cee asked.

"Different group," Andi said.

Markie laughed. "Way before your time, sweetie. They were one of the best bands ever."

"Oh." Cee Cee looked confused.

Markie continued, "I met the artist, David Rooker, when I was just eighteen and began to study with him."

Julia's head shot up. "You studied with Rooker?"

Markie nodded. "He was like a god. Older, established, his work in demand. I lived with him and studied under him...." She gave the others a wicked grin. "In more ways than one. David said I had raw talent and that I could be somebody. When you're eighteen that means a lot. When you get older, you look back and realize you already were somebody."

"Amen to that." Andi raised her refilled wineglass.

"I worked with paint, but David taught me to sculpt. Clay, metal, whatever I could find in a junk heap. I'd shape it into something. I started getting commissions for larger pieces, mostly from businesses. And David became jealous of the recognition I received. He began to put down my work and demean me. Again, when you're young and you think you're in love, you put up with that crap. I was with him for twelve years and, when I reached thirty, I stepped back and took a look at the relationship. I didn't like what I saw."

"He was an abusive bastard?" Cee Cee asked.

They all stared at her.

"I'm sorry, but I volunteer twice a month at a women's shelter," Cee Cee said, a bright flush spreading up her cheeks. "I don't have much patience for that behavior."

"I don't either, now," Markie said. "I finally saw clearly what was going on, what friends had tried to tell me for years. So, while David was away on a business trip, I packed up my art supplies, my finished pieces and my clothes. And I left."

"Good for you," Andi said reaching for a magazine to use as a fan.

Liv nodded. "No man has a right to steal your soul like that." Her voice trembled with emotion.

Andi turned to her with raised eyebrows. "And

there's a story there that we'll get to."

Gazing out toward the water, Markie said, "Art is all I've ever known. It's my life. My breath. If I can't create, I may as well die."

They sat in silence for a few minutes, listening to the break of waves on the beach below.

"I need a smoke," Markie said. "I'll be right back." Her left foot dragged slightly as she climbed the stairs. It usually hit her harder when she was tired. In her room, she dug into her duffle, removed the clear plastic baggie and a box of papers. She rolled the joint larger than usual, considering someone else may want a hit or two. She hesitated then, also considering the others might not be comfortable with her smoking. Especially not marijuana. Stuffing a lighter into her pocket, she returned to the front porch.

"Does anyone mind?" she asked.

"I don't," Andi said. "I may join you, if you can spare a cigarette."

Markie lit the joint and inhaled deeply. "Here," she passed it to Andi.

"This is marijuana," Andi said, sniffing.

Markie exhaled then. "High grade, too."

"Well, all right then. It's been a while." Andi put the joint to her lips and drew in a breath. "This is good stuff," she said in a strangled, breath-holding way. She offered the joint to Cee Cee.

"Oh…I don't think…I…um…" Cee Cee stared at the joint as if it would bite her.

"Well, don't waste it, for heaven's sake," Andi said, taking another hit. "Liv? Julia?"

"That's illegal," Julia said.

Andi gasped. "Really? Oh, no. What are we going to do? Well, we can't have this just lying around here." She took a third hit, then handed the joint back to Markie.

Cee Cee leaned forward. "I want to try it."

Andi passed the dope back to the younger woman. "You ever smoked?"

"I smoked cigarettes in high school."

"This is different. Draw it into your lungs, slowly, and hold it there," Andi said.

Markie watched with amusement as Andi taught the younger woman how to smoke a joint. One generation handing down knowledge to the next. The cannabis was taking effect, lifting Markie, giving her wings. Making her body feel uniformly relaxed. She settled back in the chair and closed her eyes.

"I cannot be a part of this." Julia's chair scraped as she stood and entered the house.

"More for us," Andi said. "Liv, want some?"

Liv shook her head. "No thanks. I've already had more to drink than I need. I think I'll take a shower and turn in."

As the three women floated on a cloud of smoke, the conversation turned philosophical, and then detoured into downright funny. Politics, religion, and past lives. Well, the past lives were Markie's. Andi said she was convinced this was her first and only life, but Cee Cee hung on Markie's words. "Oh, I hope I some day remember having been royalty. I always wanted to be a princess."

"If I've been anything in the past, it would have been a French whore or an English wench," Andi declared. "Not that I believe in that crap." She glanced at Markie. "Sorry."

Unruffled, Markie said, "There's a place in New Mexico that does past life regression therapy. Of course, it's not cheap. But you'd be surprised what you discover. I was a farmer in the 1600's in Britain. Not an easy life, I'll tell you."

Andi stood abruptly. "Am I the only one who's ravenous?"

Five minutes later, Markie, Andi and Cee Cee stood huddled around the counter in the kitchen. A bag of potato chips, a package of chocolate chip cookies, and a quart of milk sat before them.

The trio giggled while they munched their way through the snacks.

"How much of that stuff did you bring with you?" Andi asked.

Markie grinned. "Enough."

Cee Cee closed her eyes and chewed on a cookie. "Oh, my God. I can see why my kids devour these. I had no idea they were so delicious."

Markie looked at Andi and laughed. "Life is good." But the irony of her statement fell inside her with a clunk, like a boat anchor. Life was good. It had been good in the past. It was good right now, in this moment. But tomorrow, or next week, or next year? The only thing Markie feared was the unknown, the worrisome *what if.*

Chapter Four

When Darkness Falls

Julia

Julia flipped on the lights in the bedroom and frowned at all the pink. Dusty rose pink, but still very pink—the walls, the bed covering, the lampshade, the cushion on the rocking chair. It was like being dipped in a bottle of Pepto. She turned on the bedside lamp and doused the overhead, which helped soften the tones.

She felt trapped. Trapped with four women with whom she had nothing in common. Strangers with whom she could never share her secret. Some of these women were mothers. They would never understand. Eventually, someone would point out it was her turn to speak. Well, she could make something up. There was that whole menopause issue where she felt life had passed her by while she wasn't looking, and now she was sad at the chances lost forever. Maybe she could run with that story. She was a star performer in the courtroom, usually. She could act her way through this retreat. These women didn't have a clue who she was. No one had pointed a finger at her yet and said, "There's the evil witch that let that woman get away with murder—three times."

Gathering up her toiletries, she crossed the hall to the bathroom. After washing her face and brushing her teeth, she returned to her room and slipped into a pair of neatly-pressed cotton pajamas. The overhead fan pulled a cool breeze in through the window. It was almost enough to chill her.

She picked up her cell phone and stared at the screen. No messages and no missed calls. Of course not. No one was speaking to her, except those faceless people who shouted epithets as she came and went from the office. Some demanded the DA fire her for incompetence. She almost agreed with them. This retreat was nothing more than a geographic escape for her. She had zero interest in getting to know the other women or in sharing her deepest, darkest secrets and desires. Life after fifty, for Julia, was much the same as life before fifty. No new journey here. Just a short respite.

As she turned off the light and stretched out on the double bed, a shaft of moonlight, like a muted spotlight, cut across her legs. It reminded her of the searchlights in the old war movies she had seen and she shifted her legs into the shadow. Sleep snaked around her, but she fought it off. Not that she wasn't tired. But with sleep, came dreams. Well, nightmares, to be exact. Drowning children. Julia, herself, under water, the final bubbles of oxygen bursting on the surface. Her eyes fixed and lifeless.

She got up and opened her door. The house was quiet. She tiptoed to the top of the stairs. Only a small glow shone on the hardwood floor below, probably the light over the kitchen sink that someone had left on for the night. At the bottom of the stairs, she stopped and listened again, then attempted to soundlessly open the front door.

When she stepped outside and turned, a shadow caught her eye and she startled. "Oh. Who's…?"

"It's me. Markie."

"I thought everyone had gone to bed." Julia eased into one of the chairs and rubbed her arms. "It's cool out here."

"Want this?" Markie produced an afghan.

"Don't you want it?" Julia asked.

"No. I like the chill. Makes me feel alive." She handed over the blanket.

"So…you can't sleep either." Julia tucked the blanket across her chest.

"Not very well. The dope usually knocks me out for a bit, but I guess all the sugar and the talking counteracted the effects." She glanced over at Julia. "I'm sorry if my bringing the marijuana here makes you uncomfortable. I can smoke elsewhere."

"No. It's okay. I've worked in the legal system for so long, I guess I've developed very narrowly defined lines of right and wrong. I probably need to leave my job outside this house."

Markie didn't respond, just continued rocking.

"How did you get to Doylestown, Pennsylvania, from a commune in New Mexico?" Julia asked.

After a beat, Markie said, "The bus."

It took a minute to sink in, but then Julia chuckled.

"So you do have a sense of humor. There were bets to the contrary, but my money was on you."

Julia's head shot around. "People are taking bets on me?"

"Don't be offended. It shows we're interested. You're a mystery woman here. Well, you and Liv. But I think she'll open up eventually. You? I'm not so sure."

"I didn't come here to open up, to lay my life before a group of strangers for their amusement and judgment."

"Oh, Julia, there's nothing amusing about your life. And no one here is judging you. What that woman did to herself and her kids—it wasn't your fault."

Julia gasped. "How do you know about that?"

"I read the newspapers, and I watch TV. I'm a local, remember? Doylestown. Not that far outside of Philly."

Julia's heart pounded. She fought the urge to race upstairs, gather her things, and leave.

"Your secret's safe with me," Markie said. "If you want the others to know, you'll have to tell them yourself. It's not my place. But I don't judge you. I want you to know that."

A sarcastic laugh ripped from Julia. "Hah. Well, you'd have to get in line. Half of Philadelphia wants my head on a platter. If I had done my job as a prosecutor, really paid attention, two children and their mother would be alive today. She would be in jail or a psych ward, but she would be alive. And those kids…" Julia's voice cracked. She had seen the photos in the paper. A three-year-old boy and his sister, only fourteen months. Smiling. Alive. Impish faces filled with joy. She lifted a hand as if to swat away a mosquito, but instead swiped at a tear.

"The legal system set that woman free. She killed those kids and herself."

"I didn't stop her. I work for the system, and I didn't do my job." The pounding ache returned, like a jackhammer in her chest. "If I hadn't so vigorously argued against the defense claiming insanity… If I'd put justice above my winning record…"

"You can't change the past. Beating yourself up now won't make a difference. We learn from our mistakes and, hopefully, don't make them again."

"That works, unless our mistakes cost innocent lives." She stared out at the blackness. "How do I learn to live with that?"

"You just do it. You do it one day at a time, one

person at a time. You're human, Julia, just like the rest of us. We all seek forgiveness and, often, that has to come from ourselves."

"If it were only that simple," Julia murmured.

Markie steadied her gaze on Julia. "Can I ask you something? Why did you come to this retreat?"

"To get away. I'm waiting for the whole thing to die down, for people to move on. I needed to turn off the voices."

Markie's eyes widened. "The voices?"

"Not the voices in my head. The voices outside my office building, on the TV news, on radio talk shows." She lifted her head. "You can go ahead and say it—I'm running away."

"We're all running from something, Jules. And we're all running toward something."

Markie stood, resting a hand on Julia's shoulder. "Hope you can get some sleep. I'm starting to feel drowsy. I think I'll seize the moment."

"Good night." Julia tucked her legs under her and sat alone in the chill, gazing out at the ocean where a strip of moonlight cut a swathe across the water. That damned beam of light seemed to follow her, glaring at her, trying to expose her. The tears came then, and she let them fall, dripping onto the blanket that covered her. She grieved for those two children. She grieved for that mother who had lost her mind. And she grieved for herself. In this, her darkest hour, she had no one. No one to hold her, to reassure her, or to stand by her. Hell, she came to this retreat because she had nowhere else to go. She had to seek comfort among strangers.

Then she pressed her hand to her shoulder, covering the spot Markie had touched. How long had it been since anyone had touched her in a gesture of friendship? She didn't have to be so alone. All she had to do was trust. *Yeah, I'll do that.*

~ * ~

Cee Cee

Cee Cee crawled into bed and settled on the side nearest the window. But this wasn't "her" side. It was Ben's. And she couldn't get comfortable. She scooted to the opposite side and leaned up on one elbow to punch the pillow. All this empty space. Wasn't that what had drawn her here—to get space? Now that she had it, she didn't know what to do with it. Loneliness niggled at her and she pressed a palm to her abdomen. She stretched her left arm out across the vacant expanse of bed. Tears stung her eyes and she sniffled.

Lying alone in the dark without Ben made the distance she had felt between them more real. Tangible. Until now she had been able to convince herself it wasn't real. Just normal for a couple with a growing family. But now the truth burned in her chest. Her marriage was in trouble…and she didn't have the first clue of what to do to fix it.

Staring at the ceiling and the whirling shadows made by the fan, Cee Cee considered the other women with whom she would spend these days. Markie didn't mention having been married, though she had been in a relationship. Julia was tight-lipped about her life. Tight-assed, too, Cee Cee thought—and the thought brought a giggle that she stifled with the pillow. How could she feel so sad and laugh at the same time? *Must be the marijuana.*

Andi and Liv had both mentioned having been married. Perhaps one of them knew the secret to married life with children. Well, Liv was divorced. Andi might be Cee Cee's best hope. She would have asked her own mother. They had that kind of relationship. Before.

Ladies In Waiting

Before the darkness descended and stole Ruth's recognition and reasoning. Cee Cee sighed. It seemed as though everyone she loved, with the exception of her children, was being pulled away from her. And in the past year, she had noticed how Sean didn't need his Mommy so much any more.

She sat up and turned on the bedside lamp, reaching to the floor for her purse. Opening her wallet, she studied the photo of her kids. Their faces always anchored her, kept her rooted in the present. They gave her a sense of purpose. She removed the photo and stood it on the table against the base of the lamp. Then she dug back into the purse and extracted the love-worn pink bunny, turned off the light, and snuggled under the sheet. She closed her eyes and sniffed the baby scent that remained on the stuffed animal. The mantra that had played through her mind for the past four months started again: *Everything is going to be okay. It will. Really.*

~ * ~

Liv

Liv exited the bathroom and hesitated outside Cee Cee's door. If anyone recognized the muffled sobs of grief, it was Liv. She had spent innumerable nights with her face turned into a pillow, spilling out her anger, grief, and fears. Alone. She lifted a hand to knock, then thought better of it. She didn't know Cee Cee, and the younger woman certainly didn't know her. Liv knew that, on many of those unending nights, the last thing she wanted was to have someone come and sit on the edge of the bed and require an explanation. She would spare Cee Cee that particular discomfort. Hell, maybe she would climb into her own bed, bury her face in her own pillow, and join Cee Cee in her late night song of sadness.

But when she opened her own bedroom door, she

saw that her cell phone flash a signal that she had a voicemail message. She fumbled the phone on her first eager attempt to retrieve the call and it landed with a soft thump on the carpet. When she saw her daughter's name on the glowing screen, her heart quickened. She calculated the time difference. It would be early morning in London. She pressed the number and waited.

"Hi, Mom." Lauren answered on the second ring.

"Hi, honey. Is everything okay?"

"Fine. I just remembered this was your time away at that women's retreat. I wanted to make sure you got there okay."

"I did. Just this afternoon." She dropped down onto the bed.

"How are the other women? Did they recognize you?"

The heat of shame crept up Liv's cheeks. "No. I…I look different since you saw me last." She fingered her shortened hair. "I got a cut and color on my hair. And I've lost a little weight."

"You didn't need to lose weight. I'm worried about you, Mom. All this stress. I wish I could be there." Lauren's voice sounded choked.

"I wish you were here, too, but for different reasons. I miss you." Liv swallowed and then tried to make her voice more cheerful. "Maybe I can come to London for a visit in the spring."

"Derek and I will buy the plane ticket. You just say when."

"I'll buy my own ticket. And we'll see when I can come. Is Derek's family treating you well?" Liv asked.

"They're wonderful. But I still miss you. Have you heard from Nathan or Aaron?"

Liv swallowed hard again. "No. I'm sure they're busy."

Ladies In Waiting

"They're being little shits."

A smile tugged at Liv's mouth, despite the sorrow she felt. "They are your older brothers."

"I don't care what they are. I expect more of them, especially of Nate. I don't understand how he can just turn his back on you at a time like this."

Liv fingered the tufts of fabric on the bedspread. She didn't understand it herself. But she didn't want a wedge driven between Lauren and her brothers. They needed one another, especially if....

"Mom?"

"I'm here. Honey, you have to understand that this whole mess turned all of our lives inside out. Even theirs. In a way, I'm glad you're out of the country and don't have to deal with reporters and being ambushed by the nightly news."

"Oh, Mom, it sounds awful. Hold on a sec."

Liv heard murmuring, then Lauren came back on the line. "Mom, I have to run. I have an interview and Derek's dropping me on his way to the office. But I'll call you later in the week."

"Thanks, honey. It was good to hear your voice. Good luck. I'll be eager to hear how your interview goes. And give Derek my love."

"I will, Mom. Bye."

"Bye." The call ended and Liv hugged the phone against her breast as if to hold Lauren close for just a moment. She stood and set the phone on top of the chest of drawers. She pressed an ear to the wall, listening for Cee Cee's sobbing. But all was quiet.

The worst part of the whole mess for Liv wasn't all she had lost in terms of the money and the houses and the things. It was the chasm that had opened up between her and just about everyone else. At times she felt as if she wore a scarlet letter cautioning others to keep away.

Being here with four strangers, women who didn't know her story, was a relief. As long as she kept things light and on the surface, she could pretend they were friends—or could be. But living on the surface had become lonely. She felt invisible much of the time. And at other times, she tried to be invisible when stares of shocked recognition were followed by indiscreet whispers and pointing. Shame cloaked her like a second skin. She peeled off her khakis and blouse, and then her underwear, to slip into a soft cotton nightgown. But she couldn't peel off the shame. She would cover it up again tomorrow, plaster on a fake smile, and get through one more day.

Chapter Five

Houses Built on Sand

The aroma of freshly-brewed coffee and bacon wafted up the stairs to greet Julia as she exited her room. She drew in the heavenly scents, and her mouth watered. It seemed impossible she had slept for six hours without a nightmare or any other interruption. She hesitated at the top of the stairs. How would she face Markie? Had the woman been true to her word, or would Julia walk into a small, but angry and accusing group?

She found Cee Cee alone in the kitchen where bacon sizzled in a frying pan, pancakes browned on a griddle, and scrambled eggs cooked a skillet. Cee Cee gave her a youthful smile. "Good morning."

"Good morning. Can I do anything?"

"You can pour juice in the small glasses on the table. It's already mixed and in a pitcher in the fridge."

"You did all this yourself?" Julia couldn't keep the wonder from her voice.

Cee Cee grinned. "I have a husband and four kids. I do this on a daily basis."

Children. Small children. Again, the faces haunted her. "I'll get the juice." Her hand trembled as she picked up the pitcher, and she set it down again until she felt steady.

When they gathered at the table, Julia glanced at Markie. She tried to read whether or not the woman had kept her word.

Markie nodded. "Good morning, Julia. Did you sleep well?"

"I did."

Andi yawned. "Not me. I was up every hour. Sweating and panting. I used to have nights like that, but with much better reason." She took a bite of a pancake. "Oh, my. These are fantastic. Cee Cee, what's your secret?"

"Vanilla. Just a drop in the batter." Cee Cee beamed at the praise. "My mother taught me that trick."

"What does everyone want to do today?" Markie asked.

"I assume Bree will be back," Julia said.

"Maybe. If her brother needed surgery, though, we could be on our own. Her agenda said beach time this morning. We're supposed to get back in touch with our inner child, splash in the water and build sand castles."

"I didn't drive down here and spend good money to play in the sand," Julia said, immediately regretting the edge in her tone.

Andi sighed. "Well, then, you can sit on the porch and wait. Ward off any potential pot thieves, while you're at it."

"Okay, here's an idea," Liv said. "How about we leave the morning open? Each one does what she wants. Then, when Bree gets back, we'll get on to the agenda."

"Great. So who wants to go to the beach?" Andi asked.

"I'll go," Cee Cee said.

"Me, too," Markie said. "Liv?"

"I think I'll stay here for a bit. Julia and I can do the dishes since Cee Cee cooked."

Julia nodded, grateful for Liv's suggestion. She was angry with herself and embarrassed. Why was she being such an ass? Why couldn't she just relax and go along with things? If Bree was here to *lead* them and they followed a schedule, would Julia's worries magically disappear? She wasn't sure what she expected or hoped for from the retreat. Julia didn't even care for the word *retreat.* It went against her nature. She just knew that there were no crowds of people holding signs and demanding her resignation—or worse, her head. Now, if she could just breathe.

In the kitchen, she removed her sensible but expensive diamond-accented Bulova watch and began to rinse plates. She was aware of Liv clearing the cups and glasses from the table. "I'm sorry if I seem a little prickly."

"It's okay. I think we were all put a bit off guard when Bree wasn't here to direct us. We came expecting something organized—well, at least I did—and then we had to make a go of it on our own. But...may I offer a little advice?"

Julia turned and faced her. "Go ahead. Say it. I need to lighten up and give everyone a chance. I'm being intractable and judgmental and...and...stuffy. But, you know, I might have my reasons."

Liv stared at her for a moment, a smile tugging at her mouth. "I was going to suggest you simply relax and give yourself the space you need. That's what I plan to do. There's nothing magical about building sand castles. They usually get washed away anyway. I don't personally find it rewarding to build something just to have it destroyed."

It was Julia's turn to stare. "You have strong feelings about sand castles."

Liv drew in a breath and met her gaze. "Something like that." Then both women began to laugh.

"Apparently we both have our share of baggage," Julia said.

Wiping her eyes, Liv nodded, "I suppose we do. Doesn't everyone?"

Julia placed the last of the plates in the dishwasher, filled the cup with powdered detergent and turned it on. "Do you want to go for a walk and not talk about anything personal or significant?"

Liv smiled. "That sounds like a great idea."

~ * ~

Cee Cee

Cee Cee donned her bathing suit and checked herself in the mirror. She should have bought a new suit. Her belly, softened after three pregnancies—the last with twins—edged over the waistband of her bikini bottom. She poked at the dimples in her thighs. No wonder Ben had shown less interest in her lately. Sighing, she pulled on a gauzy beach robe and slipped her feet into flip flops.

She found Markie and Andi on the front porch rummaging through a box of beach toys. "What are you doing?"

"Gathering up some tools for making sand castles," Markie said. "Here, can you carry these buckets and shovels?"

"Sure. This is going to be fun. My kids do this stuff all the time when we go to the beach." Cee Cee shifted her canvas bag onto her shoulder and took the bucket handles. "Did you remember your sunscreen? Oh, and we should take some drinking water with us."

"Got it, Mom," Andi said, patting her bag. "And I packed the few cookies that were left. Man, did we eat that whole box last night?"

Cee Cee giggled. "I'd heard about munchies, but never experienced anything like that. Well, except for when I was pregnant."

The three women tossed towels over their

shoulders and strolled down the path to the beach. "Look, there's someone down there with a dog," Cee Cee said. "I thought this part of the beach was private."

"Guess he didn't get the memo. I'll clue him in." Andi kicked off her sandals and marched, barefoot, through the sand.

Markie and Cee Cee found a spot to lay out their towels and the beach toys. "Maybe one of us should have gone with her," Cee Cee said.

"I think Andi can handle herself. We're right here." Markie removed her beach robe to reveal a brightly-flowered one-piece swimsuit. She lowered onto her towel and began to slather her arms with sunscreen. "You want some?"

"I applied mine before I left the house. Thanks."

Andi returned and flopped down beside them. "He says his name is Nick and he's a friend of Bree's and that she allows him to use the beach. The dog's name is Buster. He seems legitimate—Nick, not the dog. Nick's a writer and summers here because it's quieter than some of the coastal towns, and he can get work done."

"Did you get his phone number?" Markie asked, smirking.

Andi grinned. "Yes, and I used your name."

Markie gave her a shove that sent Andi rolling into the sand.

"You two are incorrigible," Cee Cee said. "I want to be like you when I grow up."

Andi peered over the top of her sunglasses. "Then you better get started." She stood. "Know what I've always wanted to do? Swim naked in the ocean." She peeled down the bottom or her two-piece suit, then slid her fingers under the bra.

"Andi! What if Nick is watching?" Cee Cee asked. She glanced down the beach, but man and dog

47

were walking in the other direction.

Andi grinned. "Then he's in for a treat." She pulled the bra over her head, freeing her full breasts, and raced into the water. Just as quickly, she raced back to her towel, laughing. "Holy shit. That water's cold."

Cee Cee handed her a spare beach towel. "I could have told you that. We bring the kids to the beach almost every weekend."

Andi tugged her suit back on and dried off with the towel.

"You come to the beach every weekend? Where do you live?" Markie asked.

"About two miles from here." Cee Cee twisted the cap from a water bottle and took a drink. "It's sad that this is my version of running away from home. Don't be surprised if Ben and the kids show up because they miss me. Or because he can't find their clothes, shoes, or diapers." Cee Cee would be surprised to learn Ben missed her. He barely seemed to notice she was in the room, unless one of the kids needed something while he was engrossed in one of his favorite TV shows. And when she had won the argument for coming to the retreat, he had picked up the phone and called his mother for back-up with the kids.

Cee Cee lay down and soaked in the warm rays of the sun. She listened to Markie and Andi banter about Andi's love life and Markie's experiences as an artist. Memories flooded back of overheard conversations between her mother and her aunt. Her mother would have loved this retreat. She would have loved these women—even Julia.

Sleep had just begun to drag her under when a now-familiar aroma jerked her fully awake. She sat up and watched as Markie took a hit of a joint, then passed it to Andi. Cee Cee glanced around. "Aren't you afraid of getting caught?"

"By whom? There's no one here but us." Markie took the joint back and passed it to Cee Cee.

Cee Cee dragged in the pungent smoke and held it in her lungs, waiting for the buzz she had felt the night before. "Oh, this is good. I feel so…so light. Free. I can see why people enjoy this. Would you believe I've never smoked pot before?" What would she tell her kids some day when they asked if she had ever used drugs? How would she explain this? If Ben saw her now, he'd be furious.

She had come to this retreat to get space and to put things into perspective. She didn't even expect to be allowed to stay and, yet, here she was, sitting on the beach and getting high with two women her mother's age and who she didn't really know. Yet she felt as if she had known them all her life. Maybe there was something innate in women that, at some level beyond their differences, they recognized themselves in one another.

Markie lay down, and Cee Cee looked over at Andi. "Tell me about Michael," she said.

"I told you all about him last night."

"No. Tell me *about* him. What's he like? Is he sexy?" Cee Cee asked, then giggled, surprised at her own daring.

"Oh, honey. Michael is…" Andi stared out at the ocean. "He's handsome—dark hair, dark eyes, olive skinned. He's so thoughtful. Last week, he showed up with a huge bouquet of flowers for no reason at all. He just thought of me and was passing a florist's shop. Unfortunately, my daughter and my mother are both convinced he's after my money. He couldn't possibly be interested in an old lady like me." Andi opened a bottle of water and took a drink. "When my husband died, I got a huge insurance settlement. But Michael could care less.

He owns a construction company and he loves his work. He's never once asked me for a dime."

"You love him, don't you?" Cee Cee asked. Memories of how she had once felt at the mention of Ben's name sent warmth flooding through her.

Andi pulled in a shuddering breath. "I don't know."

"Yes, you do. You talk about him the way I used to talk about Ben."

"Used to?" Andi asked, facing her.

"Well, you know, eleven years and four kids later, things change. But that's life. That's why I thought this time apart might be a good thing." She sighed. "You shouldn't listen to other people. What you and Michael have is no one else's business. What do a few years matter?"

"So the honeymoon's over?" Andi asked.

Cee Cee nodded and took another hit from the joint, then giggled. "I can't believe I'm doing this. Ben would kill me."

"Think of it as therapy." Markie lifted a hand in the air, searching for the joint.

"Therapy. Yeah, that works," Cee Cee said.

The three of them finished the weed. Then they polished off the remainder of the cookies and emptied the bag of carrot and celery sticks Markie had packed.

"Time to create," Markie said, pushing to her feet. "Come on, kids, I'll show you how it's done."

They took up stations a few feet apart in the sand. Markie instructed them each to get a bucket of water so they could make the sand pliable. "If we build too near the surf, a wave could wash our castles away."

Cee Cee's chest tightened. She knew that fear of having something precious threatened with destruction. Her mother's mind had begun to crumble as if made of dry sand. Her marriage was shifting, and at any moment could fall victim to a tidal wave. She wasn't yet certain what the wave would consist of, but she sometimes thought it would be apathy. Not the overwhelming presence of any one thing, but the absence of that one key ingredient that held a marriage together. She used to believe that was love. But she did love Ben. And he loved her—she had no doubt. So what was missing? Something she had read about in some magazine while she waited for her annual pelvic exam in Dr. Kincaid's waiting room. Emotional intimacy.

"Cee Cee? You're never going to finish if you don't get started," Markie said.

Cee Cee picked up an orange plastic shovel and loaded the bucket with moistened sand. "I'll catch up." It was true, she would. She did it every day.

Each woman set about designing her own creation, stealing glances surreptitiously at one another's work.

"Ta-da!" Andi finished first, scooting back to show the others her castle.

"Ooh, nice. But your tower is…" Markie pointed. The tower on Andi's castle crumbled.

"I was going to say leaning," Markie said.

"Hey, we need judges." Cee Cee jumped to her feet. "I'm going to get Julia and Liv."

"I'm not so sure I want to be judged by Julia," Andi muttered.

"She's all right. I'll be back." Cee Cee carried her flips flops as she ran up to the steps. She dusted the sand from her feet before entering the house. "Liv? Julia? We need you on the beach."

No one answered. A check of the upstairs revealed that no one was at home. Cee Cee danced barefoot across the hot sand. "They're gone."

"Gone?" Markie asked.

"Not gone gone, but not in the house. Must have taken a walk." She sat again in front of her sand creation that oddly resembled her own house. "Why do you think Julia's so prickly?"

"She needs a good screw," Andi said.

Cee Cee stared at her, mouth open.

"What? Well, it worked for me. I was a miserable bitch. Then I started sleeping with Michael. Now I'm a satisfied bitch." Andi grinned.

"Maybe she's been hurt somewhere along the way," Markie said. "Things happen to make people that self-protective."

Andi snorted. "Protective? She would have been a good candidate for Hitler's nanny."

"Maybe Markie's right. We should give Julia a chance. Liv hasn't shared much about herself, either." Cee Cee patted the sand around the base of her castle, dug out a moat with two fingers, then filled it with water. "Done."

She sat back and waited for Markie to finish. When Markie edged back to reveal her creation, both Cee Cee and Andi oooh'd and aaah'd. The castle stood two feet high, with towers, turrets, and a gated courtyard. "That is the most impressive sand castle I've ever seen," Cee Cee said. "It's almost like the one at Disneyworld."

"You're an artist, no doubt about it," Andi added.

"Thank you. Too bad I can't preserve this, but the waves will take her away in a couple of hours."

The women sat in silent reverence, admiring their work. Until Buster raced down the beach, ignoring the shouts of his owner, and plowed through all three sand castles. He yipped and splashed in the waves, then raced back and licked Markie on the cheek.

Markie burst out laughing and hugged the beast.

"An unnatural disaster."

    Cee Cee stared at the woman. Here she was, an artist, and she could so easily let go of that thing she had painstakingly created. Cee Cee had a feeling this was the very reason she needed to be here—to learn to let go. Or, perhaps, to appreciate what she had while she had it.

Chapter Six

Getting to Know You

Liv

Liv struggled to keep up with Julia's long strides. "We're not in a race."

"Sorry, I'm used to rushing around." Julia slowed her pace. *I'm used to running the gauntlet past reporters and angry citizens*, she thought. "So, what brought you to this retreat? You seem normal enough."

"Thanks. I thought we were avoiding personal and significant information." Liv laughed.

"I'm sorry. You're right. Maybe we should just walk in silence."

Liv hesitated, then said, "I've been depressed and anxious, and my therapist recommended taking some time to sort things out. My husband—my ex-husband lost his business and, consequently, we lost everything else. Then we divorced. It's been rough, the past year." She was careful with her choice of words, hoping to keep things vague enough that Julia would conclude the economy was the issue.

"It's been a hard time for a lot of families."

Liv breathed in relief. "I'm doing all right. I have a job and a place to live. My kids are okay, so…."

"My brother had investments and got taken for half a million by an investor. Good thing he and his family had my parents' house to move into. My mother

Ladies In Waiting

passed three years ago, and then my dad went into a nursing home. The house had been empty for a year. Without it, Richard and his family would have been on the street."

Shame rose in Liv once again. Of course, Julia hadn't mentioned Adam, so it didn't mean he was responsible. "I'm so sorry." Would she ever stop feeling the need to apologize?

"Not your fault." They reached Beach Avenue and strolled along the boardwalk. "Want some ice cream? My treat," Julia said.

"Sounds good." Liv enjoyed this side of Julia. Maybe the woman was better at one-to-one conversation and overwhelmed in a group.

With double dip cones in hand, the two women sat on a bench and watched the few swimmers on the public beach. Liv considered telling Julia the truth. She was going to have to come out with it eventually. If she held back now, then shared it later in the group, Julia would probably feel slighted.

"Julia..." She started, then paused. What could she say? My husband may well have been the one who destroyed your brother's life, but please don't hate me?

Julia stared at her expectantly.

"Uh...I don't think I can eat all of this. I should have only gotten one scoop."

"Are you feeling okay?"

"Yes. Are you ready to head back to the house? Perhaps Bree has returned by now." She stood and caught a stream of fudge ripple before it dripped down her hand.

"Okay. If we follow this boardwalk, I think we can walk part of the beach to get to the house."

"Sure." She would hold her story for another time. The truth was like a sword she had swallowed, knifing into her gut. Her therapist had told her that, until she could be honest about what Adam had done and the fact that she knew nothing of his business dealings, she would continue to feel the shame that enveloped her. This retreat with a small group of strangers was to give her practice telling the story. The problem was, she would have to go to the Third World where there were no TV news reporters to find strangers who wouldn't recognize the name Adam Zacharias. The other truth—the one she tried to ignore—was that in some way, she did know something wasn't right, that the money just didn't add up. And because of that truth, she would never be free.

"Here's a path down to the beach." Julia veered off the boardwalk and into the dunes.

Liv followed, stopping to drop the remains of her soggy cone in a trash can and remove her sneakers.

They rounded a point and came up against a slatted wood and wire fence. "Well, now we know why it's a private beach." Julia glanced along the fence line. "Look, there's a weak spot. I'll bet we can climb over."

"Climb over the fence? Julia, isn't that illegal?" Liv asked, grinning.

Julia returned the grin. "I'm living dangerously. Woohoo." She tugged on the sloping slatted boards and they gave way. "I'll hold this down while you go over. My legs are longer, and I can make it over myself."

Liv tossed her shoes across, then stepped over the fence. She watched while Julia swung one leg over, holding down the slats, and then brought the other leg across.

"Trespassers, Buster."

Liv startled at the male voice and the "ruff" of a dog. Julia froze in her tracks.

The man smiled and held fast to the squirming dog's collar.

"We're not trespassing," Julia said. "We're

staying at the...the...."

"Síocháin," Liv said.

"Really? I happen to know Bree is out of town." His grin showed he was teasing. The dog emitted a whine and wriggled.

"Yes, we know. She had a family emergency. We're expecting her back today. Now, if you'll handle that beast until we get down the beach, we'd appreciate it." Julia stomped through the loose sand, staggering and righting herself.

The dog whined and wagged his tail.

"Sorry, Buster." He looked down at the dog. "I have to *handle* you."

Liv stared at the man. Sunburned nose and ruddy cheeks, wind-ruffled black hair salted with grey, wrinkled denim shirt only half-buttoned, khaki walking shorts, and bare feet. And a teasing grin that revealed dimpled cheeks. She cleared her throat. "Are you a friend of Bree's?"

"I am." Still he didn't offer a name. But, then, she hadn't, either.

She studied his features. "Do I know you?" Which she realized after the fact was the wrong question to ask. If she knew him, then he would obviously know who she was.

"I don't think so. If we had met, I would have remembered. Though..." He narrowed his gaze at her. "You do look vaguely familiar."

Liv lowered her head and glanced away. "My name's Liv McKenna."

He shook his head. "Nope, doesn't ring a bell. I'm Nick Belasco."

"The author?"

"Guilty." The dog whined again and tugged against Nick's hold.

"He wants to run," Liv said. So did she.

"Yes, and if I let go, he'll jump on you, then take off after your friend. Buster has practically no social etiquette. He learned everything from me."

Liv smiled. "Then let him go. This could be fun."

As predicted, the instant Buster was turned loose, he raced to Liv, his entire backside wagging. He sniffed her hand before standing to place his oversized paws on her shoulders and slurp her cheek.

She patted the massive head. "I like you, too. Now, go chase Julia."

The dog was off like a shot down the beach.

"Your friend's not afraid of dogs, is she?" Nick asked.

Liv shrugged. "Don't know." She shouted, "Julia, look out."

Julia turned just in time to have Buster hit her full force. When Nick and Liv caught up with them, Buster stood over a prone and sputtering Julia, happily licking her face.

"Get this beast away from me," Julia shouted as she shoved at the dog's head.

Nick called the dog and latched onto his collar. "I'm sorry."

He extended his other hand to help Julia to her feet, but she smacked it away. "I can get up myself. You know, the beach is posted *no pets allowed*."

"Julia's our resident legal consultant," Liv said.

"Buster's not a pet. He's my muse. Besides, this stretch of beach is private, and Bree allows him here."

Liv helped Julia brush the sand from her back. "I'm sorry. I put him up to letting the dog loose. If you could've seen your face, right before Buster took you down."

Julia brushed sand from her hands and the seat of

her pants. "You should at least keep him on a leash. And you…" She glared at Liv. "I can't believe you did this. After I bought you ice cream."

Liv reached out and scratched the dog's ears. "Look at him. He's harmless."

Julia's gaze locked on Nick. "Don't be so sure."

"Um…I was talking about the dog," Liv said.

"I'm going up to the house." Julia wobbled in her attempts to stomp through shifting sand.

Liv could identify. She felt as though she had been walking on a shifting surface for quite a while. She had a brief pang of guilt for setting Julia up like that.

"I met your other friends earlier," Nick said.

"Oh, they're not my friends, either." He raised his eyebrows and she quickly added. "We're all here for a retreat, but we'd not met one another until yesterday."

"What's the retreat topic?"

"It's…uh…" She hated to say a retreat for women over the age of fifty. "Women in transition."

"Transition, huh?" Nick picked up a stick and hurled it toward the water, releasing Buster. The dog raced into the surf, his tongue lolling. "What are you transitioning to?"

His word choice struck her. He had not said "from." "Who knows? Isn't that the nature of transition? We know where we've been, but we're not exactly sure where we're going." She focused on the dog. "What breed is he?"

"Part Labrador and part Australian Shepherd. You're quite the philosopher, Liv."

"Not really." She gazed up at Nick who towered over her five foot five frame. "So Buster is the muse behind all those mysteries?"

"You've read my books?"

"A few. It took me a minute to place you. Your

jacket photo is more groomed. I enjoy a good mystery." Nick dragged his fingers through his shaggy, wind-blown hair. Buster returned and dropped the stick at Nick's feet. Nick picked it up and threw it again. "Would you like to have dinner with me one night this week? We can dispel a few mysteries about one another." Then he grimaced. "That sounds like a terrible pick-up line."

"I…uh… I don't think I can. Bree has a schedule set up for us."

He grinned. "Wouldn't want to mess up Bree's schedule. If she's back."

Liv glanced down the beach toward the house. Julia had already climbed the steps and gone inside. "She's supposed to be back for lunch. I should actually go and check in."

Nick nodded. "If you change your mind, I'm staying in the cottage right back there…" he pointed "…on the other side of the fence. Bree has my phone number."

"Oh, so you trespassed to get over here," Liv said, grinning.

"How do you think the fence got in that shape?" He whistled for the dog. "Nice to meet you, Liv. I hope I'll see you again."

"Nice meeting you, too." She walked down the beach, then turned to watch as Buster leapt over the low-hanging fence and Nick followed.

As she ascended the steps onto the porch, Julia sat in one of rockers, sipping a bottle of water. "How was your date?"

A slow heat crept up Liv's neck. "Do you know who that is? Nick Belasco." She dropped into a chair and stretched out her legs.

"And I should know his name because…?"

"He's one of the most popular police mystery

authors around today. He's been on the New York Times bestseller list for the last fourteen weeks."

"Ah, well, I don't care for mysteries. My work is about untangling them."

Liv nodded. "I am sorry about the dog."

The corners of Julia's mouth twitched. "I should thank you. That was the most thorough kiss I've had in a long time."

Julia was a paradox. Just when Liv thought the woman was okay, her head would spin and she would spew out some sarcastic barb. Then, in the next minute, she would make a joke. It occurred to Liv that this was exactly how the other women might see her. Up and down. Friendly and joking, then secretive and withdrawn. If she was going to try to trust someone with her awful truth, why not these women? After this retreat, she would never see them again anyway.

Maybe tonight after dinner, she thought. "I'm going inside. Thanks for the walk and the ice cream."

In her room, Liv checked her cell phone. No missed calls. No messages. She still clung to the hope that her sons would come around, would forgive her for divorcing Adam. Lauren understood, but she lived in London. The boys had taken their father's side, accusing Liv of abandoning the man when he was at his lowest point. Well, she couldn't argue with that. Adam had hit an all-time low.

Liv knew the exact moment the fissure had appeared—the split that cracked her life into before and after. Most people would have said it was the moment Adam had been arrested. But they would be mistaken. Her life changed on a Thursday night in May four years earlier when truth twisted and burned in her stomach as if she had swallowed a live cobra. Adam had come home, giddy as a teenager, and announced he had bought a new custom-made luxury sailing yacht for only four point six million dollars. "Where are you getting all of this money?" The question had spilled onto her tongue like bile.

She bit back the question. She choked down the bile. And she swallowed the truth. Two weeks later, she and Adam went sailing.

Chapter Seven

The Start

The five women were gathered in the kitchen preparing lunch when the phone rang. Andi picked it up. "Hello?" She covered the phone. "It's Bree. She asked that we go into the office and put her on speaker. One of you get her on that phone, then I'll hang up here."

"Got it," Cee Cee called.

Andi joined them around the desk.

"Hi, ladies. You probably already figured if I'm calling, it's not good news. My brother has to have a second surgery. He's doing well, but they have to repair a badly fractured ankle. My sister-in-law is a mess, and I can't leave here."

"We understand," Markie said.

"I feel terrible because you all spent a lot of money for this retreat time, including travel. I'll reimburse you the registration as soon as I get back. And if you all send me your travel estimates, I'll find a way to reimburse that, as well."

"Bree, this is Julia Lane. You already stocked the house with food. Would it be okay if we stay here for the rest of the time, on our own?"

Andi turned to stare at Julia, as did the others.

"I'd prefer that to a refund, if it's all right with you. I just needed some time away," Julia continued.

Then Liv added, "Me, too. Oh, this is Liv McKenna. I'd like to stay, too."

"So would I," Markie said.

Bree chuckled. "Sounds like all of you are having a great time there. It's fine with me. You can lock up when you leave. I don't know exactly when I'll get back."

"We found your agenda on the desk," Markie said. "Some of us…" She glared at Julia. "…built sandcastles this morning. Maybe we can still do the activities you had planned. I can cover the Tai Chi for those who want to participate."

"Fine by me," Bree said. "I appreciate your flexibility and understanding. Each one of you will receive a gift certificate for another retreat at no cost. Anytime you like."

"Bree, we met your friend, Nick Belasco. At least he *said* he was a friend of yours," Liv said.

"Nick! Oh, yes. He spends several weeks every summer at the cottage down the road. Don't worry, he's a good guy. If anything breaks, call Nick. He can fix it."

"Good to know. We won't hold you up. I'm sure you're eager to get back to your brother. Hope the surgery goes well," Andi said.

"Thanks. Here's my cell number in case you need to reach me."

Cee Cee picked up a pen and jotted the number on a sticky note.

"Bye," the women said in unison.

"Well, let's finish lunch, and we can decide about the rest of the day." Andi picked up the agenda from the desk. "Anyone here hell bent on following a schedule?"

"Not me," Markie replied. The others shook their heads.

"Good." Andi crumpled the paper and tossed it into the wastebasket. "New rule: Every woman is responsible for saying what she wants, what she needs, and for claiming her own space when she needs it. We can each take a turn at preparing breakfast and dinner for the rest of the week. Lunch is on your own after today." She returned to the kitchen to resume tossing a salad. The others followed.

"I'm going back to the beach after lunch," Markie said. "I love lying in the sun and listening to the surf. The water speaks to my soul."

"Mind if I join you?" Julia asked.

"I'd welcome the company," Markie said. "How about you, Andi?"

"I've had enough sun for today. I'm going to curl up with a good book, maybe take a nap."

Cee Cee bit her lip, then said. "I'm going to stop by the house and check on the kids, if that's okay."

"You don't need our permission," Andi said. "Shoot, have your husband bring them to dinner. We could have a cookout."

"I don't think that's a good idea. Besides, I came here to get a break from wiping food off faces. But thanks," Cee Cee said. "I'll be back soon."

"Liv, how about you?" Markie asked.

"Hmmm? Oh, I'm going to stick around the house, too. Thanks."

~ * ~

After the others had left the house and Andi retreated to the screened-in back porch with her novel, Liv climbed the stairs to the third floor. She found the exit onto the widow's walk, hesitated, questioning if it was safe. Deciding there would be a warning sign or the exit would be padlocked if it weren't, she opened the door and stepped outside. She walked to the rail and looked down, swaying slightly from the height. Markie and Julia sat on the beach. Boats, some with billowing sails, dotted the water. She closed her eyes and imagined standing here, waiting for her husband, a ship's captain, to return from sea. On his multi-million dollar yacht. The bubble burst.

Maybe she should have waited for Adam, given him a second chance. Perhaps in time the man she had loved and married would have come back to her. Time being the key. He had been sentenced to ten years. According to his attorneys, he had gotten off easy. The last time Liv had visited Adam in prison, the day she carried the divorce papers for his signature, he looked beaten and defeated. Worn and frayed like an old pair of sneakers. She had filed for divorce after concluding that the man she had loved no longer existed. In his greed, Adam had erased all evidence of that man.

She opened her eyes. All the waiting in the world wouldn't bring Adam Zacharias back. She had to stop waiting. It was time to start living again.

Liv reached the bottom of the stairs when she heard the noise, a strangled sound which she followed to the back porch.

Andi sat, doubled over, her cell phone in her hand. "Dammit, dammit, dammit."

"Andi?" Liv stood beside her and touched her shoulder. "Andi, what's wrong?"

Andi's head shot up, her face blanched with surprise. "Wha…?"

"Is something wrong?"

"Wrong. Oh, something's wrong." She clutched the cell phone as if trying to squeeze the life out of the device. "This is what's wrong. Look!"

Liv stared at the screen bearing the photo of a handsome man and a young redhead, smiling at one another across a café table. "Who's that?"

"That is Michael," Andi growled. "My daughter sent this."

"Oh, your daughter is lovely."

Andi shook her head. "That's not my daughter. That's my replacement."

Liv stared again at the picture, then sat down beside Andi on the chaise. "You mean—that's your Michael?"

"You don't have to sound so surprised. I told you he was younger."

"I'm not surprised. I just...why would your daughter send you this photo?"

"She thinks Michael is too young for me and his interest must be in my money. And for all I know, she could be right. I'm such an idiot."

Liv sat beside her on the chaise. "Shouldn't you hear Michael's side of the story before you pass judgment? This could be perfectly innocent. Maybe it's a business dinner."

"He's in construction. That woman doesn't look like any construction worker I've ever seen."

"Oh, well, she could be a client?" Liv meant to make a statement, but it exited her mouth as a question. She was grasping at straws here.

"Katrina saw them last night at a club. Probably an hour after he told me he loved m-me. He was probably getting dressed to go out while we talked. She couldn't wait to send me the evidence." Andi dragged a hand through her short-cropped hair. "I feel so stupid, like an old fool."

"You are not a fool, and you're certainly not old. You might want to give Michael a chance to explain."

"I already know what he'll say. He'll tell me I'm being paranoid, just like he did the last time."

"The last time? This has happened before?"

Andi sighed. "More than once. I can't help myself. It's not jealousy. I just feel so insecure when I see him with a younger woman, someone closer to his age. And I assume...."

"Ah. Assumptions. They can be deadly. Call him and tell him exactly what happened. Or ask what he did for dinner last night. See what he tells you."

"You're right. I shouldn't jump to conclusions. This is exactly what Katrina wants me to do—get angry and break up with Michael. She and my mother are both convinced he only wants money. It's good to know my own family thinks I'm too old to attract a good looking guy like this. I guess it could be worse."

Liv drew in a deep breath. "Yeah, he could be in jail."

"In jail?" Andi drew back and stared at her.

"My ex-husband is in jail. White collar crime, but still.... It tore our family apart."

Andi blew her nose. "So, you divorced him?"

Liv nodded. "I returned to my maiden name of McKenna, got my first job in over thirty years, and found an affordable apartment. But I've been so ashamed."

"If it was his doing, you have nothing to be ashamed of."

"No, I suppose not."

"Lying, cheating bastards. Why do we want to believe them?" Andi asked.

"Because in our hearts, we want love to be true. Sometimes we don't get what we want."

"I had that once, with my husband. Michael looks at me the way Paul did when we were younger. I wanted that again. Ah, fuck."

"Shit," Liv muttered.

"Godammit," Andi growled.

"Son of a bitch," Liv said.

The two of them sat there, conjuring up as many curse words as possible until they were laughing.

Julia came through the kitchen. "What is going on out here?"

Liv and Andi both looked up. "True confessions," Andi said. "Michael may have cheated on me."

"And my ex-husband is a felon," Liv added.

Julia looked from Liv to Andi. "I need a drink." She turned and went back into the kitchen.

"Bring the bottle," Liv called after her.

"Hey, thanks," Andi said, giving Liv a hug.

"I should thank you. I haven't felt this good in two years. I needed to tell someone the truth." *Even if it was only part of the truth.* Liv handed Andi the phone. "Are you going to call him?"

"Maybe tomorrow. If he is cheating, I don't want to know tonight."

Julia returned with a bottle of wine and three glasses. Markie followed behind with her own glass. Just as they poured the wine, Cee Cee came in through the front door. She stood inside the kitchen and stared at the four of them. "What's going on?"

"Grab a glass and a chair, honey. We're playing truth or dare, but without the dare part," Liv said. *Part of the truth is better than all of a lie. At least it's a start.*

Chapter Eight

Finding a Rhythm

Julia awoke and blinked at the clock on the bedside table. Who the hell was playing music at six-thirty a.m.? She crawled out of bed and looked down at the front lawn where early morning light was just beginning to break. Cee Cee and Liv, still in nightgowns, followed Markie as she made slow, sweeping movements with her arms, stretching out a foot and setting it down softly, turning in one fluid motion. Tai Chi class. Cee Cee glanced up, saw her in the window, and motioned for her to join them.

"Oh, what the hell." She padded out into the hall in her bare feet and crisp cotton pajamas. Before taking the stairs, she walked to the far end of the hall and banged on Andi's door. "Time for Tai Chi on the front lawn." She smiled and waited.

"Go to hell," Andi shouted. "It's too early."

Julia laughed and strode down the hall, feeling better than she had in weeks. If she allowed herself, she just might unwind and have some fun. On the porch, she stretched and breathed in the cool morning air before joining the trio in their slow movements. Her own attempts were forced and jerky as if her joints were cemented together. She remembered how, when she was a child and made faces at her brother, her mother cautioned her face would freeze that way. She wondered now if the same thing could happen to your body when you'd held it stiff and taut for so long.

Markie came to stand beside her. "It's all about rhythm, Julia. One movement flows into the next and then the next. See?"

She demonstrated and Julia watched, knowing she would never be that graceful. Still, she stuck it out for the next half hour.

When they returned to the house, Andi sat at the table with a cup of coffee and glowered at Julia. "I thought we decided this time would be every woman for herself, no agenda?"

"I didn't want you to miss out," Julia said.

"Yeah, right. Who's taking care of breakfast this morning?" Andi asked.

Julia avoided her gaze.

"Come on, Jules. Delight us with some special secret family recipe." Andi refilled her coffee cup and headed for the stairs. "I'm going to take a shower."

"I want to call Ben and check on the kids." Cee Cee disappeared through the living room.

Markie and Liv retreated to the back porch with their coffee.

Julia stood alone and gazed around the kitchen. *Okay, how hard can this be?* She never cooked. Ever. Breakfast consisted of a bagel on the run. Maybe cereal on weekends, but she doubted pouring milk into a bowl counted as cooking. Lunch was usually delivered to the office, if she had time to eat, and dinner ordered for pickup on the way home. If anyone checked the refrigerator and cupboards in her house, they would have thought she had moved out.

She opened the fridge and stared inside. Eggs. How hard can it be to make scrambled eggs? She looked inside the carton to find three white orbs staring back at her. Well, that wouldn't work. Only a half-filled quart of milk, so that ruled out the cereal. "Shoot."

Well, she was nothing if not resourceful. She called to Markie and Liv. "Breakfast will be ready shortly. I just have to pick up a few things." Upstairs, she hastily dressed, then grabbed her purse and car keys. There had to be a place in town to get take-out.

~ * ~

Liv rinsed her coffee cup and set it on the sink for use later. She then went out the front door to retrieve the slippers she had kicked off earlier to join the Tai Chi group. She bent to pick them up and, as she stood, saw Nick approaching. It was too late to run, so she did her best to cover herself beneath the thin nightgown—one slipper across her chest and one held strategically a little lower.

"Good morning." Nick sauntered up the drive carrying a basket.

"Good morning. I was just fetching my slippers."

He grinned. "That's why I have Buster."

"Where is he?"

"I left him at home. I didn't want a repeat of yesterday, in case Julia was around." His eyes slid over her and settled on the slipper at her chest.

She met his gaze and then diverted hers to the basket he carried, hoping he would shift his eyes as well.

He held out the woven basket filled with huge, ripe strawberries. "I over-bought, and I thought you ladies might enjoy some of these."

"They look delicious." In order to accept the offering, she would have to let go of one of the slippers.

Nick seemed amused by her dilemma. "Should I carry these inside for you?"

"No! No one's dressed. I mean, they're dressed but not fit for visitors." Then she looked down at herself. "Kind of like me."

Ladies In Waiting

He strode past her. "I'll just set these on the porch." He placed the berries on the top step and turned. "Have you reconsidered my dinner invitation? I hear Bree won't be back this week. That leaves you without a *schedule*."

"Yes, well…I…uh…" She backed toward the house. "This isn't really a good time." She hurried up the steps, threw her slippers inside, and then snatched up the basket of berries. "Thanks, again."

Liv set the berries on the counter and hustled upstairs to shower and dress.

When she returned to the kitchen, Julia stood over a breakfast buffet spread out on the center island: eggs, bacon, sausage, ham, toast, pancakes, waffles, fresh melon slices, bagels, even a tofu veggie omelet noted for Markie. "Holy cow. What army are we expecting?"

"I got a little of everything. Where did the strawberries come from?"

"Nick brought them. And that was embarrassing. He caught me out on the front lawn in nothing but my nightgown."

Julia grinned. "Did it scare him off?"

"No. He keeps asking me out to dinner."

"You're going, aren't you?" Julia asked.

"Going where?" Andi walked to the sink and rinsed her coffee cup.

"Nick invited Liv out to dinner," Julia said.

"I'm not going. I'm here to relax. I'll call the others before all this food gets cold." She found both Markie and Cee Cee on the back porch. "Breakfast."

"You'll probably want to microwave your plate of food for a minute before you sit down. That's why I set it up here in the kitchen," Julia said.

"Wow, Jules. You went all out," Cee Cee said.

"I went out all right. There's a great family

restaurant in town. We may want to try it for dinner one night. The owner was so nice about preparing all of this fresh for us." Julia poured a cup of coffee. "Well, eat up."

The women moved in a delicate dance around one another as they filled plates, heated the food, and poured drinks before sitting at the dining room table.

Liv stood at the sink beside Julia. "You don't cook, do you?"

"Can't, and that's not an easy word for me to accept. It's my one flaw." She grinned at Liv.

"I would have helped, if you had asked."

"It was my turn to do something. I just..." Julia hesitated. "I want to fit in here. I'm trying to find a rhythm."

Liv patted Julia's back. "You're doing fine." Liv picked up a plate and filled it with food. She listened for a moment to the chatter of the other women in the dining room. Their voices rose and fell and blended in a harmony punctuated by laughter. Liv knew what it felt like to be the outsider, the only one out of tune. She exhaled and smiled as she joined them at the table, thinking of how she was trying to fit in and find her own balance in this group of unique women.

Chapter Nine

A Little Help From My Friends

"I think you should go out with him," Cee Cee said.

"Absolutely. Bree says he's a nice man and can fix anything," Andi added with a wicked grin.

"I don't need to be *fixed*." Heat crept up Liv's neck and into her face.

"Having a hot flash?" Andi asked.

"Perhaps I am." Liv took a long drink of her ice water.

"I think Liv's perfectly capable of making the decision about dinner without our help," Julia said.

"Thank you." Liv had apparently broken through a chip in Julia's façade and found an ally.

"Well, if you won't go out with him, I will." Andi stared at her pointedly.

"Go for it." Liv made the statement without acknowledging the jealousy that rose up in her. She had always hated jealousy. It was unattractive and made generally sane women do crazy things. So it surprised her when she felt a surge at the thought of Julia or Andi going out to dinner with Nick. Especially when Andi already had a handsome, *young* man waiting at home.

"The problem is," Andi said, "he wants to go out with you. What are you afraid of?"

"I'm not afraid." Liv lifted her chin in defiance, feeling like an adolescent.

Andi steadied her gaze on Liv. "Okay, then. Remember when we played that game of truth or dare without the dare part? Well, here's the dare. I dare you to have to dinner with Nick."

"That's ridiculous. I'm not some teenager who's going to take you up on a dare." Liv looked to the others for support, but even Julia waited. Liv's palms dampened and she felt dizzy.

"I read somewhere that menopause is like the second adolescence," Markie said. "Let's do this. Let's agree that we can each be dared to do one thing this week. It has to be something that will move us past a hurdle or force us to do something we have always feared."

Cee Cee and Julia both squirmed in their chairs. But Andi, her gaze still leveled on Liv, said, "You're on."

"Oh, for godsake. You all act like my having dinner with Nick would be such a big deal. Fine. I'll go over there right now and take him up on his invitation." She tossed her napkin onto the table and headed to the front door, but not before stopping to check her hair in the mirror in the powder room.

~ * ~

Andi slipped out of the house and down to the deserted beach. After finding a weather-worn log to sit on, she flipped her cell phone open and stared at the picture of Michael and the redhead. His possible betrayal hurt, but not nearly as much as that of her daughter who couldn't wait to tell her about it.

She gazed out at the waves that lazily rolled onto the sand, and she thought of Paul. Paul Ryan had been the love of her life. From the moment she and Paul met, Andi had never given a second glance to another man. She had loved him so fiercely that, sometimes, she ached. For a while after Paul's death, Andi had wanted to die, too. She had actually waited to die. Then, realizing that wasn't going to happen, she waited to live. The only thing that kept her going was Katrina. Until Michael.

Katrina had graduated from college and was preparing to enroll in graduate school, but after her father died, she put everything on hold. It was as if time stopped for her. Andi understood, but also knew that time had to move again, eventually. She would honor Paul by living the life she was given, and she would drag their daughter back from despair at the same time. But any change Andi made, whether it was furniture, routine, even her hairstyle, Katrina fought stubbornly. Andi had tried to explain that she wasn't forgetting or trying to replace Paul. But the girl had been close to her father and resisted change at every turn. It took Andi a full year to convince Katrina that going on to graduate school would be what Paul wanted for her. That was the only thing that got her daughter moving again.

Things seemed to be returning to normal. Well, a new normal. And then Andi met Michael, and all hell broke loose. Andi fought the urge to call Katrina now and address the ugliness of her actions in sending the picture. How had she captured the picture, anyway? Was she following Michael around, waiting for a photo opportunity?

Andi returned the phone to her pocket and drew up her knees, hugging them to her. She had been so lonely after Paul died, and she had become resigned to spending the rest of her life alone. She had told herself, in the beginning, that Michael was a fling—a purely sexual affair that would burn itself out. But, instead, he had burned himself into her, into every pore, every waking thought and, at night, into her dreams. She couldn't get enough of him, and he seemed to feel the same way. Until now.

A shadow drew her attention.

"Did you want to be alone?" Julia asked.

"No. I'm done being alone. You can sit." She scooted down the log to make room.

"Thanks for not making an issue out of breakfast," Julia said.

"What do you mean?"

"I don't...I can't really cook. I know that seems impossible. I'm fifty-four years old, and I can't prepare a simple meal. I live off of take-out."

"Why would I make an issue of that? This morning, I asked who would be taking care of breakfast. And I have to say, Jules, you took care of it in style." She grinned.

But Julia's expression remained somber. "There's something else. I want to apologize if I've been a little...or a lot...um...stuffy."

Andi snorted. "Stuffy?"

"Okay, arrogant. I can be arrogant. I don't know how to *be* with other women my age. I work in a male-dominated environment. I'm used to having to compete and defend myself."

"That actually makes sense."

"Anyway, I feel I've gotten off on the wrong foot, especially with you, and I wanted to say I'm sorry."

Andi squinted as she turned her face to Julia. "That was hard for you, wasn't it?"

"Very."

"Apology accepted."

"Thank you." Julia's chin quivered.

"You're not going to cry, are you?"

Julia stood. "Not in front of you." She walked down the beach.

Andi saw her lift a hand to her cheek and rub her eyes. She realized she and Julia weren't all that different—hard outer shells, but soft, gooey centers. Just the way Andi liked her chocolates. She and Julia could actually become friends before this retreat ended. She made a promise to back off and give the woman a break. Isn't that what they all needed at one time or another? A break?

She looked up toward the house to see Liv return. Curiosity got the best of her and she stood and wiped sand from the seat of her pants.

"Where's Liv?" she asked when she walked into the living room where all the others had gathered.

"You mean the blushing teenager who rushed upstairs to get ready for the prom?" Markie said.

"That bad, huh?" Andi tugged at her blouse as a surge of heat swept through her. She moved to the center of the room, beneath the ceiling fan, and tilted her head back. "So, what's the plan? Are we going to tease her unmercifully and make her uncomfortable? Or are we going to try to help?"

"I think we should lay off the teasing and help," Cee Cee said. "At one time or another, we all need a little help from our friends."

Andi nodded and smiled. "Friends it is."

Chapter Ten

Trust is Stranger than Fiction

Liv

Liv arranged to meet Nick at his cottage at six. She didn't need an audience for her big date—which it was not. Nick mentioned a restaurant in town within walking distance if she didn't mind walking—which she did not.

She swapped her sneakers for a pair of comfortable flats and dressed in a pair of black slacks and a vertically striped blouse because she had heard vertical stripes were slimming, and her hips needed all the help they could get. Most women who were depressed lost their appetites and, consequently, lost weight. Not Liv. She nurtured her depression and fed it well. She had put on fifteen pounds in the past year, and every one of them showed, at least to her eyes. A glance in the mirror told her she looked like a referee for the Jets. She exchanged the stripes for a soft pastel blue silk, hips be damned.

Satisfied she had done all she could with her appearance, she sucked in a breath and descended the stairs to the waiting group. The women, to their credit, each pretended to be occupied with a book, a magazine, or a fingernail, but all looked up when she entered the living room.

"You look nice, Liv," Cee Cee said.

"Thanks. I'll see you all later, then." She tried to

sound casual, but her voice shook. She hesitated at the door, waiting for someone to make a wisecrack about her date. No one did. They smiled, nodded, and said they hoped she had a nice time. Then each one went back to her distraction of choice.

Liv was surprised to find Nick waiting for her at the bottom of the driveway.

"It seemed ungentlemanly of me to have you walk to my place alone," he said.

She smiled. "Thank you."

They fell into step beside one another. Nick shoved his hands into his pockets. "What convinced you to say yes to my invitation?"

"Uh…" She couldn't tell him it was a dare issued by some of the other women. That would be insulting. "You were right. No schedule or agenda. And I haven't had a chance to see the town. I drove straight here from New York."

"You live in New York?"

"Long Island."

"I live in Manhattan. Small world."

Hopefully not too small, she thought. "How long have you been writing?'

He laughed. "Writing since I was in high school. I got my first publishing contract eight years ago."

"What did you do before that?"

"I was a cop."

"Really? Where?" Oh, God, he would have to know about Adam.

"New Haven, Connecticut. I retired and moved to New York after my first novel sold."

Liv breathed a sigh of relief. "That explains why you can write the police elements in your books so well."

"Thanks. How about you? What do you do on Long Island?"

She gave the same answer she had given the women—worked in a medical practice. No, not a nurse. "I'm the office manager." And she gave herself a small promotion.

"Have you always worked in management?"

She considered this. Truthfully, the answer was yes. She had managed a home, three kids, and Adam's business dinners and parties. That had to count for something. "Yes, I suppose I have."

When they reached the boardwalk, Nick stopped in front of a place called *The Widow's Walk*. "Here we are."

Liv read the sign. "Clever name. I was up on the widow's walk at the house yesterday. Great view from up there."

"I like this place because it's casual, they have good food, and…" He opened the door to reveal a narrow staircase. "…the restaurant is upstairs. So, great views here, too."

He cupped her elbow with his warm palm as she passed him to ascend the stairs. It was the casual kind of touch she missed.

When they reached the top, Nick stepped around her and waved to the hostess. "Do you have a table on the ocean side by the window?"

"We do for you, Nick. Right this way."

Nick held Liv's chair for her. She gazed out the window at the grey-green ocean. "This is spectacular."

"Do you like seafood?"

"I love it. What do you recommend?" she asked.

"Lobster, of course. Though the crab legs are excellent. So are the steaks if you want beef. Everything on the menu here is delicious. I know. I've tried it all. Can't you tell?" He slapped a palm to his abdomen.

No, she couldn't tell. From what she could see,

Nick was in excellent shape for a man his age, which she guessed to be just shy of sixty. "You're hardly overweight," she said.

"Well, I'm not a shadow of my former self, that's for sure. When I was a cop, I had to stay I shape. Now I'm tied to a computer most of the day."

"I hear you. I sit in an office all day long."

The waitress took their orders and then brought their drinks. Nick lifted his glass of wine and Liv followed suit.

"Here's to women in transition," he said, a twinkle in his eye.

Liv smiled and clinked her glass to his. What was she transitioning from and to? Well, she knew the from—a marriage dissolved, a dream gone terribly wrong. What was she transitioning to? A new life? A second chance?

"Liv? What are you thinking? You were gone there."

"I'm sorry." Embarrassment flushed up her neck.

He waited, obviously expecting her to say more.

"I was thinking about transitions. How they are both to and from something."

He steadied his gaze on her. "I know what you mean. When I transitioned from being a cop to being a full-time author, I had to let go of my cop identity and take on a new persona. I didn't stop thinking like a cop. That still serves me well as an author. But I had to find satisfaction and excitement in something new."

"It must have been a big change," Liv said.

"It was. But a good change. I always knew I would write, but thought it would be after I retired. Who knew that first book would take off like it did? Not that I'm complaining." He sipped his wine. "What about you? What are you transitioning from?"

How could she answer? "There was a marriage, a

betrayal, and a divorce. My daughter understands my side. The boys think I was too harsh on their father, so I don't have much of a relationship with them right now. It's sad."

"I'm sorry. An affair?"

Liv pursed her lips and shook her head. "No. He's in prison. Bad business decisions."

"Oh."

Liv stared out the window. Her heart pounded. She needed to trust someone. She turned back to Nick.

"My married name was Zacharias."

She waited for him to react.

"My husband is…was Adam Zacharias. He engineered a Ponzi scheme that cost his clients millions of dollars."

He nodded. "I saw that in the news. It had to be hard for you and your kids."

Nick was being so understanding, she had to fight back tears. "It was awful. I still sometimes think people are staring at me and blaming me for what Adam did."

Nick leaned forward and covered her hand with his. "It wasn't your fault."

"No, logically I know that. But he was my husband, and people are sure I had to have known what was going on. Where did I think all the money came from? Adam worked sixteen, sometimes eighteen hour days, six days a week. Even Sunday golf games centered on business. I thought he was successful and earning the money."

Nick turned her hand over and traced his thumb across her palm. The action would have, at one time, turned her to jelly. Now it warmed her inside—this simple, gentle touch.

"To be honest, your face looked familiar to me that day on the beach. But your hair is different. And when you said your name was McKenna, I figured I was wrong."

"And now you know." She withdrew her hand and settled it in her lap.

"I know you are a lovely woman. You're attractive and interesting and funny."

A blush warmed her face. "I'm not always all that funny."

Nick laughed. "And there it is. Liv, you need to let yourself off the hook. Adam is paying for his crimes. You've moved on and so will the public. They probably already have."

"I know several who have. You'd be surprised how something like this shows you who your friends are. And who they aren't."

"Like the women on this retreat?"

She smiled. "Like those women. Of course, they don't know any of this. They know I'm divorced and my husband is in jail, but I haven't had a chance to tell them the whole story yet."

"Haven't had a chance, or you're afraid of how they'll react?"

"There is that, too."

"And yet you told me." He sat back and gazed at her. "You know what I've learned along the way? Fear over what other people think is a lot like fear of the dark. You're terrified, paralyzed by it. Then you turn on the light and, wham, you find there's nothing there to fear. No bogeyman jumps out of the closet or grabs your ankles from beneath the bed. You just have to trust yourself enough to turn on the light."

"Trust myself? I seem to be the only one I can trust."

He nodded. "When I was a police detective, I interviewed a lot of alleged criminals. I had to sort out truth from lies. The ones who were, for the most part, being truthful were the ones who became anxious, flustered. The guilty ones were cool and calm. They looked me in the eyes. The opposite of how you'd think it would be. Of course, I did encounter the occasional psychopath. I'm fairly sure that doesn't apply to you."

The waitress served their dinners and refilled their drinks.

Liv regarded him for a moment. "Nick, thank you. I needed to tell someone the whole story, and you made it easy. I am anxious and flustered most of the time. I guess it's guilt by association."

"You still have an appetite, or did our conversation kill it?"

She looked at the lobster on her plate. "Oh, I have an appetite." She was amazed she did. Usually talking about Adam and her family made her feel sick inside. But not this time. This time telling the truth had set her free.

After dinner, Nick bought them gelato on the boardwalk and they walked slowly back to the retreat house. For this one evening, Liv felt normal, just a woman having dinner and a nice evening out with a man. She exhaled and gave way to a smile.

Chapter Eleven

When the Bubble Bursts

Liv—1982

"You've done well for yourself, Liv. Adam has proven to be quite a catch." Liv's best friend Caroline sipped champagne.

"He works so hard. I barely ever see him." Liv took a drink of the ginger ale in her glass.

Caroline laughed. "Well, you've seen him at least once in the last seven months." She nodded at Liv's expansive middle. "Maybe he'll have more time once the new company is up and running."

"Maybe. And what are you talking about, anyway? You snagged the best looking doctor on Long Island."

Her friend sighed. "Yeah, I did. By the time we pay off his loans for medical school, it'll be too late for me to have a baby, though. I talked to John about investing with Adam but he says we have to have something to invest first. Adam sure is good at what he does, though."

"My mother finally stopped complaining about me marrying 'an accountant.' She could not grasp the difference between that and an investor. The new BMW we gave her for her birthday seemed to change her tune. She's even dropped the disgusted look when she reminds me Adam is ten years my senior."

"A gift like that would make me sing an aria from *Madame Butterfly.*"

Liv sighed. "I worry about Aaron, though. He hardly ever sees his father. And now we have another one coming along. I always thought…."

Caroline looked at her, eyebrows knitted together. "Is something wrong?"

"No, not wrong. Just not quite right. I didn't expect to be a stay-at-home mother whose husband worked sixty-hour weeks. That's all." She set the empty glass on a nearby table. "Excuse me. Bathroom break."

In the bathroom, Liv looked into the mirror, into her own eyes. Things had happened so fast—her pregnancies, Adam's success, the new cars, new house. The new friends—people Liv didn't know. People who made her feel a little uncomfortable with their pretentious lifestyles and better-than-others attitudes. Liv was one of the 'others.' At least until she had married Adam. No point wondering about *what ifs* now. Maybe Caroline was right—things would settle now that Adam had everything he had worked for all those late nights—success and wealth. He just wanted the best for her and the children and she had no right to criticize the way he provided for them.

~ * ~

1991

"Where are you? I need you here," Liv hissed into the phone between contractions.

"I told you, I can't get home. I'm in Atlanta. How did I know this baby would come a week early? Besides, you have your mother there with you. It's not like you haven't given birth before. Twice."

Liv bit her lip as another contraction rolled through her.

"Liv, we have to get you ready for delivery. You'll have to get off the phone now," the nurse said.

Her mother took the phone. "Adam, your child is coming into this world. Wherever you are, I hope it's worth missing this." She ended the call, then clutched Liv's hand. "It's his loss. Don't worry about that now. Just focus on having this precious baby."

When at last the doctor placed a wailing little girl into her arms, Liv wept openly. The tears were a mixture of joy and sadness. Joy that she had this beautiful little girl after having two sons. Sadness for Adam that he'd missed his daughter's arrival. Sadness that making money was more important to him than his daughter's birth.

Later that evening, Adam appeared in the doorway to her hospital room, a huge bouquet of yellow roses in hand, along with a wrapped gift. "I'm sorry. What else can I say? She was early."

Liv stared at him, setting aside the gift he had handed to her. "You are honestly going to blame your daughter for you missing her birth?"

He laid the bouquet on the foot of the bed and sat on the edge, smiling. "We have our little girl." He leaned forward and kissed Liv on the cheek. Just like that, any argument ended. Liv's feelings had been ignored, as always. "Open the box."

"I don't want this, Adam. I don't want the jewelry and the cars and the big house. I just want you to be a part of our lives."

His face darkened. "I am a part of your lives. You and I created our three children together, as I recall. I work hard to give you the best—a gorgeous home in a great neighborhood. The best private school. Travel to anywhere in the world. Jesus, Liv, what more do you...."

He was cut off by the opening of the door and a nurse entering carrying Lauren, who whimpered. "Time for someone's dinner." The nurse handed the red-faced infant to Liv and left the room.

Liv opened her gown and the baby immediately latched onto her breast to nurse. Adam sat again, tracing a fingertip along the baby's cheek. "She's so beautiful. Thank you."

"She is. She has your chin, I think." Liv stared down at their daughter.

"She also seems to have my appetite. Speaking of which, I came here straight from the airport and haven't eaten. Do you mind if I grab a bite and come back?"

Liv shook her head, never taking her eyes away from her daughter. "Go."

While she had to admit that she enjoyed the luxuries Adam's success afforded her, her life was in her children. She vowed to do everything in her power to give them balance as they grew up. She had seen too many of their friends' children grow up to be spoiled brats who believed they were deserving of everything and had to work for nothing. That wasn't how Liv had been raised and it would not be how her children would behave.

After the baby finished nursing and slept in her arms, Liv picked up the wrapped package and opened it. Another diamond tennis bracelet. Bigger diamonds, but not much different from the last one Adam had given her. This had become her life—bigger and, supposedly, better with her husband's growing success. She wasn't certain about the "better" part, but she had been conditioned not to question. Adam would look hurt, then rage at her about how ungrateful she was. From the generous allowance he gave her every month, she managed to give something back through donations to the women's shelter, the homeless shelter and soup kitchen, even a scholarship fund at the private school Aaron and Nathan attended.

These offerings assuaged her guilt and, in some way, she believed, redeemed both herself and Adam.

~ * ~

2010

"Here we go again, folks. Another financial mogul arrested for an alleged intricate Ponzi scheme that bilked his clients out of millions, leaving them in financial ruin. This time, police have taken well-known New York investor, Adam Zacharias into custody following a lengthy investigation. Our own Mike Branson is on his way to Central Park West where federal agents are reportedly about to serve a search warrant to Zacharias' wife to search their apartment. We'll interrupt local programming and update you as the story unfolds."

Liv watched the screen in horror as detectives led Adam from his office in handcuffs. He looked much older than his fifty-nine years. She turned off the TV and froze when the knock sounded on the door of the penthouse.

A second louder knock jolted her into action. Their maid stared from Liv to the door and back to Liv. "Shall I answer?"

Liv nodded, then waited.

Two men in suits accompanied by uniformed police officers entered the apartment. One stepped forward. "I'm Agent Carlson with the FBI. You are Olivia Zacharias?"

Liv nodded again, unable to speak.

"This is a warrant for search and seizure in this residence. Is there anyone else here?"

Liv shook her head. "It's just me and Selena, our maid."

"Are there any explosives or weapons in the apartment?"

"Explosives? Of course not."

"Any weapons, ma'am?"

"None that I know of." She began to tremble violently.

"Is there a safe?"

"Yes, in Adam's den. He uses that room as a home office."

"Do you know the combination?"

"Yes. It's...."

"I'll need to ask you to open the safe for us, then you'll both have to leave. You can wait outside with Officer Denton." He nodded toward a female officer in a blue uniform.

"Of course."

After shakily punching in the combination and opening Adam's safe, Liv returned to the foyer where the young officer waited. Officer Denton escorted Liv and Selena out into the hallway between the apartment and the elevator. Liv rested her forehead against the marble post, letting its surface cool her. Her mind whirled. Should she have resisted admitting them? Should she have called their attorney first? Well, Hal was probably busy with Adam.

Liv turned to the policewoman. "Do you think they would give Selena her purse and coat so she can leave?"

"I'm sorry, but neither of you can leave just yet. You can't remove anything from the apartment until they've finished." Her expression softened. "I'll ask if they'll bring a few chairs out here for you. Do you need a glass of water?"

"Thank you. I am feeling a little weak."

The officer spoke to someone inside and, a minute later, two of the dining room chairs appeared followed by two glasses of water. Liv sat and the young officer handed her one of the glasses.

"Thank you," Liv said.

"You're welcome." The police woman resumed her position, standing between Liv and the door to the apartment.

"Excuse me," Liv said.

The policewoman turned. "Yes?"

"I...I've never been arrested before. Is there someone I should call?"

"You're not being arrested. They just have to search the apartment. But is there someone you'd like to call?"

Liv thought for a moment. Her first instinct was to call Adam, but that was obviously out of the question. Lauren was in London with friends. Aaron—she should call her eldest son. "Yes, I'd like to call my son."

"Do you have a cell phone?"

"It's on the kitchen counter."

Again the police woman went to the door and returned quickly. "They have to hold onto your phone. Here...." She removed a cell phone from her pocket. "You can use mine."

Liv stared at the phone. "That's okay. I don't remember the phone number. I'll make the call later." She shivered, feeling more alone than she had ever felt. This could not be happening. What had Adam done? What had he done to them?

The elevator door opened and two more men in suits emerged carrying armloads of boxes. In a matter of minutes they carried filled boxes out of the apartment and back to the elevator. Agent Carlson advised her not to attempt to leave the state and that she would, no doubt, be called in for an interview. When the agent and police left and Liv was free to return to her home, she stepped inside and immediately burst into tears.

Drawers had been emptied onto the floor. Furniture cushions were turned over. Books had been removed from shelves and tossed into a pile. The place looked as if it had been ransacked by thieves.

Selena wiped at her own eyes and waited for instructions.

"You might as well go home, Selena. I'll call Aaron and go to his place this evening."

"No. We will clean this mess up together." Selena began to replace the cushions on the white brocade sofa.

Liv shook her head. "We can't clean up this mess." The words held deeper meaning than Selena would understand. "Just go home. I'll call you. Don't worry, you'll still get paid." And Liv hoped she would be able to keep that promise.

She stood alone in the middle of the disaster area that had been the master bedroom and punched Aaron's number into her phone. His phone rang several times, then her call went to voicemail. After two attempts, she called Nathan.

"Mom, are you okay? I tried to call you," he said.

"Oh, Nathan." And she broke down.

"I'll be right over."

Liv poured a glass of brandy, uprighted a chair and waited.

"Jesus, what the hell did they do in here?" Nathan waded through the rubble.

Liv looked up at him. "Where is your brother?"

"They took him in for questioning because he worked closely with Dad. I expect they'll call me to come in, too."

Staring across the room to the window and the fading light, Liv asked, "Is it true?"

Her son hesitated, then said, "I don't know."

In the weeks that followed, Adam was formally

charged with securities fraud, investment adviser fraud, and money laundering. More charges were pending further investigation, but these were enough to put him behind bars for a long time. He had managed to keep both Aaron and Nathan out of jail by taking full responsibility. But the shadow had already been cast on both of them and on Liv. She was grateful that Lauren would be in London for the next seven weeks.

Liv made several attempts to visit Adam in jail. He refused to talk with her. When he appeared in court, he never glanced her way. Caroline tried to comfort her by suggesting it was Adam's way of protecting her. Pushing her even farther away did not feel like protection. It felt like rejection.

When Liv signed the divorce papers a year later, after Adam's conviction, the sadness and fear gave way to a measure of relief. She had lost just about everything—her husband, her home, financial security, her dignity, and her sons. Caroline had talked her husband into giving Liv a job in his medical practice on Long Island. Aaron and Nathan had turned on her when she filed for divorce, accusing her of abandoning their father. What hurt the most was that Adam had apparently taken a vow of silence in the matter and let her take their punishment. Only Lauren stood by her.

A few months after the divorce, Liv knew it was time to look forward. She picked up the magazine, studying the advertisement. This retreat would be her next step—*Embracing the New You: Reinventing Yourself After Fifty*. Then the irony made her smile—a *retreat* in order to move forward. She had to back up, perhaps to get a running start.

Chapter Twelve

Girls Gone Wild

Andi closed her book and sighed. "What are *we* going to do this evening?"

Markie peered at her over a pair of reading glasses. "What would you like to do?"

"I don't know. Have some fun. It's way too quiet here."

"It's a retreat," Markie replied with a smile.

"We could go out for drinks and dinner," Cee Cee suggested. "I know a place outside of town that I've always wanted to try. It's kind of plain, though."

"You mean like a diner?" Markie asked.

"No. More like a biker bar. It's called *The G Spot*."

Julie glanced up from the newspaper, eyebrows raised.

"Now that sounds like my kind of place." Andi leaped to her feet. "And we don't even have to dress. Well, except for you, Jules. You could probably dress down a little."

Cee Cee stood. "Come on, Julia. It'll be fun. I'll even drive my soccer mom van."

"I'm in," Markie said. "Julia?"

"Oh, all right. I have to eat, and we've already established that I can't cook." Julia folded the newspaper and set it on the coffee table.

"You want to change into jeans?" Andi asked.

"We'll wait."

Julia glanced down at her beige linen slacks. "What's wrong with these?"

"They scream *stuffy rich white lady from Philadelphia*," Andi said.

"I am not rich. And I don't own a pair of jeans. This is me—take it or leave it." Julia stood with her hands on her hips.

"Okay, but don't complain to me when somebody sloshes beer all over your two-hundred-dollar pants," Andi grumbled.

"They were only one-thirty-nine. And if you're going to abuse me all evening, I'll just stay home." But Julia was already settling the strap of her leather shoulder bag onto her shoulder.

Cee Cee held up a hand. "Here's what I tell the kids—Don't make me call a sitter. Now, we call a truce and play nice or we don't go at all."

Both Andi and Julia stared at Cee Cee then laughed. "Yes, Mother," Andi said.

Twenty-five minutes later, they pulled into the parking lot of a clapboard building topped by a flashing red sign announcing *The G Spot.* Motorcycles lined the side of the building. Cee Cee headed toward the back of the lot and managed to squeeze the van into a narrow space between a pick-up truck and the dumpster.

"Are you sure this place is safe?" Julia asked.

Cee Cee shrugged. "I've never heard of a murder taking place. I suppose it's safe."

"Great," Julia muttered as she slid more than stepped out of the van.

Andi hopped down and looped an arm through Julia's. "Don't worry Jules. If trouble breaks out, I'm sure you can handle it. After all, you're 'an officer of the court.' You can at least provide enough of a distraction for the rest of us to get to the van."

Cee Cee sent Andi a warning glance. "What did I tell you?"

Andi stopped and hung her head. "Sorry." Then she grinned and resumed walking. "Let's go in there and raise some hell. I want to dance."

"Oh, good lord." Julia paused and waited for Markie. "You okay?"

"My leg fell asleep in the van. I'm fine."

"A little dancing will loosen that right up." Andi opened the door to admit the other women. A smoky cloud wafted out the door.

Julia waved a hand in front of her face. "I thought smoking was illegal inside bars and restaurants."

The cloud was followed by a tidal wave of bass and drums.

"It's just a fog machine," Cee Cee shouted. "There's a live band on stage. Isn't that great?"

"Whoopee," Julia said.

Their entrance drew stares from the much younger crowd at the bar.

"You ladies lost?" A young man in leather, a blue bandanna around his forehead, stepped in front of them. He towered over Andi, Cee Cee, and Markie.

But Julia stepped forward and glared down at him. "Why would you assume that?"

He returned her stare. "You don't look like the *G Spot* type, that's all."

"Really? I'll have you know we ladies knew about the G Spot long before you were even a consideration. Excuse me." She brushed past him and signaled for the others to follow. "There appears to be a free table back in that corner."

Once they had pushed aside the empty beer bottles and arranged their chairs around the table, Andi applauded Julia. "You must really be something in a courtroom. Hat's off to you, Jules."

Cee Cee laughed. "Did you see the look on his face? You left him speechless, Julia."

"I doubt that. He probably just came to the end of his vocabulary and had nothing more to contribute." Julia grabbed a wad of napkins from the holder and sopped up the wet rings on the table top. "This is disgusting. Do you see a waitress?"

Andi slipped away to the restroom and pulled her phone from her purse. No call from Michael. When she returned from the ladies room, the band launched into Springsteen's *Hungry Heart*. It was as if a tornado whipped through the bar and tossed Andi back thirty-plus years.

~ * ~

Everybody's Got A Hungry Heart

Andi—1981

"Andi, come on. Shore traffic's a nightmare and we want to get to Wildwood before midnight."

Andi leaned out her bedroom window to see where Jen waited beside her new cherry red Camaro. "I'm coming. One minute." She stuffed the spare bikinis into her bag and zipped it shut. She grinned, remembering the last trip down the shore when she ended up short on underwear and never did find that lost pair.

At the base of the stairs, she dropped her bag and headed to the kitchen, "Ma, I'm leaving. I'll be back on Sunday."

Her mother hugged her. "You girls be careful. And don't do anything...." Then her mother frowned. "Ah, hell. What's the use? You're past twenty-one. Do what you're gonna do, but be careful."

Andi grinned. "I will, Ma." She snagged her bag on the way to the door and hurried to the car where her two best friends waited.

After stowing her bag in the trunk that Jen slammed shut, Andi opened the front passenger door to find Kath already seated there. "Hey, I always get the front seat. You know I get car sick."

"I left a plastic bag back there for you. Puke away. I'm tired of sitting in the back and missing half the conversation."

Andi closed the door and slid into the back seat. "I hope I projectile puke on the back of your head." But she couldn't stifle the grin that tugged at her lips. They all knew her car sick claims were bogus. She just liked to ride up front. "Okay, Jen, put the pedal to the metal. We're late and I'm not getting any younger here."

Both women turned and glared at her, and she laughed. She was always late and they both knew to expect it. Andi knew they always told her to be ready half an hour earlier than they really wanted to leave. It was a game the three best friends had played since junior high school. They forgave one another's faults.

"Good thing it's your birthday weekend," Jen muttered as she worked the car into traffic.

"Yeah, imagine. Twenty-two and still single. I gotta do something about that soon." Andi settled back into the leather seat.

Traffic inched along for the next half hour. Springsteen blared from the cassette player. Impatiently, Jen made a quick right and headed inland. "I'm going to find a way around this. The whole weekend is slipping away while we drive behind these tourists."

Sliding across the back seat, Andi grabbed at one of the front headrests. "Easy on the turns. Or do you want me throw up on your upholstery?"

Ladies In Waiting

"Sorry, I just have no patience for this traffic. I'll cut back toward the shore at Mays Landing." Jen gunned the engine and made a left, heading south once again.

Andi leaned forward between the split seats of the Camaro. "Hey, did I tell you guys I have an interview at the middle school in Beachwood? Seventh grade."

Kath turned in her seat. "I fail to understand why you want to teach. Spending the entire day in a classroom taming other people's kids—I don't get it."

"It sure beats spending the day with my hands in someone else's mouth cleaning their teeth. That's just gross."

Kath grinned. "I don't plan to spend my life as a dental assistant. You should see the new dentist Dr. Mills hired to replace old Doc Bailey. Paul. He's fresh out of dental school and has the most gorgeous blue eyes..."

Andi never heard the rest of the comment. Everything exploded around her and then the world went black.

~ * ~

Andi wandered from one of the viewing parlors at Moretti's Funeral Home across the hall to the next parlor. She winced as the crutches dug into her armpits. People from both grieving families mingled in every available space. Andi spotted her mother sitting with Kath's mom, an arm around her shoulders while she sobbed. None of this seemed real. Anxiety gripped her as breathing seemed impossible.

A hand grasped her elbow. "Are you okay?"

She looked up into clear blue eyes. *The most gorgeous blue eyes....* "I have to get out of here," she croaked.

"No problem. Let me run interference." He walked in front of her and excused their way through the crowd.

When at last they stepped outside onto the porch, Andi leaned against him and drew in a deep breath.

"Thank you."

"You must be Andi."

"You mean, *the one that survived*?"

"Kath's other best friend. You and Jen were all she talked about, how you all were going to celebrate your birthday in Wildwood."

Andi nodded, gulping down the horror she felt.

"I'm sorry for your loss."

She looked up at him. "Who are you?"

"I'm sorry. Paul Ryan. I worked with Kath for a short time."

"She mentioned you just before…."

The door swung open and Andi's mother came out onto the porch, dabbing at her eyes. "Oh, there you are. We should go. You need to rest your leg, tomorrow will be a long day."

Andi couldn't imagine tomorrow being any worse than today had been. She had faced the families of her two best friends as the only survivor of the accident. She has listened to the story being told over and over—a car full of college kids, drinking, in a hurry to get to the beach. If she had been in the front seat, she would have been dead. And Kath would be here now, living through this hell instead.

"Let me help you to your car," Paul said.

"We walked. It's just a block. You could help me down the steps though. I'm not very good on these." She nodded down at the crutches.

"I can do that." He took the crutches and handed them to her mother, then lifted Andi into his arms as if she were feather-light. "Hold on."

She did as she was told, looping an arm around his neck. He was deceivingly strong for his thin build.

Easing her to her feet at the bottom of the steps, he waited until she had the crutches in place again. "I could drive you both home."

Her mother shook her head. "She's not ready to get into a car again. But thank you."

He gazed back at Andi. "Will I see you at the funeral?"

Andi nodded. "I'll be there."

~ * ~

1983

Andi steadied herself as her Uncle Tony looped his arm through hers. "You ready for this? Not too late to change your mind."

She grinned. "I'm ready, Uncle Tony."

"You know, if he don't treat you right, he'll have me to deal with. Same as if your father was here."

A lump formed in Andi's throat. Her father wasn't here. He wouldn't walk her down the aisle or caution his son-in-law about taking care of her or see his grandchildren. But his younger brother had stepped in the day after he died and had been there for Andi and her mother for the past four years. "Paul's a good man, Uncle Tony. Now let's get down the aisle before he thinks I changed my mind." She looked up and locked eyes with Paul.

After the funerals of her two best friends, Paul had become her rock. It was only a matter of months before they spent all their time together, and then he proposed. They worked through her issues of surviving the accident and then moving on and being happy. Paul even went to two therapy sessions with her. He adored her, and Andi knew it. She loved him with every beat of her heart and she hoped he knew it.

When Paul took her hand and smiled, everything

faded away and it was just the two of them.

In the following year, Paul shared her grief over two miscarriages. She worked and cut corners with their household budget to help him open his own dental practice. When she became pregnant a third time after being told it probably wouldn't ever happen, he insisted she stop working and stay home.

Andi thought Paul would explode with joy when their daughter was born. They agreed on the name Katrina Jennifer as a way of remembering her best friends Kath and Jen. When Kat was six months old, Andi returned to her teaching position. She and Paul settled into what appeared to be the perfect family life with their new daughter. At least by her standards. They worked together for their family. Occasional arguments were easily resolved.

Kat entered her teen years and Andi soon realized she could neither do nor say anything with which her daughter would agree. Kat was Daddy's girl and this became a source of tension between Andi and Paul. She was actually jealous of her daughter's relationship with Paul.

Then in 2010, after twenty-seven years of marriage, Andi found herself alone. It had been a warm spring Saturday morning. Paul left at 7:30 a.m. for his run. He had kissed her cheek and said he'd be home in an hour and would then take her out to breakfast. When he hadn't returned by 9:15, she tried his cell phone. The call went to voicemail. Irritated that he didn't consider she might be hungry, she toasted a bagel and ate half.

When the doorbell rang at a little past ten and she opened it to find a police officer, she knew. Time blurred the following weeks—the funeral, the meeting with their attorney, Kat's anger directed solely toward her. A widow at fifty. Wasn't fifty a turning point? A time for self-examination and change—positive change for women? Andi wanted to rewind the past few weeks, to go back and stop action. She should have grabbed Paul's hand when he climbed out of bed for his run, pulled him to her and made love. She should have insisted he forego the run and take her out to breakfast. She should have stopped him, then maybe he would be alive. Or perhaps he would have collapsed in their bed after sex or slumped over at the Waffle House.

If one more person had told her it was God's will, she would have screamed. She would cheerfully strangle them. Perhaps it would prevent her from lashing back at Kat. The hurt and loss in her daughter's eyes killed Andi and there was still nothing she could do or say right. If anything, Paul's death drove a wider wedge between them at a time when they needed one another the most.

Most days, Andi stayed at school as late she possibly could. The house was too empty, too quiet. The bed too big. She moved into Kat's former bedroom, something her daughter made issue of when she came home for an infrequent and obligatory visit at Christmas. Andi found her daughter asleep on the loveseat in Paul's den the next morning. Right after Christmas, she called contractors to expand the den into a downstairs bedroom. She hired Michael DiGiorno.

"Hey, Andi?"

Andi blinked at the faces of Julia, Markie and Cee Cee. "What?"

"You phased out on us for a few. Where were you?" Cee Cee asked.

Forcing a half-hearted smile, Andi said, "Love that song—*Hungry Heart*. The Boss always takes me back." She stood and picked up her glass. "Anyone need a refill?"

Thirteen

Markie

Markie sat on the edge of her bed and stretched. Pins and needles prickled down her arms and into her hands. When she stood, her left leg wobbled. She sat down again and then rose a second time, waiting to gain balance before she took a step. It was her turn to prepare breakfast. She carefully descended the steps, keeping a grip on the hand rail.

After starting the coffeemaker, she removed a carton of eggs from the fridge. Then she decided to experiment, put the eggs back and withdrew two packages of firm tofu. She cut up peppers, onions, and tomatoes. The tingling in her hands forced her to use extra care. She could easily lose her grip on the knife. She could easily lose her grip on a lot of things.

Cee Cee was the first to join her. "Smells wonderful in here. Can I do anything to help?"

"Toast the bagels?"

"Sure. Have you seen Liv this morning?"

Markie shook her head. "You're the first person I've seen this morning. Do we know for sure she came in last night?"

Cee Cee gasped. "You don't think she spent the night with Nick, do you?"

"Would that be so terrible? She's a grown woman, after all. And single." Markie stirred the concoction in the skillet.

"Maybe I'm a little jealous." Cee Cee sighed.

"You? You have a husband at home. What do you have to be jealous about?"

When Cee Cee didn't respond, Markie turned to look at her.

Cee Cee stared at the toaster.

"Hey, did I say something wrong?"

"No." Cee Cee shook her head. "Nothing wrong."

Liv entered from the back porch. "Good morning."

Markie nodded. "Good morning."

"I was walking on the beach," Liv said. "I got up early for Tai Chi, but no one else was up."

"I'm sorry. I should have left a note for you that we weren't meeting this morning," Markie said. "We had a late night."

Andi dragged into the kitchen, but smiled when she saw Liv. "Well, well. Look who's back from her date. Come on, spill. We want to hear all about it." She proceeded to the fridge, opened the freezer and leaned forward.

"Oh, no. I'm sure Bree left something on the agenda for this morning," Liv said. "And, for the record, I'm not just back from my date…er…dinner."

Markie dished up breakfast, handing a filled plate to each woman. "Here you go. Enjoy."

They were all seated when Julia joined them. She eyed the plate suspiciously, then lifted a fork full of what everyone assumed to be scrambled eggs. "What is this?"

"Breakfast," Markie said.

One by one, the women forked up the concoction and stared at it. "These aren't eggs," Andi said.

"It's scrambled tofu with veggies. Taste it. You just might like it," Markie said. "And the soy could help with your hot flashes."

"I'd rather melt." Andi dropped her fork with a

loud thunk on the plate. "Pass the bagels, please."

Liv took a tentative bite. "Mmmm, this isn't half bad."

Markie laughed. "Thanks, I think."

Cee Cee was next. "A little softer than scrambled eggs, but tasty. I'll bet my kids would eat this if I didn't tell them what it was."

Julia continued to stare at her fork.

"Come on, Jules. It's not poison," Markie said.

"Fine, I'll try it." Julia removed a tiny bit of tofu from her fork with her teeth and shuddered. "There, I tried it." She set down her fork and reached for the bagels.

Markie bit her lip to hold back the tears—another side effect of her episodes—difficulty controlling emotions. She pushed up from the table and, as she turned, rolled on her ankle, going down hard.

"Oh, my god." Liv knelt beside her. "Don't move."

Markie groaned. "I'm okay. Just give me a minute." She caught her breath, then slowly sat up. "See, I'm fine. Nothing hurt but my pride." She rubbed her twisted ankle.

"You sure? That was a bad spill," Liv said.

"Just give me a hand up."

Liv took one of Markie's hands and Cee Cee took the other. Markie stood and gripped the back of a chair, working her foot to ensure the ankle was okay. "Thank you. I'm just clumsy sometimes. I'm sorry about breakfast."

"No, I'm sorry," Andi said. "I was rude. I should be grateful you prepared something."

Cee Cee hugged Markie. "The tofu is fine. Come on, sit down."

Markie accepted the glass of water Liv offered.

But her hand shook, and she set the glass down again before anyone else could notice. "Please, finish your meal. I'm fine." When they were all seated again, she said, "Okay, Liv. Tell us about your date."

Liv nodded as if she recognized the plea Markie conveyed that the attention be redirected from her. "We had dinner at a great restaurant in town. It's called *The Widow's Walk*, and it overlooks the water. Nick is an interesting man. He used to be a cop, which explains the credibility in his books." She frowned. "You all must have turned in early. I was home by nine-thirty, and the house was already dark."

Andi and Markie exchanged glances.

Cee Cee burst out laughing. "We went to a bar in Wildwood. We didn't get home until one-fifteen. We were speculating that you had stayed with Nick all night."

Liv's mouth dropped open. "I barely know him. And I can't believe you went without me. Or that I didn't hear you all come in." She glanced at Julia. "You went, too?"

Julia pursed her lips. "Why is that so surprising?"

Andi grinned. "Yeah, Julia even got hit on—by a younger man. Of all people, he picks Jules."

Julia blushed. "He was not hitting on me. He simply asked if he could buy me a drink. Which I, of course, refused."

"Of course," Andi said. "Wouldn't want to sully that straight-as-an-arrow reputation of yours. Even though having a drink with a younger man is not against the law."

Julia's color deepened and she met Markie's gaze. Then she turned back to Andi. "Look, just because your boyfriend decided to play with someone his own age, don't take it out on me. Maybe if you grew up, you'd attract a man with some maturity."

Andi got to her feet, leaning forward and bracing her hands on the table. "What did you say?" The air crackled with tension.

Julia mimicked the stance from the opposite side. "I said perhaps if you ceased such adolescent behavior as getting drunk and dancing on a table, you might find that others look at you with some measure of respect and take you seriously."

Cee Cee whipped her head back and forth, watching the two as if it was a tennis match. Markie held up a hand. "Stop it, you two."

Liv narrowed her eyes at Andi. "You were dancing on a table? I'm sorry I missed that." She grinned. "Next time, I'm going out with all of you."

Markie snickered, and Cee Cee broke into laughter.

Andi and Julia stared one another down. Then Andi said, "You could have at least introduced me to the guy."

In seconds, all of them were seated again, and laughing. Even Julia.

Markie wondered if studies had ever been done about estrogen levels in groups of women. She had heard jokes about the heightened testosterone in a room filled with men and the potential for violence. But she would bet no group of men would stand a chance with this crowd of females. And she rather liked the idea. Being with these women gave her strength and a sense of belonging. "Okay, so what's on today's agenda?"

Cee Cee ran to the office and returned with the schedule.

"I thought I destroyed that," Andi said.

Smoothing the crumpled paper on the table, Cee Cee said, "I pulled it from the trash. Just in case. It says this morning is writing letters to our younger selves about what we've learned about life."

"Hah, I'm not touching that one," Julia said.

Cee Cee continued, "And this afternoon is alone time, followed by a weenie roast and bonfire on the beach. That's when we're supposed to share our life lessons with one another."

"Good God. Markie, bring your stash. I'll check the wine supply." Andi picked up nearly empty plates.

Undaunted, Cee Cee said, "There are journals for us on the credenza in the office. I'll get them. I can't wait for this. Of course, you all have a lot more learnings to share."

Markie and the other three stared at her.

"I mean, you're old...er...you've had more...um...."

"Experience?" Julia suggested.

"Yes. Experience. That's the word I was looking for." Cee Cee grinned.

While the others cleared the table and cleaned up the kitchen, Markie slipped outside and carefully made her way down to the beach. The fall had shaken her. Not so much the falling down, as the fact that her legs had just given out beneath her. It had happened before, and that had sent her for tests and resulted in a diagnosis. The numbness and lack of control was occurring more frequently. And the thoughts of what might await her in the coming months terrified her. She stood on the beach and glanced back at the house, then gazed out at the ocean. What if she sat down on the sand and couldn't get up again and the tide rolled in and...?

She lifted her face to the sun and clutched the crystals she carried in her pocket—one for emotional wellbeing, one for physical health, and one for the freedom to let go. No stranger to letting go, she closed her eyes and breathed in the salty air, traveling back in time and remembering.

~ * ~
The Summer of Love

Markie—1967

"Karen! Dammit, I have to go to work. Get out here and watch your sister."

Karen stared down at the sketch she had been doing. She would have to finish it later. She emerged from her bedroom and watched her mother apply heavy makeup. Her mother's almost outdated beehive hairstyle and revealing miniskirt made Karen's stomach twist. At thirteen, she now understood what it meant when neighbors snickered about her mother.

"Why do you have to go out tonight?" Karen asked.

"If I don't dance, we don't eat."

Her mother barely made enough money as a dancer at a club. Karen knew most of their money came from what her mother did after the dancing ended. She stared at her four-year-old sister. "Aunt Hannah says Carly and I can come and stay with her for the summer."

The stare she received from her mother made her take a step back. "Your Aunt Hannah would just love to get her hands on you girls. Do you think I'd ever see you again?"

Karen bit the inside of the her lower lip, resisting the urge to ask, "Would that be so bad?"

Her mother tugged on a pair of shiny knee-high white boots and gave herself an appraising look over in the mirror. "Don't open the door for anyone and make sure your sister's in bed by ten. Got it?"

Karen nodded. Even she knew ten o'clock was late for a four-year-old to go to bed. She watched her mother hike the chain-link strap of her purse onto her shoulder and close the door.

Carly looked up from the page she was coloring. "I want ice cream."

Her younger sister favored their mother—fair-haired, light-skinned, and self-absorbed. But, then, she was only four years old. Karen resembled their father's Romanian heritage with her dark hair and deep brown eyes. He claimed his family descended from Gypsies and Karen used to love his stories. Her father was the one person who believed in Karen and encouraged her art. Her mother called her drawings a waste of time.

Her father died two months after enlisting in the Army and being shipped off to Vietnam. Karen was sure she would never get over the grief that overwhelmed her at times. Nights were the worst and she tended to stay up and watch TV at least until her mother returned in the early morning hours with a 'friend.'

Later that night, after she managed to get Carly to stay in bed, Karen watched a TV news special about San Francisco and what was being called *The Summer of Love*. She saw women walking around in long skirts and wearing flowers in their hair. In other parts of the country, people were rioting and protesting the war. But in the streets of San Francisco, people were laughing, singing and dancing, handing out flowers. Karen wished they could live in San Francisco.

She lay in her bed almost sunken into sleep when the door to her bedroom creaked open. She almost gagged at the odor of her mother's breath on her cheek—a blend of whiskey and cigarettes and something more pungent. She squeezed her eyes shut, pretending to be asleep.

Karen got up to use the bathroom, glancing at the clock beside her bed. Six-fifteen in the morning. When she reached the bathroom door, a long-haired naked man stood relieving himself in front of the toilet.

Karen gasped. The man glanced at her and grinned. "Hey." He finished, shook droplets of urine from his penis, and turned toward her. It would have been a shock if this was the first time she had encountered a naked man in their apartment. She walked past him to the toilet and flushed.

"I was gonna do that." He leaned back against the sink, totally unconcerned about his nudity. "You don't look much like your big sister."

Her mother always introduced her and Carly as her younger sisters. "I look like my father. He's a war hero."

The man snorted. "War hero. There aren't any heroes in this war."

Anger burned in Karen's chest. "Are you finished? I need to use the toilet."

His lingering gaze down her body thinly-clad in a short cotton nightgown made Karen's skin prickle. Her Aunt Hannah called her an "early bloomer" when she took her shopping for her first bra. The gazes of the men her mother brought home often fixed on her chest, just like now. She watched as he ran his tongue along his lower lip and his penis twitched.

Her mother appeared in the open door. "You two having a convention in here? I have to piss."

Karen's stomach roiled in disgust. She hated it when her mother used that kind of language. She skirted the man still standing at the sink and brushed past her mother. She could hold it. In her room, she sat on her bed with her knees pulled up to her chest. If she had anything in her stomach right now, she would vomit. She had to get out of there and she had to get Carly out, too. But at thirteen, Karen could hardly take off with her sister in tow.

After her mother left that evening, Karen settled her sister on the sofa beside her, a bowl of popcorn between them. "Carly, you like Aunt Hannah, right?"

Carly smiled. "I love Aunt Hannah. She gives me candy and stuff."

Karen smiled back. "Yes, she does. She loves us both very much. Did you ever think about living with Aunt Hannah instead of living here?"

Carly's smile faded to a frown. "But what about Mama? Would she live with Aunt Hannah, too?"

"No. Mama would have to stay here. She has her…job. Remember the pictures Aunt Hannah showed us of her house in Napa and the vineyards? It would be fun to live there, right?"

"I guess so. Are we going to see Aunt Hannah?"

Karen knew Carly would never go without her. "Yes. I'm going to call her now."

She dialed the phone with a shaking finger. Aunt Hannah was her father's younger sister. After he died, she made it a point to stay in touch with Karen and Carly, even though their mother didn't seem to like it very much. Karen knew Aunt Hannah gave their mother money for them—money they never saw.

When her aunt picked up the phone, Karen told her everything about the men coming home with her mother and the man that morning whom she had encountered in the bathroom. She added her own story about the man coming into the bedroom she shared with Carly and staring at them both.

"Oh, God. Oh, Karen. I'm going to get you girls out of there."

"You have to come now. Mama's out, but she'll be back and she'll bring him or another man with her. I'm scared for Carly."

"Pack some things for both of you. I'll be there in

a little over an hour. Don't open the door for anyone until I get there."

"Okay. Thanks, Aunt Hannah." Her voice trembled. "I didn't know what else to do."

"I'm glad you called me, sweetheart. I'll take care of you both. Just hang on until I get there."

Karen hung up the phone. If she went with Carly, her mother would confront her about the lie she told. If Aunt Hannah called the police, they would question her until they got the truth. The man had not come into their bedroom. Then the police would give her and Carly back to their mother with a warning. But if Karen wasn't there to tell anything different....

She set down the packed suitcase beside her baby sister. "Aunt Hannah will be here soon to get you. If I'm not back, be sure to give her this envelope. I have to go and tell Mama where we're going. Lock the door behind me and don't let anyone else in, except Aunt Hannah."

Carly's eyes widened with fear. "I'm afraid to stay alone."

Karen shoved a love-worn stuffed dog into her sister's arms. "I'm leaving Bobby the Beagle with you. He'll protect you until Aunt Hannah gets here." She hugged Carly hard, then stood and settled the canvas strap of a duffle bag onto her shoulder. The dog was the last gift from her father before he shipped out. But it gave Carly comfort. The child huddled on the sofa hugging the animal to her and clinging to the envelope. The note Karen had written simply stated she was leaving and would be in touch and asking her aunt to please take care of Carly.

Karen bent and gave her sister another hug. "Be good. Now come and lock the door behind me."

Only after she stepped out into the hall and heard the click of the lock, did Karen give herself permission to

Ladies In Waiting

cry. She pulled out the roll of bills she had taken from her mother's underwear drawer and counted them again. She had stuffed forty dollars into the envelope for Carly and had one-hundred-eighty-six dollars for herself. She exited the building and walked the four blocks to the bus station. In the restroom, she pulled up her hair and wrapped it in a scarf in the manner she had seen on those women on TV. She padded one of her mother's bras—something her mother rarely wore anymore—and applied light makeup. She could pass for sixteen easily.

The night clerk at the bus station counter gave her a quick second glance, but sold her the two tickets. "You know, your mother should be the one to buy these."

"I know, but she's in the restroom. Cramps." She shrugged. "You know how it is that time of the month."

The man behind the counter grimaced. "No, I don't. And I don't need to know." He shoved the tickets across the counter to her.

When her bus arrived, Karen tossed one ticket into the trash and climbed aboard. San Francisco wasn't that far from Sacramento, but she was pretty sure she could get lost easily in the city.

On the bus, she was seated next to an old woman who smelled a little like tuna fish. But she found comfort in the woman's presence.

"Are you traveling all by yourself?" the woman asked.

"Yes. I'm on my way to San Francisco to spend the summer with my aunt."

"I'm Adelaide. And you are…?"

"Ka…uh…Markova Leonte. Everyone calls me Markie, though." In that instant, she became her great-grandmother.

~ * ~
Six Months Later

"Wow, Markie. You are good." The girl who called herself Summer stared over Markie's shoulder. "That looks just like Boyce." Summer plopped down on the pillow beside Markie. "By the way, Boyce says we're going to New Mexico and check out a commune there. You want to come with us? Lucy, Mitch and Evan are coming, too."

Markie's breath caught. *Leave California?* "I…uh…"

Summer stood. "Think about it. We're leaving in two days."

Markie leaned back against the wall of the sparsely furnished room she shared with three other people. She had called her aunt once to make sure Carly was safe. When Carly got on the phone and cried for her to come to Napa, Markie couldn't take it and hung up. She couldn't go back, and she was afraid to stay in San Francisco by herself. She had been lucky that Boyce and Lucy had found her and invited her to stay with them and the others. She was pretty sure Lucy knew Markie wasn't sixteen, but they lived a life where no questions were asked.

Before she could set aside her drawing and stand, Evan came into the room. "Watcha' doin'?" He glanced down at the sketch. "I should ask." He dropped down beside her. His long blond hair hung around his shoulders and a light beard shaded his tanned face. His blue eyes sparkled as he smiled. "You're coming to New Mexico with us, aren't you?"

At that moment, she would have said yes to going anywhere with Evan. She smiled and warmth flooded her cheeks. "I guess so."

He nudged her with his elbow. "Good. I'd miss you."

"You would?"

"Sure." He reached out and she thought he was going to hug her or pull her close and kiss her. Instead, he ruffled her long hair. "You're a nice kid. And I love your artwork."

Markie stared after him as he left. *Kid?* Evan was all of nineteen. And he was her first crush. He was nothing like the men her mother had brought home. Evan was gentle and smiling and respectful. He never made her feel uncomfortable. Of course she was going to New Mexico.

~ * ~

Four Years Later

Taos, New Mexico

Markie's colorful skirt swirled around her ankles as she walked through the outdoor art exhibit. Some day she would have her own paintings on display like this. She stopped in front of a metal sculpture. The sign at the base said *Conflict*. She studied the piece, drawn in by the intricacies in the weaving of the metal.

"What do you think?"

She startled at the deep voice erupting by her right ear. "It's amazing. It looks woven together. I've never seen a metal sculpture done quite like this." She turned around and stared into dark gray eyes the color of storm clouds.

The man smiled. "Thank you. I'm David Rooker."

She tore her gaze from his to look at the plaque beneath the sculpture. Artist: David Rooker. "You did this?"

He pressed a palm over his heart and the gray eyes lightened. "Ouch. You didn't know me?"

Heat warmed Markie's cheeks. "I'm sorry. I work

more with paint. I'm Markie Leonte."

"Leonte?"

"It's Romanian."

"Ah…a gypsy?"

She grinned. "My great-grandmother's name. The family changed it to Lyons. But, yes, a few generations back we were gypsies in Romania."

"And what about you? You still have gypsy blood? Wanderlust?"

She was mesmerized by his deep gray eyes, the timbre of his voice. "I guess I do. I wandered from California to New Mexico."

David threw back his head and laughed.

His laughter rumbled through Markie like a freight train, shaking loose a multitude of feelings.

She spent that night with David and remained under his mentoring as well as in his bed for the next twelve years. She was in love with him and in awe of his artistic talents.

One evening in the spring of 1972, she watched a story on the national news about a massive fire at a winery in Napa. Horror shot through her as the reporter announced that three people died—the owners Hannah and Timothy Donaldson, and their son, Ricky. A niece, Carly Lyons, was hospitalized but expected to recover. The grief leveled Markie. She couldn't share it with anyone, not even David. It would expose her lie. She retreated to her studio workroom where she spent day and night staring at blank canvas. David came to the door only once—to tell her he was leaving for a few days.

She called the hospital in Napa, but couldn't get any information on Carly. She then called Child Services, but the person she was connected with started to ask too many questions and offered no answers to hers. She could only gather from the brief conversation that Carly had survived and was in foster care. A quick assessment of her lifestyle and her age told her she would not be a good candidate as parent. Besides, if Carly remembered her at all, Markie doubted her sister could ever forgive her for running away.

Hollowed by grief, Markie's work took an abstract turn. Oddly enough, a local gallery owner loved it, saying it would have high appeal. Even David, upon his return, remarked on the emotional quality of the new work. Praise that was short-lived.

As her own talent emerged and the demand for David's work diminished, he became critical and withdrawn. He graduated from alcohol and marijuana use to experimenting with harder drugs like LSD. His work suffered and Markie's concern was translated into "criticism"—something David Rooker would not tolerate. His abusive outbursts and veiled threats escalated.

~ * ~

1984

Markie sat one evening and looked around her. David was everywhere, in every corner of their spacious adobe house. Her work was relegated to the small spare bedroom in the back. She had moderate success and was known locally, but in the past few years had very few requests to exhibit her work. One sympathetic gallery owner had finally told her it was because of David—that he had threatened to pull his work from the local galleries if they displayed Markie's paintings. This was the last straw. She chided herself for waiting so long and possibly missing her chance to become known as an artist in her own right.

David had gone to Phoenix for a week to set up a display of his work. Markie packed up her paintings and smaller pieces of sculpture and left them with a friend she could trust. She got on a bus and headed east. Several days later when she reached Philadelphia, exhausted and just wanting off the bus, she decided this was the place for her to settle. Preferring a small town to the city, she found an apartment in Doylestown. Her friend in Taos shipped her paintings and sculpted pieces to her. David could easily have found her. He simply didn't look.

 Markie soon built a name for herself. She wasn't known worldwide, but she managed to make a modest living from her art and found peace in the small town. She made friends easily and those friends made her a part of their families. Markie had never looked back after leaving Sacramento and had no clue if her mother was dead or alive. She still ached with grief and guilt over the loss of her aunt. Markie had sent Carly to live in the place where she very nearly died. And she was too much of a coward to go back and claim her now.

 Markie vowed that she would never have children. She wasn't mother material. She would dedicate herself to her art.

~ * ~

 The screech of gulls diving for tidbits on the sand jerked Markie back to the present. She squinted into the sun reflecting off the water, and then plopped down in the sand and pulled the journal from her skirt pocket. Her entries might be her greatest work of fiction. The life lessons she had learned would be far too painful to commit to paper, much less to share around a camp fire.

Chapter Fourteen

Cee Cee

Cee Cee sat on the front porch with her feet up on the railing and the journal in her lap. She stared at the blank page. Where could she start? Everything was such a mess. If she had the words to make sense of it all, she wouldn't have needed to be here.

She couldn't sit still, so she shoved the pen into her pocket, tucked the journal under her arm, and started walking. The sun was warm on her back, but an ocean breeze cooled her. She hadn't started out with a route in mind and was surprised when she found herself standing behind a tree across the street from her own house.

Ben would be at work, and his mother would be looking after the three younger kids. Sean would be at Little League baseball practice. Cee Cee felt a pang of guilt, realizing her need for time away had disrupted the lives of two other people. Then she wanted to slap herself. Those were Ben's children, too, and his mother adored her grandchildren.

The front door opened and Benji raced to his grandmother's Subaru. Margie Carter emerged, one of the twin girls clinging to each of her hands and toddling beside her. Cee Cee remained hidden, observing while her mother-in-law buckled the kids into their car seats and pulled from the drive.

When the coast was clear, she tiptoed up the driveway and removed the spare key from beneath the ceramic frog. She stepped inside the house as if she were a burglar casing someone else's home. It smelled of the cinnamon and vanilla potpourri she kept on the mantle above the fireplace, out of the reach of tiny fingers.

Cee Cee walked around, touching the framed photos, studying the faces of Ben and the kids. Even her own smiling face. She had not had a minute alone in her own house in over four years, since Benji had been born. She picked up an apple from the kitchen counter and rubbed it on the front of her tank top.

The phone rang, and she startled. She reached for it, then drew her hand back, remembering she wasn't supposed to be there. She climbed the stairs and visited the boys' room first. Margie had cleaned. Cee Cee was embarrassed by the fact that she was not a meticulous housekeeper. Cleaning meant that clothing didn't cover the floors and dust didn't coat the tabletops. She vacuumed once a week, unless one of the twins upturned a plant or stomped Cheerios into the carpet.

The girls' room was so orderly that Cee Cee's heart quaked at the possibility they didn't live there any more. She couldn't imagine life without her babies. Which is why the thoughts she had been entertaining—no, the thoughts that had been plaguing her—were so disturbing.

In the master bedroom, the one she shared with Ben, she fell on her back across the bed. The room smelled of him, of both of them. His woodsy aftershave, her after-shower body spray and scented antiperspirant. She stared across the room at the collage of photos of her, Ben, and the kids. Their faces stared back, accusingly. *You don't love us anymore.*

Cee Cee curled into a fetal position and sobbed. Once she exhausted her grief, she sat up and opened the journal in her lap to put all of her feelings into words. How would she ever explain this to the other women?

Ladies In Waiting

How would she explain it to Ben?

The slam of a door and the pounding of feet jerked her awake. She had dozed off and hadn't a clue what time it was. The journal thumped onto the floor as she sat up and blinked, unsure of her surroundings.

Benji raced past the room, stopped and ran back to the open door. "Mom, you're home!" He flung himself onto the bed and into her lap. "I missed you."

"I missed you, too." Tears blurred her vision as she kissed the top of his head. "I just stopped by to get something I need." When she looked up, Margie stood in the door way with two fidgeting little redheads in matching powder blue outfits that made their eyes look big as the sky.

As soon as their grandmother released her hold, both girls scrambled up onto the bed and hugged Cee Cee. "Mama back," Katie said.

Beth patted Cee Cee's cheeks with both her sticky palms. "Mama."

Cee Cee hugged the girls close, breathing in their sweet, powdery scents.

"We just ran to the grocery store and had lunch at the DQ," Margie said. "Is your retreat over already?"

"No, I just came by to get something. But I'll put them down for their naps while I'm here."

"I'll be downstairs, then." She hesitated. "Cee Cee, is everything all right? You look as if you're upset."

Cee Cee swallowed hard and nestled her face in Katie's red curls. "Everything's fine." She set the girls down beside her. "Okay, you guys. Nap time."

"I'm too big to take a nap," Benji whined.

"Don't be silly. Even Daddy takes a nap sometimes. Come on." She carried the girls and nudged Benji toward his room. He was probably right. Four years old was stretching it for an afternoon nap. She knew his

125

nap time consisted mostly of play in his room, but at least he was quiet about it.

This time, however, he issued a half-hearted complaint as she removed his sneakers, but his eyelids drooped when his head hit the pillow. The girls were another matter. They had started to talk at eleven months—just sounds, but a language they seemed to understand. Cee Cee would often waken at night and hear them across the hall babbling away to one another. Quieting them so they would sleep was always a challenge.

She got the girls settled into their cribs and, once they were chattering softly to one another, tiptoed from the room. She smiled, knowing the twins would always have each other—a closeness other sisters couldn't even understand.

Margie stood at the sink peeling potatoes when Cee Cee entered the kitchen. "Thanks for helping out while I'm at the retreat."

"You know I love to be with the kids." Margie set down the peeler. "How is your mom doing? Any news?"

Cee Cee shook her head. "Dad says she has good days and bad. Ben and I are going to take the kids up there in a couple of weeks. I hope it's not too much for her."

"I can stay with them, if you and Ben want to go alone," Margie offered. "Might be good for the two of you."

Cee Cee wondered what her mother-in-law had observed. What she really wanted was to go to Maine by herself, to slip back into her childhood home with her parents, take a step away from everything. Her mother's early onset Alzheimer's had been a shock to all of them. Cee Cee knew it was only a matter of time before she lost her mother completely to the disease. She needed to be a child with her mommy again for just a little while. "We'll see," she said. "I'll talk to Ben."

Margie dried her hands and crossed to her, pulling her into a hug. "I'm sorry about what's happening to your mother. You know you can count on me with the kids any time." She drew back and looked Cee Cee in the eyes. "And you can talk to me if you need to. About anything else?"

No, I can't, Cee Cee thought. How can I talk to you? How can I tell you that my mother's illness is only one of my problems? That I'm having doubts about your son, my marriage? "Thanks, Margie. I have to head back now."

"Okay, honey. I hope you get what you need from this week." Margie gave her a squeeze before letting her go.

If only I knew what I need. For months she had felt as if she was waiting for something—something to happen or to change. But it never did. She hated that she had this deep desire to just run away, to become invisible and leave her life behind. Maybe Liv or Markie would take her home with them. Could someone still be adopted at thirty-two?

Chapter Fifteen

If I Knew Then What I Know Now

Andi and Liv followed the instructions left by Bree and stacked kindling and small logs in the stone ring on the beach. When Cee Cee and Markie reached the top of the wooden steps with the cooler, Andi hurried to take it from Markie. "I'll get this."

"I've already got it. I'm not an invalid," Markie snapped.

Andi flinched and then backed down the steps. "I was just trying to help. I'll get the blankets."

"Julia's bringing them," Cee Cee said.

"Okay, then. Let's see if Liv and I can get a fire started." Andi squatted down beside Liv and the two of them struck match after match until the kindling caught.

Markie set down her end of the cooler and nudged Andi with her foot. "I'm sorry."

"No problem."

Julia dropped the stack of old blankets and quilts onto the sand and wrapped her jacket around her. "It's chilly out here."

Liv looked up. "Don't you have a sweatshirt or heavy sweater?"

"I'll be fine."

"No, you won't. I'll be right back." Liv brushed sand from her palms and strode toward the house.

By the time Liv returned, Andi had a fire blazing and the others had spread out the blankets and skewered hot dogs on the sticks Cee Cee had gathered earlier. Liv handed a heavy gray sweatshirt to Julia. "Put this on. It should fit okay."

"Thank you."

The five of them sat in a semi-circle around the fire.

"This brings back memories," Markie said. "When I was a little girl, my dad used to set up a fire ring in our back yard and my sister and I would roast hot dogs and toast marshmallows. And my dad would tell scary stories."

"My brother was a Boy Scout and I envied him because he got to camp out and I didn't. When I was six years old, I dragged the blankets off my bed and built my camp on our back porch." Andi leaned back on her elbows. "But I didn't realize the door had locked behind me. At the first sound of rustling in the bushes, I was ready to go back to my bedroom. I woke up the entire family and half the neighborhood pounding on the door and screaming for help. My mother was furious with me. I'm sure it was more panic at realizing what could have happened if I'd wandered farther than the porch." She sat up and turned her stick to evenly brown the hot dog.

"I went to summer camp once, but I missed my parents so badly, they never sent me again. I think the counselors called them every other day so I could hear their voices," Liv said.

"How old were you?" Cee Cee asked.

"Eight. It was the first time I'd ever been away from home for more than an overnight." Liv smiled. "How about you? I'd peg you for a Girl Scout."

Cee Cee tucked her red curls under the hood of her sweatshirt. "And you'd be right. I love hiking and camping. Spending a night outside, under the stars, is pure heaven to me. I may bundle up, keep the fire going, and sleep here on the beach tonight."

"Are you nuts? It gets cold out here at night. And what if the tide comes in?" Andi asked.

"It doesn't come up this far." Cee Cee took in a deep breath. "Just listen."

They all quieted. The waves rolled in with a rush and then receded with a hiss. Overhead, a full moon lit the beach. Night birds sang in the distance.

"Oh, shit." Andi lifted her empty stick from the fire. "My weenie fell off."

Julia snickered and soon they all roared with laughter.

"Now that's a tragedy," Markie said. Since pork byproducts and nitrates didn't appeal to her, she munched on carrot sticks and whole wheat crackers. "There are more in the cooler."

When they had eaten the first course, Cee Cee set their sticks aside. "Before we toast marshmallows, I think we should share from our journals. I misplaced my journal, so I wrote this out again on note paper."

Andi, who had laid on her back and gazed up at the stars, said, "Sure. You go first."

"Okay." Cee Cee crossed her legs and unfolded several sheets of yellow legal paper. She produced a small flashlight and aimed the beam at the page.

Liv glanced at her. "You really were a Girl Scout. Prepared for anything."

Cee Cee cleared her throat. "Here goes. Dear Younger Me, I know you can't wait to grow up, but I have to tell you it's not all it's cracked up to be. It looks like fun from where you're sitting, but believe me, it's not that easy being an adult. You're going to have to make tough choices and let some things go. Things you might really want." Her voice quivered and she paused. "You're going to marry Ben. I know that sounds

Ladies In Waiting

awesome to you. But marriage is not easy. And people change. You'll change. And he'll change. And then there will be the kids. Four of them."

She smiled. "They're beautiful. But they can test my...your patience, too. They will need you, all the time. And Ben...Ben likes to have things his way, so you have to compromise a lot. And he's so damned stubborn." She looked up at the others. "Sorry.

"Anyway, what have I learned? Well, I've learned that you should really think about the big decisions, the life-changing decisions you make. And you should be very certain about commitments before you make them." Her voice softened. "Otherwise, you end up with doubts and regrets."

Cee Cee folded the sheets of paper and squeezed them in her hand. "That's all I have," she murmured.

In the flicker of firelight, Andi could make out Cee Cee's profile. The girl bit her lower lip, and her eyes glistened.

Andi poured a glass of wine, lifted it to Cee Cee with a nod and took a big gulp. "I'll go next. I didn't write this out. But if I could warn my younger self of anything, I would tell her to be cautious with her heart. Don't just give it away to anyone. Choose wisely and don't expect to find that great love in your life more than once." Andi paused for another swallow of wine. "You'll find that love. And always value your friends. Cherish every minute because everything will be taken from you far too soon." She choked on the last words.

Markie reached over and touched her hand. Andi did not pull away, though she wanted to. She allowed that simple sign of understanding to give her the courage to continue. "You're going to get lost along the way. I'd like to tell you that you find your way out of the maze, but to be honest...." She stared into the fire. "I'll have to get back to you on that."

She squeezed Markie's hand, then pulled away. "Who's next?"

Markie withdrew a joint from her pocket and lit it. The orange tip glowed in the dark. She drew in a deep breath, then passed the joint on. When she exhaled, she opened the journal on her lap and reached for Cee Cee's flashlight. "Markova—you took the name of your great-grandmother. She was a woman of strength who survived poverty and persecution. She came to this country as a child and with nothing but the clothing on her back. She learned the customs and the language and built a life for herself, created a legacy. You bear that legacy. You will need her strength, her determination to survive. It's important for you to know that she is a part of you and that you will have what you need when you need it."

She reached for the joint and took another hit before continuing. "You are an artist. You may have to learn new ways of creating your art, but it's in you. It's the one thing no one and nothing can take from you. There are many ways to get to the same place. You can run. You can walk. Or you can crawl, if you have to. You will be tempted to give in to fear. But you can't. It will cr-cripple you." Markie handed the flashlight to Liv. "That's all."

Andi had lain down and now turned her face to look up at Markie. She expected to see tears for some reason, but what she saw was determination on the woman's face. She thought about what Markie had shared and the fall she had taken earlier, and she wondered.

Liv shifted position, drawing up her knees and hugging them to her chest. When Markie offered her the flashlight, she shook her head. "I don't need to read this. I've had this conversation with myself a hundred times when I've looked back to see where I might have done something differently, changed the outcome of my life. I see that girl I used to be, the one who fell in love and believed in a fairytale." Liv smiled sadly. "She was so naive, so trusting. She gave up everything for the dream. And it was a good dream—until it became a nightmare."

She looked to Andi. "Give me a hit of that stuff." She drew in the smoke and coughed, passing the joint over to Cee Cee. She waited a moment, hoping to feel the high. "That girl had everything she wanted—a loving husband, three smart, funny, wonderful children, homes—plural—money, social standing. She had the American Dream."

Liv glanced at each of them. Markie gave her an encouraging nod. Liv continued, staring into the fire, "Dear Olivia, you'll marry a man who loses his soul to greed. A man who takes your love, your heart, and smashes it to pieces like it means nothing. You'll lose your soul, too, in the process. You'll give away your dreams to fulfill his." Tears filled her eyes. "And after it all falls apart and your life is shattered, you'll want to disappear, to become invisible because of the shame. But you have to know that your only sin is loving someone so blindly that you can't see the darkness in them." She glanced up at the others. "If I could tell that girl anything, I would tell her to pay attention. To keep her eyes open. To think, not just follow along and believe Adam's stories of good business deals and winning markets. Don't let yourself drown in his wake."

Andi sat up and cocked her head. "Wait a minute. Liv, are you talking about...?"

Liv nodded. "I was married to Adam Zacharias."

After several minutes of silence, Liv said, "Doesn't anyone have anything to say?"

Julia tilted her head back and drained her wine. "I

can top that."

They all turned to her with piqued interest.

"My grandfather was a lawyer. As was my father and my mother. When I was a child, I just knew I'd be a lawyer. It was like taking up the reins of the family business. I always had a sense of justice, of right and wrong, and believed that people should take responsibility for their actions. Just ask my brother. I regularly reported on his behavior when we were kids." She extended the glass toward Andi for a refill.

Julia sat cross-legged, cradling the glass of wine. "I would tell that girl with high ideals and narrow parameters regarding justice that she might want to be more flexible, to see things from more than one view. Otherwise...." She paused.

"Otherwise, she may miss important facts, truths that change the way things should be done. Sometimes justice is blind to those truths, unyielding. I was blinded by my determination to serve justice." She lowered her head. "And it cost the lives of two innocent children."

Cee Cee gasped.

Liv stared wide-eyed across the fire at Julia.

Andi checked Markie for a reaction, then realized the woman was not the least bit surprised by what she had just heard. She already knew. "Julia, what are you talking about?"

Julia hunched her shoulders, sinking into the sweatshirt. "I work with the DA's office in Philadelphia. I was the prosecutor in the Amanda Lansdale trial."

"That's the woman who allegedly killed her husband. She was set free, drowned her two kids and killed herself," Cee Cee said in a near whisper.

Julia nodded. "I screwed up. I put winning and being right over true justice."

Markie reached over and patted Julia's knee.

"You couldn't have known. You were just doing your job."

"Maybe there are more important things in life than doing the job," Julia murmured.

The women sat in silence. Andi added another log to the fire and watched the sparks rise, twinkle, and then fade like tiny stars. "Am I the only one who feels like something should happen now? Like I'm waiting for something miraculous to occur?"

"Not the only one," Liv said.

Andi reclined on her elbows and gazed up at the clear sky, at stars sparkling like scattered diamonds. "If I'd known then what I know now, I wonder if I'd have done anything differently." She took the stub of the joint from Markie and sucked in the pungent smoke then coughed as she exhaled. "Probably not."

Julia rubbed a sleeved arm across her face. "I would." She glanced down at Markie. "Do have another one of those...cigarettes?"

~ * ~

The women dragged their beach gear and the cooler. Markie led them in a sing-along of Dylan's *Rainy Day Women*. Cee Cee led the way up from the beach and turned to shine the flashlight on the steps for the others to follow. When they all reached the top, the women stopped and sang together, "Everybody must get stoned."

As they approached the house, a shadowed figure stood at the foot of the porch steps. "Cee Cee?"

Cee Cee gasped. "Ben? What are you doing here? Oh my God, it's one of the kids." She passed the flashlight to Andi.

"The kids are fine. My mom's with them. But you and I have to talk," he said. "About this." He held up the journal.

She remembered then that the journal had fallen

onto the bedroom floor. She had put the kids down for their naps and talked with Margie for a minute, forgetting to go back for the book.

"Hi, you must be Cee Cee's husband. I'm Andi."

"I'm sorry." Cee Cee introduced Ben to each of the women. He nodded cordially, even accepting Markie's hand.

"We've heard a lot about you," Markie said.

"I can imagine." He shifted his gaze back to Cee Cee.

"I'll be inside in a minute." Cee Cee turned back toward the beach and Ben followed.

"Wait. You should take this." Andi tossed her the flashlight.

"Thanks." Cee Cee had to run to keep up with Ben as he strode purposefully to the steps and down to the dark beach. "Ben, that journal is part of the retreat exercises."

He turned and the moonlight gave his face a bluish tint—deathly. He held up the journal. "I'd ask you to explain this, but I can't imagine you can come up with an explanation. You're high, for godsake."

"No, I...."

"You reek of weed."

"I just had a little."

"What? You didn't inhale? It's more like you forgot to exhale."

His words struck a chord in her. That was exactly how she felt—as if she had been holding her breath for a very long time.

"I'm sure your friends up there—who, by the way, are your mother's age—got a good laugh out of your story."

"Ben... First of all, I didn't share with them what I wrote in the journal. Not all of it."

Cee Cee recognized the twitch in his jaw. It meant he was measuring his words and controlling his emotions. "Is this really how you feel? Trapped? Like our marriage is a mistake? What do I say to the kids—sorry, guys, but Mommy changed her mind. She sends her *regrets*."

Cee Cee bit her bottom lip and her throat tightened. She had used the word regret. Her voice came out in a squeak. "That's not what I meant. I love the kids."

Ben's shoulders dropped and he gazed out at the ocean. "So it's just me."

"I...." She couldn't finish the sentence. She thought she loved him. Of course, she loved him. He was her husband. But their life together had become mundane, predictable. They moved around one another like pieces on a chess board. Something was missing.

"What? Nothing to say? Maybe you can write it all down and drop it in the mail." He shoved the journal at her and started up the beach.

She raced after him. "Ben, wait!"

"For what? For things to get even worse? For one of us to change again?" He whirled around. "I'm stubborn—remember? I thought I knew you, Cee Cee. I thought we were in this together for life." He clambered up the rickety steps.

Cee Cee reached the top in time to see the taillights of his truck disappear down the dark drive. She stood there, stunned, not sure what to do. Should she go home and try to explain? Did he need time to cool down? She sucked in a quavering breath and headed toward the house.

Chapter Sixteen

"You okay?" Liv asked from the shadows on the porch.

Cee Cee slumped down in a chair next to her and covered her face with her trembling hands. "I don't know. I went by the house earlier and that's where I misplaced this." She held up the journal. "Ben found it and read what I'd written. God, it must have sounded awful to him out of context."

"Was it what you shared with us earlier?"

"That and more. I summarized with you all. For some dumb reason, I thought writing out all my thoughts and feelings in this journal would be helpful. It's…pretty bad. He's hurt. I've never seen him so hurt." She hunched over and cried. "He's a good guy. I just don't know if I love him any more. I think I do, but…. What the hell is wrong with me?"

"Oh, honey." Liv reached over and took her hand. "I'm sorry."

Cee Cee squeezed Liv's hand. "Thank you. It wasn't until I started to talk to my younger self about marriage and my life that I realized a part of me isn't happy. I'm on autopilot. I just go through the motions every day. Feed the kids, clean house, do laundry, cook, feed the kids, cook again, bathe the kids and put them to bed. I feel like I got lost."

Liv nodded. "I know. It happens to a lot of us. I was lost, too. I was Mrs. Adam Zacharias. Olivia—Liv—was nobody apart from him. I didn't know that had happened until Adam was in jail and I was alone again.

The hell of it is, I still love—loved him."

"What would you have done differently?" Cee Cee asked.

Liv rocked in the chair for a moment. "I wanted to own a flower shop. It's funny, really, because we lived in an apartment most of our lives. Central Park West. The extent of my gardening was done in flower pots on a balcony. I used to love to garden at our summer house, much to the dismay of the landscapers Adam hired." She faced Cee Cee. "What dream did you give up?"

Cee Cee hunched over again, her arms wrapped across her middle. "I wanted to be a nurse. Everyone says I'm really good to have around when someone's sick. I was planning to go to nursing school, but I didn't have the money. I moved down here from Maine and took a job for a summer. Then I met Ben. And the rest, as they say, is history."

"It's not too late, is it?"

"We have four kids. If I told Ben I wanted to pay for nursing school, he'd have a fit. I was going to go back to work when I found out I was pregnant with the twins. Now that they're toddlers, I've considered asking my mother-in-law to babysit so I can look for a job. I've tried to talk to Ben about nursing school, but all he ever says is we have to wait. Wait until the kids are older. Wait until we have enough money—which we never will with four kids who will go to college. Wait, wait, wait."

"And the marriage?"

Cee Cee sighed. "I love Ben. I know I do. I'm just not so sure I love *us*—him and me together. I know marriage is work, and the honeymoon has to end eventually. I never thought we would get into this kind of rut. And now that he read what I wrote, God only knows what will happen. I didn't know if I should go after him, or give him time to cool down." She looked up at Liv.

"He's a good man."

"Then don't give up on him too quickly. And don't give up on yourself, either. If you want to get a nursing degree, there's got to be a way to do it."

"Says she who does not own a flower shop." Cee Cee grinned. "Maybe you should take your own advice. I saw a book on one of the shelves inside titled *It's Only Too Late If You Don't Start Now*. Maybe that's advice for both of us."

Liv chuckled. "Maybe so." She stood and squeezed Cee Cee's shoulder. "I'm turning in. It's been a long day. Are you going to be okay?"

Cee Cee reached up and patted Liv's hand. "I will be. Thanks."

Tears stung her eyes as Cee Cee sat alone and recalled some of the things she had written in the journal. They were her thoughts and feelings, but would have sounded so harsh and hurtful to Ben. She felt guilty. But why? All she had done was express her true feelings. She hadn't blamed him. If anyone, she blamed herself. And the writing exercise seemed harmless enough. Until she really got into it. Who the hell ever said truth set you free? Committing the truth to paper had only dug her into a deeper hole, and she didn't have a clue how she would climb out. Ben was always the one to give her a hand up when she needed it.

~ * ~

Cee Cee—1998

"Don't look now, but that guy's back and he's watching you."

Cee Cee glanced quickly over her shoulder long enough to see the lanky, dark haired boy break into a broad smile and wave. Heat raced up her neck and into her face. She collected plates from a vacated booth and hustled to the kitchen.

Her best friend Traci followed. "He's cute. You should talk to him."

"I didn't come here this summer to meet a guy. I'm here to make money for school." Cee Cee deposited the dirty dishes next to the dishwasher. "If you think he's so cute, you talk to him."

Traci grinned. "Okay, I will."

As she took another lunch order, Cee Cee couldn't help but glance across the diner to where Traci stood smiling up at the boy. He looked over Traci's head and his gaze connected with Cee Cee. He was cute, probably a couple of years older than she and Traci. His jeans were streaked with dirt and he looked as if he'd been working outdoors.

"Add a chocolate milkshake to my order, too, please."

Cee Cee tore her gaze from the boy and back to her customer. "Anything else?" She double-checked the order and delivered it to the kitchen.

Traci came up behind her and slid her order slip onto the counter. "This is to go, Mike." She nudged Cee Cee. "His name is Ben. He's twenty-one and works for his dad in a landscaping business. He asked for your name, if you were with anyone, and if I could introduce him. He's got it bad, Cee."

"I told you I'm not interested."

"Well, you better get interested before eight tonight, because we're going to a beach party Ben is having. It's farther down the shore in Cape May."

"Traci…" But her friend was already gone, delivering a lunch order. Well, just because Traci told Ben they would both be there didn't mean she had to go. Traci was a big girl. She could manage on her own. But they had promised each other to stick together this summer and watch one another's backs. This was the first time either of them had ventured this far from home on their own. Traci's mom had a college friend who lived in Wildwood and offered to let the two girls occupy her furnished garage apartment while they worked at the Surfside Diner for their first summer after graduation from high school. Wildwood seemed a world away from Camden, Maine in so many ways. The only similarity was summer tourists.

    When their shift ended, Cee Cee gathered up her purse and waited for Traci. "Hey, Trace, I'm really tired. I don't want to go to a party tonight. Let's catch a movie, my treat."

    "I'm going to the beach party, with or without you. I didn't come to Wildwood to dish up burgers and watch movies. We're at the beach. Where it's actually warm enough to wear a bikini and there's enough sand to dance on. And we always do what you want."

    Cee Cee had to admit that she had taken the lead in the two weeks they'd been there, deciding how they would spend their free time. They had seen three movies, driven down to Cape May for a day, and visited two museums and a few art galleries. When she thought about it, Cee Cee felt like she was forty instead of eighteen. Reluctantly she gave in. "Okay, I'll go. But if it gets too weird, we're leaving. Agreed?"

    Traci grinned. "Define weird."

    "You know exactly what I mean—drinking or drugs, guys getting too pushy or feely."

    "Agreed."

    The soft glow of sunset cast the sky in an orange-gray haze when she and Traci parked the car and found the section of beach where Ben had directed them. A bonfire sent up a plume of smoke and flames. A dozen silhouetted bodies danced in the firelight.

"I thought fires weren't permitted on the beach," Cee Cee said.

Traci shrugged. "Maybe he got a permit or something."

As they approached, Ben turned and grinned. "You made it." He spoke to both of them, but his eyes fixed on Cee Cee.

Traci stood between them. "Ben, this is Cee Cee. Point me in the direction of something cold to drink, then I'll leave you two to get acquainted."

Ben showed her where the cooler was stashed and introduced her to one of his friends, a guy with bronzed skin and sun-bleached hair. Then he turned back to Cee Cee, offering her a Coke. "This okay, or do you want a beer?"

"The Coke is fine, thanks." She glanced toward the fire. "Is that legal?"

"It is here. This is a private beach." He waved toward a house sitting on higher ground back from the sand. "That's my family's beach house."

"Oh."

"I'm glad you came. I'm sorry if I made you uncomfortable in the diner. I wasn't stalking you, I promise. I always pick up lunch there for the crew."

"The crew?"

"Landscaping crew. My dad owns the business and I work for him. We have jobs all along this section of the shore."

"So you grew up here?"

He nodded and took a draw on his beer. "I did. How about you?"

"Maine." She pulled the tab on the soft drink can and sipped.

"Nice. I went on a hunting trip with my dad and uncles once up to Maine."

She frowned. "I don't approve of hunting."

"Well, I'm not very good at it. I didn't shoot anything. And it's cold in Maine."

Cee Cee grinned in spite of herself. He was charming and seemed harmless enough.

He nodded down the beach. "You want to take a walk?"

A nearly-full moon had risen and sent a bluish-white glow over the ocean and across the sand, lighting the beach. "Okay."

"Traci told me the two of you are here for the summer. What are you going to do after that?"

"Nursing school. It's all I've ever wanted to do."

They walked in silence for a few minutes until Cee Cee became aware that they had rounded a curve in the beach and were out of sight of the others, including Traci. "Maybe we should head back?"

"If you want." Ben paused. "Look, you don't know me. But I'm a good guy." He lifted the beer bottle. "I never drink more than two of these. I'm not dating anyone that I'm cheating on right now. I come from a nice family and I'm a hard worker." His gaze locked with hers. "I guess I'm trying to say that you'll be okay here, and so will your friend. I just had to talk with you, is all."

Cee Cee held his gaze. He had the bluest eyes she'd ever seen and they shone in the moonlight in stark contrast to his dark hair. "I'm not looking for a guy right now. I mean, I'm going to school in a few months."

"So you can't just enjoy the summer with someone?"

"Are you suggesting…?"

He lifted his hands, palms facing her. "No, wait. I didn't mean that the way it may have sounded. I'd like to get to know you. Go to a movie, have dinner, walk on the beach. That's all. There's just something…." He reached out and carefully lifted a strand of hair from her face, tucking it behind her ear.

His touch sent a shiver through her—a pleasant shiver.

Taking a step back from her, Ben gazed out at the water. "So, would you like to have dinner with me tomorrow evening? You choose the place."

Cee Cee studied his face. He was more of a man than a boy, but there was something about him that pulled at her. "Okay, but you'll have to choose the restaurant. The only place I know is the Surfside, and I'm more than happy to get out of there when my shift is over."

His smile lit up his eyes. "Great. Let's head back before Traci comes looking for you or calls the police to report a kidnapping."

By the end of the summer, Cee Cee was head over heels in love with Ben and totally confused as to what to do about it. She was returning to Maine, ten hours away, and starting nursing school. She had one week left with him.

Then the phone call came that changed everything.

Cee Cee sat in stunned silence. Within fifteen minutes, Ben responded to Traci's call and was sitting next to her. "Cee Cee, talk to me. What happened?"

Fat tears streamed down her cheeks. "My house is gone."

He slid an arm around her. "Tell me what happened. Is everyone in your family okay?"

"They said the fire started in the attic after a lightning strike. My parents barely made it out." She sniffled and he passed a wad of tissues Traci handed to him. "Our dogs didn't get out. Oh, God. We lost everything."

Ben held her while she sobbed. When she

finished, he hugged her then said, "Why don't you get dressed and I'll drive you up there so you can see your parents? I'll just run to my place and pick up a few things."

He had been her rock. Her parents loved him and her father expressed his gratitude that Ben had brought Cee Cee home rather than letting her drive alone. They had spent the night at a hotel—Cee Cee sharing a room with her mother and Ben sharing one with her dad. Cee Cee returned to Wildwood to finish out her last week of work. She would need the money more now than ever. With the loss of their home, even with insurance, her parents told her she would have to postpone school for a year. She applied for loans, but it wouldn't be enough.

And, once again, Ben came to her rescue. In the winter months, his father had a contract for snow removal for the city. They needed a dispatcher in the office and Ben recommended Cee Cee for the job. With no other prospects, she accepted.

Cee Cee fit easily into the Carter family and into Ben's life. One year rolled into two and the next thing she knew, Cee Cee was walking down the aisle at St. Ann's Catholic Church to become Mrs. Benjamin Carter.

In her new role as wife, setting up their new home in Cape May, Cee Cee let the dream of nursing school slip away. The first couple of years were spent working hard and building their dream house. And then when she became pregnant, she focused all of her energy and attention on becoming a good mother.

She helped Ben establish his own landscaping business in Cape May. He took to the role of loving husband and father so easily, insisting on getting up for four a.m. feedings with Sean and even helping with the household chores after working all day. They were a team. When had it all changed?

~ * ~
2008

Ben sat in the den poring over a spreadsheet on the computer. It had been a slow season and money was tight.

Cee Cee hesitated in the doorway before approaching him.

He glanced up. "What?"

"I need to tell you something."

"I'm almost done here. Can it wait?"

She walked to the desk and stood beside him. "How bad is it?"

"We're not destitute, but it's going to be a tight year."

Cee Cee bit her lip, trying not to cry. This should be a joyful moment for both of them. She ran her fingers through his thick hair. "Ben?"

He looked at her and must have seen the distress on her face. "What's wrong?"

"I...I'm pregnant."

He didn't respond, just continued to stare. Then he drew in a deep breath and leaned his face into her abdomen. "How far along?" he asked, his voice muffled.

"About six weeks."

Rising, he drew her into his arms. "It'll be okay."

She began to cry. "You could be happy, you know."

"I am happy." He kissed her temple. "I'm sorry if I'm not jumping up and down right now. It's the business, that's all. We'll make it okay." He held her face in his hands. "I love you. You know that, right? I'll take care of us."

And he did. He picked up extra work wherever he could find it. He stubbornly refused to allow Cee Cee to look for work. He came home late most nights and dog tired. He was gone early nearly every morning. Sean would come downstairs in his pajamas and ask, "Where's daddy?" and it would break Cee Cee's heart.

Then Benji was born and Cee Cee was on her own with baths and feedings and doctor's appointments. Ben had his role as provider and Cee Cee had her role as mother and homemaker. And that was that.

When Benji was two years old, Cee Cee got sick and knew immediately. She was pregnant again. And when an ultrasound confirmed she was carrying twins, she was terrified. But by then, Ben's business had picked up and they were doing well financially. He was elated about the babies.

Cee Cee was happy, but she wouldn't use the term 'elated.' Something had been tugging at her lately. Something elusive and just beyond her reach. Something she couldn't clearly describe but that she knew wasn't *this*—a part of her life now. Something that shook her to her core and made the foundation beneath her feel like the sand on a hot, dry day.

While she huddled now on the porch of the retreat house, an ocean breeze kicked up, ruffling through her hair and causing a shiver. She suddenly knew what had been missing. It wasn't about Ben or her marriage or her family. *She* was missing—a part of her that she had set aside. It just happened that that part of her wanted her own career, wanted to be a nurse. But, first, she had to find a way to explain all of this to Ben so she didn't sound crazy and he wouldn't feel rejected. She felt sick at the thought that her marriage might now be damaged beyond repair.

Chapter Seventeen

Breaking News

The house was quiet, the front door closed. Everyone seemed to have turned in for the night. Julia crept down the creaking stairs and slipped through the kitchen and into the office. She turned on the computer and waited while the screen blinked to life. Not knowing exactly what Philadelphia news was reporting about her had been driving her crazy, but she could never get solo computer time, and she was afraid to turn on the TV news.

She located the WPVI-TV website and searched her name. And she gasped. Her photo splashed onto the screen with the headline: *Lead Prosecutor Disappears Following Botched Trial*. She clicked for the video, turned the volume down and leaned close to the monitor speakers. "Julia Lane, lead prosecutor for the Philadelphia District Attorney's office, has seemingly disappeared. Our attempts to reach Ms. Lane at her residence and at the phone numbers provided by an unnamed source have failed. The DA's office refuses to comment on Ms. Lane's whereabouts, but sources tell us the District Attorney Thomas Wilder has asked police to look into Ms. Lane's disappearance. A check of Ms. Lane's mailbox revealed several days of accumulated mail. We'll provide more information as it becomes available. Again, if you have seen Julia Lane, please contact Philadelphia police."

"Oh, my God. I forgot to place a mail hold." She sat back in the chair. "They think I've disappeared—or worse." A smile tugged at her mouth. "They think I've disappeared. What if I actually did?" The thought of never going back, of making a new life for herself far from the debacle that threatened to devour her sounded appealing. Sure, some would see that as running away. But sometimes it was just smart to turn and run. Self-preservation. Fight or flight—and she was so tired of fighting. She fought all the time in the court room.

She typed Philadelphia Inquirer in the browser box and hit enter. The early edition of the newspaper opened on the screen. The story of Julia's disappearance appeared under the headline: *Foul Play Feared in Assistant DA's Disappearance.*

"Foul play? They think someone killed me?" Well, it wasn't out of the realm of possibility, given the anger of the mob that had last chased her car from the court house parking garage. Then she thought of her brother. He must be frantic. Well, maybe not frantic, but a little concerned. Or he could be calculating his good fortune since he was listed as her beneficiary on a hefty life insurance policy. In any case, she would have to call him first thing in the morning. It dawned on her that she hadn't turned her cell phone on for a few days. All calls would have gone to voicemail.

She closed the internet browser and shut down the computer. As the screen faded to black, Julia once again weighed the benefits of doing the same thing—fading into oblivion. But she only had two hundred dollars in cash, and any attempt to access her bank account or use credit cards would draw attention. She sighed. It had been an enticing dream for a few minutes. She would, she supposed, call the office in the morning to let them know she was alive.

Ladies In Waiting

Three a.m. and still sleep eluded her. Julia fetched the heavy afghan from the sofa and stepped outside, closing the door softly behind her. She stood facing the ocean where a narrow beam of blue-white moonlight cut a swath across the water. Closing her eyes, she breathed deeply. But when she exhaled, bottled up emotion pushed a sob from her. She clutched the blanket around her shaking shoulders as hot tears flowed.

Julia was not used to being out of control of anything. She maintained strict routines in her life, took charge in her work, and kept her personal business to herself. Now she realized that all she had accomplished was to become predictable, to face high expectations in her job with no emotion, and to find herself with no friends and few acquaintances. This sent a new wave of sadness washing over her. The pit of despair seemed bottomless.

She rummaged in her pockets for tissues, but her search came up empty. "Dammit." When she turned the doorknob to go back inside, the door refused to budge. She turned the knob a second time and pushed with her other hand. Locked. Julia hesitated, then used her sweater sleeve to wipe her face.

A check of the windows on the ground floor and of the kitchen door gave evidence of someone's diligence. The house was locked up tight. She stumbled around the back of the house and noticed the small shed about twenty yards away. Opening the door, she peered inside. Once her eyes adjusted, she spied an aluminum ladder leaning against one wall. She dragged it from the shed and set it against the front porch roof of the house. Andi's windows were open, and one opened onto the porch roof. She just had to get to the roof without killing herself.

Julia stood on the first step and tested the ladder's

stability. She had never been fond of heights. *Just look up and keep moving*, she told herself. When she reached the top, she paused, uncertain of how to get her body onto the roof without knocking the ladder over. She swung her left leg up and to the side, then lifted the rest of her body over the top of rung of the ladder, landing on the shingled roof with a thunk.

The surface was rough and still warm from the sun. Julia got onto her hands and knees and inched her way up to the window. She now had two choices—call to Andi and waken her for help or work the screen loose and slip inside, then tiptoe to her own room. She put her fingertips under the bottom of the screen and lifted. It gave way and popped loose. Easing the screen down to the floor, Julia worked her right leg over the windowsill. But she forgot to duck and smacked her head on the raised window.

"Ouch!"

Light filled the room.

"Julia? What the hell are you doing?" Andi sat up in bed and clutched the sheet to her chest.

Julia rubbed at her right temple. "I'm sorry. I got locked out."

"How did you get up here?"

"I found a ladder. The downstairs windows were all locked. I didn't want to wake everyone."

"So you chose me. Well, are you going to straddle the windowsill all night, or are you coming inside? And put that screen back or the mosquitoes will eat me alive."

Julia set her right foot firmly on the floor, eased her body inside and then bent to retrieve the screen. "I'll put this back in place and be on my way."

When she had the screen secured and turned around, Andi was staring at her. "What were you doing outside at three in the morning?"

"I couldn't sleep. I needed some air."

Andi tucked the sheet under her arms and sat back on her pillows. "Thanks. Now I'm awake, too." She cocked her head. "Can I ask you something?"

"Uh...okay." Julia stopped midway between the bed and the door.

"What are you doing here—really? You act like you're pissed off half the time because you have to be here. Unless this is some unusual community service sentence for cat burglary, I don't get why you're here."

Julia pressed her lips together and took a breath. "Same reason you are—trying to get a better handle on things. I'm sorry I woke you, and I'm sorry if I seem angry. It's not you or anyone else here."

Andi sat up and pointed to a chair. "For chrissake, sit down. We're both wide awake." She narrowed her eyes. "Trying to outrun guilt?"

"I'm not... I'm...." Julia deflated, dropping into the overstuffed chair in the corner. "I'm so damned tired."

"A minute ago you said you couldn't sleep."

"Not that kind of tired. I checked the Philadelphia news online earlier. The police are looking for me."

Andi swung her legs over the side of the bed and stood. "What?"

Julia glanced at her standing there naked. "Oh, for godsake, put something on."

Andi grabbed for a silk robe and cinched it at her waist. "Why do the police want you?"

"They think I've been kidnapped or...or killed."

Now Andi paced in front of her. "Want to explain why they think that? Is someone trying to kill you?" She whirled to face Julia. "We could all be in danger if that's the case."

Julia let out a weary sigh. "No one's trying to kill

me. They're just wishing me dead. I left town rather abruptly and didn't tell anyone where I was going or for how long. I did leave word at my office that I'd be taking some time off, but then I forgot to put my mail on hold. And with those angry crowds shouting for my head...." Julia stood and retrieved a tissue from the box atop the nightstand.

 Andi slapped the bed beside her. "Sit."

 When Julia sat, Andi patted Julia's knee. "It was not your fault. That woman was insane."

 "Yes, and I fought against an insanity plea, and then she wasn't convicted and locked up."

 "Is that the first case you ever lost?"

 "No, but it's the last. I'm resigning. I won't be able to work effectively as a prosecutor any longer."

 Andi shook her head. "Martyrdom doesn't become you, Julia."

 "You think I'm being a martyr?"

 "Yes, I do. Sometimes we heap blame on ourselves so others won't have power over us. It's a control thing. We beat 'em to the punch. As long as you're blaming yourself, all those other people can't touch you." Andi sat back, resting on her elbows. "I do the same thing all the time. I beat myself up because Michael is so much younger than I am. If I say it first, then anyone else who says he's too young for me is telling me something I already know. Takes the sting out of their comments."

 Julia thought for a moment. It was out of character for her to turn tail and run. She had faced angry mobs before either because she won or lost a case. The difference in this case was the kids. Innocent lives had been snuffed out. Now that she thought about it, the defense attorney had been greeted with the same hostility. "You're right."

Andi straightened. "Excuse me?"

"You are right. It's sad, so very sad, that those children lost their lives. But sometimes the justice system fails. Sometimes we do our best and it's not good enough. And sometimes it's too good. Either way, there is the risk always that an innocent person will be found guilty, and the guilty person will be set free. It's a subjective system that isn't perfect."

Andi stood and applauded softly. "Well, counselor, you have the speech you need to make at your press conference."

Julia snatched up another tissue and wiped her eyes. "Thank you."

"You're welcome. Now, you think you can sleep?"

Julia shrugged. "Maybe."

"Good, because I'm exhausted and about ready to melt. So this robe is coming of in ten seconds and I'm getting into bed."

Julia made it to the door in five seconds or less. "Thanks, Andi. Goodnight."

"Three, two, one…" Andi untied the robe and laughed as Julia fumbled with the doorknob and exited into the hall.

In the hallway, Julia leaned against the wall and drew in a deep breath. In the span of one hour, she had overcome her fear of heights—in the dark, no less—and had gained perspective about her work and herself. Andi was the last person Julia would have thought would be helpful to her. Maybe she wasn't so very different from these women after all. Perhaps she just needed to give them a chance. Perhaps she needed to give herself a chance.

Chapter Eighteen

Footsteps

Julia—1986

Julia entered her father's law office. "Dad, we need to talk."

Without looking up, he asked, "Why? Something wrong with the office I've set up for you?"

"No, it's not that. It's...I...."

Her inability to finish the sentence got his full attention. "What's going on?"

She dropped into one of the chairs in front of his desk. "I've had an offer from the District Attorney's office."

"That's ridiculous. You're not a prosecutor."

Julia hesitated, then said, "But what if I want to be a prosecutor?"

Her father remained eerily quiet, staring at her. Then he shook his head. "This is about Ellis Graham, isn't it?"

Julia sat up straighter. "This has nothing to do with Ellis. I don't know how to say this without hurting your feelings."

"Please don't spare them now. Do you have any idea how much I've invested in making you the attorney you are today? Not just money. Time, mentoring from some of the finest lawyers in Philadelphia. This is a family owned practice. You have an obligation."

"I don't want to be the one to turn criminals back out onto the streets," she said.

"Don't mince words. You do realize I've dedicated my life to ensuring alleged criminals have due representation?"

"I'm sorry." Julia closed her eyes. "I knew you'd take this personally."

"Of course I take it personally," he barked. "You're my daughter. I was counting on you to come into the firm that has been the Lane family firm for over sixty years and keep up our tradition of excellence."

"I will maintain the Lane tradition of excellence in law. I'll just be doing it from the other side of the table."

He stared at her, defeat pulling at the corners of his mouth. "You're going to do this no matter what I say, aren't you?"

She nodded. "I have to, Dad."

He stood and rounded the desk, sitting on the edge. "Why are we just now talking about this?"

"I was afraid of how you'd react." She paused. "One of my profs at Penn invited me back to help out with a mock trial. I took on the role of the prosecuting attorney. It was such a rush. I felt…powerful. Who knows, in a few years, I could become the DA."

"A few years? Julia, I know passing the bar is exciting. It's an accomplishment and you should celebrate. Enjoy this time. But don't get carried away."

Tears stung the backs of her eyes. "You just can't believe in me, can you? If you were having this conversation with Richard, you'd be slapping him on the back, offering him a cigar, and planning to prepare him to become a senior partner in the firm."

"Yes, I would. And I'd groom you in the same way if you joined this firm. Without the cigar, of course."

He narrowed his gaze. "At least give me the courtesy of honesty and tell me how Graham comes into play."

Julia sighed. "I won't lie. Ellis and I have gone out a few times."

"I know."

She drew her eyebrows together. "How do you know?" she asked, certain her father had a spy watching her.

"He's the only man I've met who can make you smile just by walking into the room."

Warmth flooded Julia's face. "That's not true. I know another man who has that affect on me." She smiled and batted her eyelashes at her father.

He laughed. "I could never say no to you from the time you were old enough to point at what you wanted. If you're serious about switching teams, I'll support you, of course. And if you're serious about Ellis Graham—I'll fire him."

Julia gasped. "Dad!"

"I'm joking." He stood and pulled her up, taking both of her hands. "I was looking forward to working with you every day. Now I hope to God I never have to go up against you in court. I'm not at all sure I'd win."

"Thanks, Daddy."

He stared into her eyes. "You haven't called me that in years." He kissed her forehead. "Go on now, get the criminals off the streets. And tell Mark Rogers if he doesn't treat you right in the DA's office, he'll be answering to me."

~ * ~

1990

"Julia, please don't make this more difficult. We haven't really been in a marriage for months, and you know it."

She stared at Ellis. When had he become a complete stranger to her?

"Please say something."

"Go to hell." She whirled around and hurried up the stairs to their bedroom, slamming the door behind her and turning the lock. Leaning back against the door, Julia fought to control her breathing. She and Ellis had been married now for two years. They had agreed to put off having children while both focused on their careers—hers in the DA's office and his as a defense attorney with Lane and Associates.

And now he wanted a divorce to marry another woman who was carrying his child? Nausea rolled in Julia's stomach and she raced to the master bathroom, kneeling in front of the toilet. Empty after several minutes of retching, she slumped against the wall and let tears flow.

Ellis pounded on the bedroom door. "Come on, Julia, open the door. We're both adults. Be reasonable."

Reasonable? Adultery was reasonable? She wearily got to her feet and stood at the sink to rinse her mouth. She lifted her gaze and stared into the mirror, seeing a stranger looking back at her—a mad woman with disheveled blond hair, red-rimmed eyes, and a puffy face. She jerked a tissue from the holder on the sink and blew her nose.

Julia unlocked the door and ripped it open. "You son-of-a-bitch. Get some clothes and get out of here."

Ellis seemed to shrink before her. "I didn't plan for this to happen."

"Clearly you were thinking with your small head, the one where your brain apparently does reside. I hope your whore has a good job because I can assure you, come Monday, you will be unemployed."

He opened his mouth to say something, then

closed it again. He pushed past Julia and retrieved a suitcase from his closet. "I'll come back for my things while you're at work on Monday."

"The hell you will. You'll come when I'm here. I want to see everything you remove from this house. Don't bother taking your key. I'll have the locks changed an hour after you leave."

He dropped the shirts he held into the suitcase and faced her. "Do you want to know why I turned to another woman?"

Julia weighed the question. Did she want to know?

Ellis didn't wait for her to decide. "Because she doesn't give a shit about the law, court proceedings, arguments, which judge is an asshole this week. Jesus, Julia, every conversation with you is like a damned debate. We can't even have sex without arguing who's going to be on top. And for your information, you're not all that good at it, especially not when you're on top." He grabbed a fistful of boxers from a drawer and jammed them into the suitcase. "It's like being ridden in a fucking rodeo." He disappeared into the bathroom and returned with his toiletries. "You don't need me. You don't need anyone. You get off in court. Sex with me is just obligation. Don't worry about calling your father. I'll tender my resignation first thing Monday morning."

Julia stood motionless. She felt skewered. But after he brushed past her and she heard the front door close, she felt something else. Relief. It was over. Now she could focus on her work and stop pretending to want to share her life with Ellis. The fact that his other woman was pregnant was the biggest hurt of all, since it had been at his insistence that they delayed having a baby. But a child wouldn't have changed anything, just added complications.

Ladies In Waiting

She walked into the bathroom, removed the packet of birth control pills from the medicine chest, and emptied it into the toilet. She flushed and watched the tablets circle in the whirlpool and disappear.

In the library, she thumbed through the phone book until she found a locksmith on twenty-four hour call. "I need to have the locks at my house changed tonight."

"Sure. Give me the address. Break in?" he asked.

"More like a break out."

~ * ~

1998

Julia remained in the bathroom stall, eavesdropping on the gossip going on at the sinks.

"I was shocked when Rogers lost the election, weren't you?"

"Yes, but his track record has been slipping the last year. That Hawthorn case is what took him under."

"What do you know about the new guy—Wilder?"

"He moved here from Pittsburgh. I heard he graduated from Harvard and knows Mark pretty well."

"That sucks, when one of your own friends unseats you."

Tired of waiting for them to leave, Julia flushed the toilet. The gossipers scurried out of the room before she emerged from the stall. She had done her homework on Thomas Wilder—Juris Doctorate from Harvard Law, married with two children, stellar career statistics as a prosecutor in Pittsburgh. She had found everything but his height, weight and favorite color. She was prepared to meet Mr. Wilder.

The man who introduced himself to Julia a few days later was nothing like what she expected. His shock of unruly black hair and piercing blue eyes mesmerized her.

"Miss Lane?"

"I'm sorry?"

"I said it's a pleasure to meet you. I've reviewed your records and I have to say I'm glad you're on my side."

Julia hated the rush of heat to her face. The blush was the one thing she could not control. "Thank you. It's a pleasure to meet you, too. You have an impressive win record also."

He grinned. "Someone's been doing homework."

The heat intensified. "I like to be prepared."

He cocked his head to one side. "And were you?"

"Not completely." She regained control of what she thought were her senses but were, in reality, her hormones. "You're taller than I anticipated."

He laughed and the laughter rumbled through her. She reminded herself this man was both married and her boss.

"Well, I look forward to working with you. When you leave, would you see if Art Simmons is available and ask him to come in next?"

"I'll do that." She sent Simmons in and then returned to her cubicle. *Is this guy going to meet individually with all two hundred plus Assistant DA's?*

It impressed Julia that, by the end of the two months, Thomas Wilder had done just that. He had personally introduced himself to each and every Assistant DA and most of the support staff. And he earned Julia's full respect.

~ * ~

2006

Tom sat across from her at a corner table at The

Jury Box, a local hangout for attorneys just a block from the courthouse. He rolled a sweating bottle of beer between his palms. "If you'd ever have asked me if I'd be divorced, I would have said you were crazy."

"I'm so sorry, Tom. I know how that hurts."

He looked up. "You do?"

She didn't talk much about her personal life in the office. "It was a very long time ago after a very short marriage. But it hurts, I know."

He nodded. "We're trying to keep it civil for the sake of the kids. They're grown, but it's still hard for them." He took a draw on the beer.

Julia studied the lines that had deepened in his face and now understood why. She knew Mary Beth Wilder, had been to their home for parties. They seemed happy. Just further evidence to Julia that your work was the only thing that wouldn't betray you in the end. The DA's office was her spouse, her lover, her best friend. Clearly, she had made the right choice.

Tom smiled. "I shouldn't be dumping my problems on you. I'm your boss."

"We're off the clock. If you need to talk any time, you know where to find me." She glanced at her watch. "Which reminds me. I need to get back to the office and finish preparing for court in the morning."

"It's nearly nine p.m. Don't you have a date or a dog to get home to?"

Julia shook her head. "Dogs are too much trouble. So are dates." She stood and slipped the strap of her purse over her shoulder. "I'll see you tomorrow."

Back at her desk, she found herself unable to concentrate. All she could think of was that Tom Wilder was getting a divorce which would make him available—and her heart would start to pound. *Get a grip, Julia. The last thing you need in your life is a complicated relationship with a man on the rebound. A man who also happens to be your boss.*

Chapter Nineteen

Julia paced the Pepto pink bedroom, cell phone in hand. What was she going to do? If—and it was big if—she still had a job, she needed to clear up this misunderstanding with Thomas Wilder. She punched in his personal cell number.

Her call went to voicemail. She cleared her throat as if preparing to give a closing argument. "Tom, it's Julia Lane. I saw the news reports last night, and I'm afraid there's been a big misunderstanding. I've not been kidnapped or murdered. I simply went out of town for a few weeks. I had arranged the time off at the office, so I thought you knew. But I forgot to put my mail on hold and, well, with the animosity directed toward me, I can see where one might conclude...."

Her phone beeped an incoming call and she glanced at the screen. It was Tom. She pressed the talk button. "Tom, I was just leaving you a message."

"Julia, are you all right? Where the hell are you? The police are questioning your neighbors."

Heat enveloped Julia's face. "I'm so sorry. I'll call the Philly police and let them know I'm alive and well."

"Are you?"

"Pardon?"

"Are you well? That last case was tough on you. So was the press. And what happened after... I know how you must be feeling. I'm concerned about you."

"I'll be fine, Tom. I know this kind of thing comes with the territory. I've been the target of anger before, but not outrage like this. I came to a women's retreat in Cape May for time away and to regroup."

"Maybe you should spend some time with your family, too."

"I don't have... I...uh...I'll consider that." Time with family. He made it seem so simple. Being around her brother was never easy. He loved to argue with her, and would probably take on the voice of the angry mob just to play devil's advocate. Julia was very much alone in this. She swiped at a tear that escaped, despite her clenched jaw and determination she would not cry.

"Julia, we need to talk."

She sucked in a breath. *Here it comes. I'm fired.*

"Can it wait until I get back to Philadelphia?"

"I...uh...suppose so. Do you need anything?"

"Thanks, but I'm fine. Really. I'll be back in Philly in a week or two, and I'll call." She had no clue where she would go after this retreat, but she had no plans to return to Philadelphia at the end of the retreat. Maybe she could pay Bree to let her stay here another week.

"What's the place like where you're staying? Relaxing?"

She glanced around her hot pink room. "Sort of." *With the lights off.*

"Good. Well, I'll see you when you return to the city. Call if you need anything."

"Thanks, Tom."

She ended the call and stared at her phone. There was something different in Tom's tone. They had worked together for the past fifteen years. He was professional and work-oriented. Always. But just now, he seemed to genuinely care that she was all right. She shrugged it off as him being a good boss looking after an employee. Perhaps he was concerned she would file, claiming a stress-related disability.

There was a time when Julia allowed herself a brief fantasy of a relationship with Tom Wilder. He was four years her senior, handsome, intelligent, and divorced. Attractive and available. But Julia had set a hard and fast rule for herself about never getting involved with co-workers, much less with her boss. As effectively as poking a straight pin into a balloon, she deflated that fantasy. Besides, it wasn't as if Tom had ever given her thoughts any encouragement.

After reassuring the Philadelphia police that she was in fact fine and had not been kidnapped, Julia sighed and slipped the phone back into her purse.

When Julia entered the kitchen, Cee Cee smiled up at her from the table. "Hey, do you know how to ride a bike?"

"Is this a riddle?" Julia poured a cup of coffee and sat down.

"No. I went exploring and found a half dozen bicycles in the back of the garage. They must be for the use of guests. I thought we could take a bike ride, all of us, after breakfast."

Julia hesitated. She hadn't been on a bicycle since college. But it sounded like just the kind of challenge she needed right now. "You know, that would be fun."

Cee Cee lifted both eyebrows. "Really? You'll do it?"

"Yes. I'm in. Do any of the bikes have a basket? We could pack up a picnic and bike down to the beach beyond the boardwalk."

"Two of them have baskets." Cee Cee set her empty cup in the sink. "I'll make breakfast. The others should be coming down soon. We'll need to clean the bikes up a bit. They don't look like they've been used since last year."

"I can do that while you cook. I saw a bucket and some rags in the laundry room." She ignored the surprised look Cee Cee gave her. If the girl lifted her eyebrows any higher, they'd disappear under her hairline.

Something had snapped in Julia since last night. She had been here for four days and was just now beginning to feel like she belonged. Perhaps it was the knowledge that someone out there cared about what happened to her. Not the police. They had to care, or at least to question. The women she had met here cared about one another, and she knew they would include her if she allowed them. And Tom Wilder cared. That thought brought a half-smile to Julia's face.

She retrieved the bucket and rags from the laundry room, poured a couple capfuls of Mr. Clean into the bucket and added hot water. If she knew how, she would have whistled as she headed for the garage. Skipping was out of the question. She'd spill the water.

~ * ~

Like Riding a Bike

Five gleaming bicycles sat in a row inside the garage.

"Are there helmets?" Liv asked.

"You're not supposed to fall over," Andi said, choosing a blue and white Schwinn.

Markie stared at the bicycles. She had loved bike riding and still had a bike in her own garage at home. But now the bike presented a daunting challenge as she wondered if her legs would have the strength to make the ride through town and back.

"Ready?" Cee Cee put a hand on Markie's arm.

"Maybe I'll stay here, pass on the bike ride."

"Please come. Look, on Bree's agenda we were scheduled for a bike ride and picnic. I know we've abandoned that agenda, but it sounds like such fun. A chance to feel like a kid again. Didn't you and your girlfriends go biking together when you were a kid?"

Markie smiled at the memory. "We did. There were three of us who were like sisters back then. We'd take off on our bikes and spend the entire day pedaling and talking, mostly about boys."

"Oh, please tell me we don't have to talk about boys," Julia groaned.

Liv chuckled. "Of course not. Now we talk about men."

Andi balanced on her bike. "You get to go first. We want to hear more about your dinner date with Nick. And why there hasn't been a follow-up."

Cee Cee used a bungee cord to secure a small cooler filled with drinks in the basket on her red bike. "Okay, ladies. Ready to roll? Now remember, we ride to the left, facing traffic. I do this with my kids all the time, so just follow me."

Markie watched the women, one by one, kick off and settle their feet onto the pedals of their bikes. She swung one leg awkwardly over her pale green bike and pushed off, praying she would make it.

A steady breeze lifted her hair and her spirits, and Markie felt as if she were soaring. Drivers slowed and passengers smiled and waved as the convoy of middle-aged women on bicycles pedaled by. In the front of the line, Cee Cee held up a hand to signal a stop. "Everybody doing okay?"

"Great," Andi said.

"Fine," Liv added

"How much farther?" Julia asked.

Markie slid from the bike seat and stood. Her legs trembled and numbness tingled in her feet. She steadied herself with the handlebars and shook each leg to stimulate the blood flow. But she knew the muscles were reacting to the exercise. "I think I've had enough. I'm going to head back. You girls go on."

"You okay?" Liv asked.

"I'm fine, just tired. I'll see you all later back at the house." She checked for traffic before walking the bike across the road and heading toward the retreat house.

She made it about a mile and was half way up the hill just shy of the driveway when her legs gave out. She stretched her left foot down to prevent her fall, but her weakened muscles let go and she tumbled into the weeds alongside the road, the bike landing on her still-tender ankle.

"Ouch!" she cried out. She sat up and pulled her foot from beneath the metal frame, scanning the road in each direction. Not a single car in sight.

~ * ~

Liv lowered the kickstand on her bike and swiped a hand across her damp forehead. "Whew, that was a workout. And we have to repeat the trip to get home."

"I can pedal back and get my van, then come and pick up the rest of you," Cee Cee said with a grin.

"Smart ass," Andi muttered. "Just because you're younger."

"And I have to keep up with four kids," Cee Cee added.

The women sat in the shade of an oak tree in a hidden cove at the far end of a sandy beach. Cee Cee passed sandwiches around. "Do you think Markie got back okay? One of us should have gone with her."

"She's fine. We were only a mile from the house. It's too bad she turned around, though, because she would love this spot." Andi lifted her face to the breeze and closed her eyes.

Liv nodded. "It is beautiful here. How did you

find this place?"

"It's my hiding place," Cee Cee said. "My in-laws live down the beach, just beyond those dunes. This is the beach where I had my first unofficial date with Ben. When I have a chance to get away by myself, which isn't very often, I come down here to think."

After they had eaten, Andi and Liv kicked off their shoes and walked on the beach. Cee Cee packed up the trash and drink bottles. Julia perched on a large rock in the shade and stared out at the water. She looked up when Cee Cee approached. "Thank you for bringing us here."

"You're welcome." Cee Cee plopped down beside Julia. "Can I share an observation?"

"Sure."

"You seem more relaxed today, almost like you want to be here."

Julia chuckled. "Maybe because I've realized that being here with all of you is good. I need to apologize, but I think I'll save that for dinner when I can say it to everyone at one time."

Cee Cee nudged Julia's knee with her own. "You don't owe anyone here an apology. It's kind of hard to believe the five of us came here complete strangers just four days ago. And look at us now."

Julia glanced down at Cee Cee and grinned. "Yeah, look at us."

Andi and Liv returned from their walk. "Should we head back?" Liv asked.

"Sure." Cee Cee stood with ease.

Julia groaned as she straightened her legs, bending to rub her knees. "Oh, God, give me strength."

Andi laughed. "What's the matter, Jules? Feeling your age?"

Julia limped to her bike. "Every damn minute of

it."

As the bikers crested the hill before the driveway, Cee Cee brought her bike to an abrupt stop. "That looks like the bike Markie was riding."

"It is. Oh, my God. You don't think she got clipped by a passing car, do you?" Andi was off her bike and searching the tall grass. "Markie?"

Liv uprighted the bicycle. "The bike doesn't appear to be damaged. Maybe something went wrong and she left the bike and hiked home."

Unable to gain momentum on the incline, Julia walked her bike up the hill at a quick pace. "I'll check the house."

The other women followed, Andi awkwardly pushing both her bike and Markie's.

Nick sat on the porch, with Buster lying at his feet. He stood when the women approached, and Buster let out a muffled 'ruff'.

Julia dropped her bike and headed up the porch steps. "Is Markie here?"

"She is. Had a little mishap with her bike, and I brought her to the house."

"Where is she?"

"Inside, icing her ankle. I didn't want to leave her alone until someone else was here."

Julia hurried past him and into the house, followed by Andi and Liv.

"Thanks, Nick." Cee Cee stopped to ruffle Buster's ears. "Is she okay?"

He shrugged. "She says she is, just turned her ankle. But…." He glanced at the door, then motioned for Cee Cee to follow down the steps. "She couldn't get her legs under her. They seemed to be weak. I practically had to carry her up here."

"Oh. Well, she took a fall the other day. Maybe it

weakened her ankle. It was nice of you to stay here until we returned."

"No problem. If you need anything, just call me. And...maybe you could remind Liv about my invitation for the boat ride? For all of you?"

"I'll remind her. That sounds like fun."

He snapped his fingers at the dog. "Come on, Buster. Let's go home."

Inside, Markie sat on the sofa with her left leg elevated and the ankle wrapped with a makeshift ice pack—a bag of frozen peas—and towel. She seemed embarrassed by all the attention, so Cee Cee didn't ask her to explain one more time what had happened.

"Some people will do anything to get a guy to pick them up," Cee Cee chided.

"This will teach me to pay attention to where I'm going," Markie said.

But Cee Cee thought about the ways her mother had laughed off her forgetfulness for the past year before she was diagnosed. "I'm going to make lemonade. Want a glass?"

"Thank you." A glance at Markie's face told Cee Cee she was being thanked for more than the offer of refreshment.

Chapter Twenty

What Are We Waiting For?

"The topic Bree has listed for tonight is *What are we waiting for?* Anyone game for that one?" Andi asked.

"We're all waiting for something all the time, aren't we?" Julia asked. "How unique is that?"

Markie gazed hard at the flowers Cee Cee had arranged in the center of the dining table. "Sometimes we wait for something that we know will never happen. And sometimes what we are waiting for looms over us like a shadow about to swallow us whole."

Andi turned and stared at her. "That sounds philosophical and just a little bit foreboding. I vote we have this discussion." She stood and began to clear the table. "I'll make coffee. Markie, you might want to bring along some of your special blend for this conversation."

Julia stood. "I might need another hit of that stuff myself."

"Uh-oh, Julia's got something big to share if she's willing to break the law to spill it," Andi teased.

Dusk sent a soft yellow glow of sunlight across the waters of the Atlantic beyond the beach below. Andi set the tray of cups on the wicker table and settled into one of the rockers. The women filled their cups and balanced plates with the apple pie Cee Cee had baked.

A pleasant breeze carried the scent of ocean and mingled with the spicy aroma of the warmed dessert. Markie elevated her swollen ankle on the other low wicker table Cee Cee slid her way. "Thanks."

"Well, here we are—waiting," Andi said. "Who wants to go first?"

"Let's just enjoy our dessert and the sunset," Liv suggested.

Cee Cee giggled. "We're all very good at waiting, that's for sure. Or is it procrastinating?"

~ * ~

Liv

When they had each finished dessert and sat in silence, Liv straightened in her chair. "Okay, I can't take this any longer." She glanced at each of the other women. "Want to know what I'm waiting for? I'm waiting for what comes next. I never expected to find myself in the situation I'm in—divorced, struggling financially. Alone. In my life before everything turned upside down, I rarely had to wait for anything. The only waiting I did was when I was pregnant with my children, and that was a joyful waiting. Well...." She grinned. "Until the last three or four weeks. But now I feel as though I live every day waiting for that proverbial other shoe to drop, for something to pull what I have left out from under me."

Even as she said the words, an icy cold hand seemed to clutch her insides, and Liv shivered.

"Oh, Liv. That sounds nerve-wracking," Markie said. "But I know what you're saying."

Liv nodded. "It is. I chose this retreat because I thought I could get away from the stress, but it's always with me, just below the surface. I...." Her voice broke, and she blinked. "I'm afraid of something I can't see most of the time. Reminds me of childhood fears of the bogeyman in the closet." She remembered Nick's words about fear and sucked in a breath. "I guess I'm waiting for the morning when I wake up and I'm not afraid.

When I feel normal again, like life is okay, if not truly good." She dabbed an invisible spot on her pant leg with a napkin. "And I'm waiting for my sons to call."

Cee Cee, who sat closest to Liv, reached over and squeezed her hand. "I'm sorry. All that happened because of your divorce?"

Liv looked up. "Since the divorce. A lot of things led up to it. The boys feel I abandoned their father. They can't see the way his actions betrayed me and a lot of other people." She reached for her coffee and lifted the cup with a trembling hand. "Sorry. I'm sure Bree intended this exercise to be positive and uplifting."

"Screw uplifting. We've all reached the point in life where the only thing uplifting is a ninety-dollar bra." Andi nodded to Cee Cee. "Except, maybe, for you."

Cee Cee pressed one palm across her breasts. "Are you kidding? After nursing four kids? And Ben wants another baby? In his dreams."

"If they had to give birth, there isn't a man alive who'd want a baby," Andi said. "I haven't met one yet that could survive childbirth. Ouch, it hurts, it hurts. Make it stop," she whined. She sobered and turned to Liv. "Sorry, I didn't mean to make light of what you're going through."

"No problem. I wish I could make light of it or find some light in it. I'd hope to see that light but, with my luck, it would be the proverbial freight train coming through the tunnel. I almost hesitate to say this, but…I'm so tired of waiting. I want to *do* something to change my life. I want to be back in control."

"What's stopping you?" Julia asked.

Liv shrugged. "I am, I suppose."

"Then take a step and do something. What would that first step be?" Markie asked.

"I'm not sure. Maybe I'd call my sons and make

them listen to me and hear my side of the story."

"Then that's what you have to do. Even if they don't listen. Even if they hang up. At least you've taken a step forward," Andi said.

Liv nodded and swallowed the golf-ball sized lump in her throat. "Maybe I should remind them of the hours I spent in labor just to bring them into the world." She grinned. "A little guilt couldn't hurt."

~ * ~

Cee Cee

"Ben barely survived my delivery of our kids," Cee Cee said. "The nurse had to get him a chair the first time. They were afraid he'd pass out." She sighed. "Want to know what I'm waiting for? I'm waiting for the day when all my kids are in school." She held up a hand. "I know, my mother-in-law is horrified that I'm wishing away their childhoods. But I just want some time for me. And maybe I should feel badly about that, but I don't. I love my kids. I always thought we'd have two—a boy and a girl. We got two boys. Then I got pregnant again, and we had the twins—both girls. Now Ben thinks we should go for at least one more. I swear, if he had his way, we'd have kids hanging from the rafters."

Cee Cee sat back in her chair. "I'm tired. I'm only thirty-two years old, and I'm so damned tired." She looked at them hopefully. "Tell me that's normal and it passes."

"I only had one child at home, so it's hard for me to say," Andi offered.

"I always had help," Liv said. "We had a nanny. Something I regret now. I should have spent more time with my kids. I was too busy with events, clubs, my husband's business entertaining. I wish I could take it all back."

"Now I feel guilty," Cee Cee said. She had planned to approach Ben about hiring a nanny, at least part time for the twins while the older children were in school this coming year. She wanted to do something. She wanted to go back to school herself, get her nursing degree.

"Oh, no. I didn't mean that for you. Things are different today than when my kids were growing up. Parents both have careers," Liv said.

"I've decided to go back to school, regardless of what Ben thinks," Cee Cee blurted. Then she studied each of the women for a reaction.

"Good," Julia said.

Liv turned to face her. "If that's what you want to do, you should do it. There are ways to get grants for schooling. Especially for women who have been homemakers and are trying to return to the workforce. I know because I served on a board Adam set up…well, that fund is now bankrupt."

"I already checked into nursing programs nearby. And there are grants and loans I can apply for."

"I can loan you the money," Andi said as casually as if she were saying *I'll get you another cup of coffee.*

Cee Cee's head whipped around. "What?"

Andi shrugged. "I said I can loan you the money. You can pay me back later, or not."

"But that could take years," Cee Cee said. "And you don't even know me."

"So. Look, I've got plenty of money. Hell, I know all I need to know about you."

"Are you serious?" Cee Cee asked.

"Yup. You would have to figure out child care. How about your mother-in-law?"

"She's already said she would take the kids any time." Cee Cee practically bounced in her seat, then suddenly stilled. "I can't accept your offer. It's very generous, but...but there's more to it than what I've told you." She sucked in a deep breath and exhaled. "Lately I've been thinking about...about a d-divorce. Which may be definite now that Ben read that journal entry. I tried to talk to him last night, but he just said he was busy with the kids and we'd talk when I got home." Tears stung her eyes and she bit her lip.

"Oh, honey." Markie reached over for Cee Cee's hand.

Despite her efforts, the words ripped from deep inside her. "I...just...don't...know...if... Ben...st-still...loves me." Her words were punctuated by gulping sobs. "Sure, he wants more kids, but I think it's just a way to k-keep me at home—barefoot and pregnant. And then there's my m-mom."

"What's happening with your mother?" Markie asked.

Cee Cee sniffled and reached for a paper napkin to blow her nose. "She was diagnosed with Alzheimer's a few months ago. She's only fifty-seven."

"Oh, Cee Cee. I'm so sorry." Liv got out of her chair and stooped to wrap Cee Cee in a hug.

Cee Cee sank into the warmth of Liv's embrace. "Thank you. It's just all too much. I feel like I've lost Ben, and now I'm losing my mother to that hideous disease. I can't seem to find myself, either. And I'm sick of being called Cee Cee. It makes me feel like I'm twelve years old. My name is Clare, dammit." The eruption of anger shook her, and Cee Cee looked up at the other women.

Liv stood beside her, eyebrows raised. Julia and Markie simply stared, but Andi's mouth quirked up at the corners.

"It isn't funny," Cee Cee said.

Andi straightened her face. "No, Clare, it is not funny. So you start from there, by reclaiming your name. You've been waiting for something to change. But you're the only one who can change things. Just like Liv said. Take one step forward."

Clare thought about her mother's condition and understood what Andi meant. She wouldn't have the power to change that, but she could decide how they went through that dark journey together. As for Ben, that was going to require some thought and more than a little soul-searching. She knew she loved him. She just didn't know if she could continue to live with him. Not with the way things were now between them.

"Thanks," she said weakly.

Andi smiled. "You are very welcome—Clare."

~ * ~

Andi

"Am I the only one craving a glass of wine? Coffee just isn't going to cut it for me." Andi got to her feet. "I'll be right back. Markie, I know you have a joint in your pocket. Now would be the time to light up."

She returned with a bottle and five glasses, filling each one and offering them around.

Liv chuckled, accepting the glass. "If this keeps up, we can meet again next year in rehab."

When Andi sat down again, she slipped her cell phone from her pocket and glanced at the screen.

"Guess we know what you're waiting for—a phone call," Julia said.

"I spend a lot of hours waiting for Michael to call or waiting for Michael to return my call. Until now, I thought the only thing I was waiting for was for the hot flashes to end." She waved a hand in front of her face. "But I wait for Michael. I even wait for him to say it's over and to leave me." She sipped the wine. "I've never been good at waiting. I know that surprises you all, to learn I'm impatient."

"I'd never have guessed." Julia grinned.

"You know, nothing will ever come close to the day I waited for Paul to return home from his run. One hour, then two. Then the police at the door." She shook her head. "I imagined him having run into a friend and stopping at Starbucks as he often did at the end of his run. I imagined him finishing the run and just lounging on a bench by the water. I never imagined him lying on a deserted path, dying alone."

She gulped down her wine and refilled the glass. "After that day, I stopped expecting good things to happen. It was as if a light was turned out in my soul, and I could only see darkness. So I imagine the worst with my daughter, with Michael, with my job. I think I got involved with a younger man because he's not as likely to die while jogging and leave me alone. Not that that's true. He could fall off the scaffolding at a construction site."

A familiar fear danced up her spine. "If Paul could die at fifty-three, why can't I?"

"You think you're going to die?" Liv asked.

"I just think it's more possible now than I thought it before. Paul and I were supposed to grow old together. I've been forced to face my mortality, along with menopause. I'm determined to squeeze every last bit out of life now. My daughter thinks I'm a slut."

Clare gasped. "She said that?"

"No, not in so many words. I know it's hard for her. I'm not the mother she grew up with—doting, always available to her. Paul's death left a huge hole in our lives, and it created a gaping chasm between us. Instead of doing everything I could to bridge that chasm, I've started off on a new life for myself."

"As it should be," Liv said. "I'm trying to do the same thing. My sons can't understand it, but I hope some day they will."

Andi hadn't talked about these feelings with anyone, hadn't admitted them to herself, much less spoken them aloud. She sounded like an old woman, like someone who had given up on life. She had never found bitterness to be attractive in anyone. Was that what Paul would have wanted for her—to give up? He was a man who always embraced life, welcomed every day with a smile and a positive attitude.

"Ah, it's the wine talking. I need to shut up now. I'm depressing myself. God, we're a gloomy bunch. All of us waiting for something bad to happen. Or for just *something* to happen. Whatever became of hopes and dreams?" She lifted her glass. "How about you, Jules? What are you waiting for?"

A car slowed at the end of the drive, then backed up and turned in. The headlights swept across the women's faces, and Andi shielded her eyes. "Who could that be?"

"Maybe Bree came back," Clare said.

The car stopped, the lights went dark, and the door opened. A tall man climbed out and stood behind the open door. "Is Julia Lane here?"

Julia abruptly passed the joint back to Andi, choking and waving away the smoke. She shot to her feet. "Tom?"

The man closed the car door and waved, approaching the porch.

Julia descended the steps and met him before he reached the house, steering him back toward his car.

Andi lifted an eyebrow. "Well, maybe we just found out what Julia's been waiting for. Or should I say whom?"

Chapter Twenty-One

Be Careful What You Wish For

Julia's heart raced as she guided Tom back toward his car. She turned her head and exhaled heavily over her shoulder. When they reached the car, she asked, "What's happened?"

"Nothing," he said. "I was worried about you after we talked. So I figured I'd drive down here and see for myself that you're okay. A woman at a diner out by the highway told me how to find the retreat house."

"You were worried about me?" The 'me' came out as a squeak and Julia swallowed. She glanced up at his angular face, half in shadow and half lit by moonlight. Of course she had noticed before how handsome he was, but now she noticed in a different way. And it made her feel uncomfortable, and just a little giddy. "Why?"

Tom leaned back on his car, hands shoved into his pockets. He steadied his gaze on her face. "I've never known you to retreat, to run from anything. You're a warrior. When you took off the way you did...."

"You told me to take some time off. Remember? I figured you wanted me out of the DA's office because I'd put us in such a bad light with the public. So I got out of town." Her hands trembled and she clasped them together to still them.

Tom gave her a rueful grin. "I told you to take time off so you could escape those daily hecklers. I hated to see what those crowds were doing to you." He removed one hand from his pocket and lightly touched her cheek. "I'm sorry if you felt like you were alone in this, Julia. That was my fault. I wasn't sure what to do for you, and you didn't seem to want or need help."

She was sure the heat from his fingertips would burn indelible prints into her skin. Resolving not to cry, she bit hard on her lower lip, but the tears spilled down her face anyway. Embarrassed, she turned her head and swiped the moisture away.

He leaned closer to her and sniffed. "Is that...?" His eyes widened. "Have you been smoking marijuana?"

She took a step back. "Where would I get marijuana? It's illegal," she countered, scowling. "Why are you here? We talked on the phone and you knew I was fine."

He glanced over her head to the audience of women on the porch. "Can we maybe take a walk on the beach? I have some things I need to say to you. In private."

"If it's about my job, I understand. I'll tender my resignation as soon as I return to the city."

"It's not about your job, Julia. Will you please just give me a few minutes and listen?"

Julia nodded. "Sure." She kept her gaze fixed on the wooden stairs that led to the beach, not giving the curious women on the porch a glance. She knew she would have some explaining to do later, and she dreaded that conversation.

"Julia!" Cee Cee ran down from the porch, holding something in her hand. "If you're going down to the beach, you might need this." She slapped a small flashlight into Julia's palm.

"Thanks." Julia accepted the light and kept walking. Why did she feel like a self-conscious teenager on her first date? "Be careful, Tom. These steps are a little shaky in places."

When they both reached the bottom, Julia turned off the flashlight. The moon hung bright in the sky and cast a silvery glow across the beach. Julia stepped out of her sandals, allowing her feet to sink into the still-warm sand. The action made her feel naked and vulnerable, and she was about ready to slide her feet back into her shoes when Tom kicked off his docksiders, removed his socks and bent to cuff up his pants. "It's a beautiful night."

Julia fell into step beside him, her fingers tightly clutching the flashlight. "I never really looked at the ocean before I came here. I'd seen it, of course, but never *looked* at it. It's funny and kind of sad—the things we take for granted. Know what I mean?"

He stopped walking and stared into her eyes. "I know exactly what you mean."

For a heartbeat, Julia thought he was going to kiss her. But he resumed walking. The back of his hand brushed against hers. "Sometimes we take for granted the beauty that's around us. I know I have."

Julia laughed. "Beauty? In the Philadelphia DA's office?"

"Not to wax poetic, but beauty is all around us. We just have to take the time to look. You said that yourself." He stopped and turned to face her. "Take you, for example."

"Me?"

"In the years we've worked together, I've come to count on you to always be there, to be strong, to be a winner. I failed to really see you, Julia. I failed to see the woman behind the attorney." He lifted her free hand and squeezed it. "And in the days since you've been gone, I've realized what I missed."

Julia's breath caught as Tom lifted her hand and kissed first the back of it, then the palm. A shudder rolled through her. *I should say something*, she thought, but no words came.

Tom tugged her closer, so that only a thin wall of heated air separated their bodies. "I need to know if you feel the same way. If you think there's a chance for us."

"Us?"

"You and me."

Julia's body swayed and Tom's arms wrapped around her. She allowed him to draw her closer until her cheek settled on his shoulder.

"It's a simple question, Julia. If you like, I can offer arguments." His breath ruffled the hair at her temple.

She breathed in the spicy scent of his aftershave. "We work together."

Tom chuckled. "That's what I'm hoping for." He tightened his hold and kissed the top of her head. "We can deal with the office politics later."

"If I no longer worked as a prosecutor, it wouldn't be an issue." The words were out before she had time to process them.

Tom held her away from him and studied her face. "Are you quitting?"

Julia sighed and dragged a hand through her hair that blew across her face. "I don't know. I've had some time to think and I've realized I'm tired of fighting. Maybe I should give up law altogether."

She turned to walk, but Tom held her fast to the spot. "Julia, you've dedicated your life to the law. You could just walk away from that?"

"What has it gotten me?" She pulled away and trudged down the beach.

Tom hurried after her. "What would you do? Where would you go?"

The questions stopped her in her tracks because

she didn't have a clue about answers to either.

Tom caught up with her and turned her to face him. "I'm not saying you shouldn't quit. But you need to give this a lot of thought."

Julia bristled. "It's hardly a decision I'd make lightly. Practicing law is all I've ever known, all I have." With the admission, the full impact of her aloneness struck her.

Clutching her hand, Tom said, "It's not all you have. You've got me—if you want me."

Julia blinked, expecting the action to clear the vision before her and wake her from a dream. Before she could respond, he lowered his lips to hers and kissed her lightly. When Julia opened her eyes, Tom's eyes locked on hers.

He raised an eyebrow. "No objection?"

She held her breath, fearful that if she exhaled the apparition of Tom Wilder would fade and she would find herself alone on the beach. How the hell had she come to this? A minute ago, she was filled with dread at the thought of eventually returning to Philadelphia, resuming her work. Had Tom just suggested they engage in a relationship? *Suggested, hell. He'd just offered himself on a platter.*

She exhaled and smiled, feeling her insides loosen. "No, counselor. No objection." This time she tilted her face up and met him for a kiss that curled her toes in the sand.

They stood gazing out at the ocean, Julia with her head on Tom's shoulder. Tom's hand rested familiarly on her hip.

"I did not see this coming." Julia said. If she had, she would likely have summoned up a strong argument against why they could not have a relationship. For once, Julia was happy to have been taken off guard and rendered speechless.

"Surprised me, too. So, now what?"

She whipped her head around to look at him. "I thought you had a plan or something."

"Not beyond finding you and confessing my feelings. In my mind, I pick you up and carry you off behind a sand dune to ravage you."

"You carry me?"

"In my mind."

"In your dreams." Julia laughed. Her heart threatened to beat its way out of her chest as she took his hand. "I don't know about the ravage part, but I do happen to know where there are sand dunes within walking distance."

~ * ~

What the hell just happened? It wasn't her only flaw, but at the moment, her most annoying—overthinking. Each time Julia closed her eyes, she relived the past two hours and the image of the taillights of Tom's car as it disappeared down the driveway. Following their time on the beach spent confessing, then murmuring, then mildly arguing, then making love, then shaking sand out of clothing and other places, then awkwardly walking back to the house, Julia now sat alone on the porch and battled her own mind. Not that she was certain she was in her right mind. If she had been, she would have thought twice before making love in the sand. She had sand everywhere, in every uncomfortable crease. Then there were the mosquito bites.

She scratched at one of the welts on her inner thigh, grateful the other women had given up their watch and turned in before she and Tom climbed the steps from the beach. Confusion swirled in her brain and she was in no position to offer a play-by-play or answer questions. She told herself she was too old for this, but when she remembered Tom's lips on hers, his fingers as they tenderly explored her body, she flushed and nearly giggled like a teenager. So this was love.

If only she could turn off her thoughts. Unfortunately, the list of all the reasons why a relationship with Tom Wilder was wrong and could not possibly work out ran in her mind like a Times Square ticker. Over and over and over—*It can't work...It can't work...It can't work...*

She squirmed and felt the abrasion of sand in her panties. At the age of fifty-four, Julia Lane had sex on a public beach. No, a private beach. That fact didn't lessen the act. Her grin broadened into a chuckle. This Julia was new to her. So why did this Julia feel more real than the Julia she had known for the past fifty-plus years? Would she have to sacrifice one to hold onto the other? If so, which Julia would she choose?

Chapter Twenty-Two

Clare

Standing before the mirror, Cee Cee stared into her emerald green eyes—eyes that Ben used to say reminded him of the ocean. "I dub thee Princess Clare of Cape May." She grinned, then remembered that her prince wasn't speaking to her right now. Anxiety clenched her heart and she checked her cell phone for the umpteenth time. No calls, no texts. No nothing.

She pulled back the cool sheets and slid between them. The bed felt huge and empty and, more than anything, she wanted Ben beside her. But at what cost? How long could she fake being happy? Would she eventually become a bitter, resentful woman?

She got up and moved to open the window. Julia stood on the beach with the man who had come looking for her. For a minute, Clare watched them draw close, then separate, walk a bit further, come together and, finally, kiss. Clare sucked in a breath. Until now, she hadn't really seen Julia as a woman. Julia rather struck her as a robot, one of those Stepford wives but programmed to attorney mode.

Clare smiled as she thought of Julia's tough armor being shattered by that seemingly unending kiss. My God, would they ever come up for air? She was glad she and the other women agreed not to wait up for Julia's return. Let her have her privacy. Besides, she was sure Andi would force the story out of Julia in the morning.

The couple moved further down the beach toward

the dunes and Clare lifted the window to admit the evening breeze. She returned to her bed and lay down again. She set the alarm on her phone to wake her at five. She would slip out, go home and make breakfast for Ben and the kids. Then she and Ben would have a talk before he went to work. She would make him listen and everything would be fine.

And it was fine until *Viva la Vida* by Coldplay blared from her cell phone on the nightstand. Clare sat up, disoriented as she fumbled for the phone. She pressed the talk button. "Hello?"

"Cee Cee, it's me. You've gotta come home."

Now she was fully awake. "Ben? What's wrong?" Even as she asked the question, she tossed the sheet aside and stood.

"Both the twins are sick, I think, and they're crying for you. I can't get them settled down. It's late and I hate to call my mother."

"I'll be right there." She ended the call and grabbed up her shorts and tank top from the chair. As quietly as possible, she hurried down the stairs and out the front door.

Ben paced the kitchen, a twin in each arm. Both girls were crying, red-faced, and snotty. Clare dropped her purse and keys as her babies both reached for her. She sat down and took them into her arms. "Shhh. It's okay, Mama's here." She pressed her lips to first Katie's forehead, then to Beth's. "They each have a fever. Probably teeth coming in. Would you take Beth for a minute?"

She bent and stuck a finger into Katie's mouth and felt around. "Yep. New teeth."

Ben gave a sigh of relief. Clare glanced up at him. He wore a pair of drawstring pajama bottoms and nothing else. Moisture—a combination of baby tears and snot—

gleaned on his chest. His rumpled dark hair stood out from his head. "I didn't know what was wrong with them."

Clare hiked Katie into her arms and stood. "I have some gel for their gums upstairs in the medicine cabinet along with baby aspirin." She passed Katie back to him. "I'll get those and you can get their sippy cups filled with some water. I don't want to take them back upstairs until they quiet down, or we'll have Sean and Benji awake, too."

She climbed the stairs and retrieved the medications from the bathroom. Before returning to the kitchen, Clare quietly opened the door to her sons' room. Sean lay sprawled across his bed in a pair of pajama bottoms much like his father's. Benji curled into a ball around a well-worn stuffed lion. Her heart clenched. Her boys. Well, two of them. The biggest boy was in the kitchen, bewildered and adorable from sleep. She eased the door closed and headed back down the stairs.

"I give them half a dropper of the liquid aspirin first. It's flavored. Then I have them take a sip of water." She administered the aspirin to first Beth, then to Katie, who was less compliant and spit the first dose back onto Clare's tank top. She ignored the purple spot. "Now you just squeeze a dab of this gel onto your fingertip and rub it on the gums where the tooth is trying to come through." She did so with Katie and the child almost immediately stopped crying, nestling her head against Clare's chest.

Clare watched as Ben repeated the process with Beth.

They sat at the kitchen table, each soothing a child, until both girls' eyelids drooped and their breathing deepened.

"Let's see if we can get them into their cribs without waking them up." Clare eased to her feet and Ben

Ladies In Waiting

followed.

Once the twins were settled, Clare stepped back from the cribs and turned toward the door. She wasn't sure of what to do. Should she just stay for the few hours remaining of the night? Should she leave and return to the retreat house? Was this a good time to try to talk with Ben?

They exited the room and Ben whispered. "I'm sorry to have to call you this late."

She turned to face him. "I'm their mother. Why wouldn't you call me? I was just a few miles away."

He nodded and studied her for a moment. "What's happening to us?"

Clare gazed up at his handsome features now pinched with fear. "I don't know. Let's go downstairs before we wake them again."

In the kitchen, she poured a glass of water from the pitcher in the fridge and sat down. Ben sat across from her. "I actually hesitated to call you tonight. I wasn't sure if it would be okay."

"Oh, Ben."

"I don't want to lose you, Cee Cee. But, dammit, we have a marriage and that takes two of us."

"I agree." She reached for his hand. "I don't want to lose you, either, but we have to talk."

For once, Ben remained silent and listened as she told him about her dreams, her fears, and the future she wanted. He seemed to start breathing again when she said, "That future includes you and our children. I can't imagine living without you or them. But I need something for me, too. Can you understand that?"

"I thought our marriage and our family was that something. You're a wife and a mother. What more do you want to be? A freakin' astronaut?"

"Lower your voice or the kids will be awake."

She picked up a discarded twist tie that lay on the table and wrapped it around her fingertip. "Ben, I love being a wife and a mother. But...look, you're a husband and a father. And you also have a business you run. What if I want to work at something else, too?"

"Then who takes care of the kids? That's your job."

She bristled. "Caring for *our* children is both of our responsibilities."

He stood and began to pace. "We talked about this before we got married. I would work to build the business and you would take care of our home and children. That's what we agreed on."

"That's what *you* agreed on, as I recall. I told you then that I wanted to go into nursing. You said, 'Maybe later when we have kids and they're in school.'"

He threw up his arms. "Exactly. And the twins aren't in school yet. So why are we having this conversation?"

"Because I want to have it now. I want to go to nursing school." Emotion clogged her throat and the words came out in a croak. "Just for once, I want you to listen. And I want what's important to me to matter to you. Look at me, Ben. Look. At. Me."

He stared at her. "It's those women at that retreat, isn't it? They're filling your head with all kinds of ideas. I can hear it now—Oh, Cee Cee, you could be so much more. There's no limit to what you could do, if only...."

"Stop it!" she shouted, then cringed and listened for one of the kids to cry out. But silence hissed in the air. "Just stop it," she said, feeling drained. She covered her face with her hands. "This isn't getting us anywhere. We're both exhausted."

He met her eyes. "I thought this is what marriage was supposed to be—I work to support you and the kids, you stay here and care for them, cook, clean house....Well, that's what my mom did."

"That's what your mom *chose* to do. You haven't given me a choice, not really. Yes, I chose to have babies with you, and I don't regret that for a minute. But I lost something important along the way."

"What's that?"

"Me. A part of myself that I also need to nurture. Ben, I've felt like I'm drowning here."

Ben sucked in a breath. "Being with me has been that bad? Isn't it a little late after twelve years and four kids to decide this isn't the life you want?"

Clare saw through the anger in his eyes to the fear her comment had unearthed. "No, listen. This isn't all about you. I played a part, too. It's not like these past four days have given me this great revelation. I've known for a while, but now I can put words around the feelings. It's not that I don't want or need what I have with you and the kids. I just need something more."

She folded her hands on the table and sat up straight. "I'm going to nursing school. I know it will be a struggle at first, financially, but I've explored some options for loans. And before you tell me all the reasons I can't, I'm telling you right now it is not optional. I'm doing this, not just for myself, but for us and our family."

"So what I think about this doesn't matter. You've made up your mind."

"Yes, I've made up my mind. And, yes, what you think matters. But maybe this time you don't get to have the final say." She stood and picked up her keys. "The girls should be fine now. Be sure to tell your mom about the teething and she can give them more medicine after ten. I'm going back to the retreat house." She stopped by the door and turned. "And when I come back home, I'd appreciate it if you would please call me Clare. I'm an adult." She closed the door before he could respond.

Chapter Twenty-Three

The Other Shoe

Liv stared in horror at the headline on the computer screen: *Class Action Suit Filed Against Zacharias' Wife and Sons.* Her mouth went dry and her heart slammed in her chest. Breathing became an almost impossible task. She was being sued? What the hell did they think they'd get? She had already lost everything.

"Oh, God. Oh, God." She thought of Nathan and Aaron then. Did they know? Scrambling to her feet, she raced upstairs to her room. Once she had her cell phone turned on, the voicemail indicated six waiting messages. And the battery power indicator blinked orange—low battery. "Shit." After ripping through her purse, her suitcase and the drawers that held her clothing, she concluded she did not have the charger.

She nearly missed a step midway down the stairs and managed to catch herself with the handrail. In her car, she fumbled in the console, removed the charger and plugged in the phone. *Charging.* Terror of what the waiting messages might announce made her palms sweat. She bit her bottom lip and listened to the first message.

"Mom, it's Lauren. I just got off the phone with Nathan. Are you okay? Call me, please. It doesn't matter what time."

"This is Aaron. You need to call Hal Siegler right away. We've got a problem."

No greeting. No, 'Hi, Mom.' No, 'How are you?'

The formality of her eldest son's call sparked a thorny ache beneath her breastbone.

She skimmed the other messages. Three marked 'private,' and two calls from the Ray Brook Correctional Facility in Upstate New York. Liv's hand shook as she thumbed through her contact list to find Attorney Hal Siegler. She identified herself, asked to speak with Hal, and was put on hold.

"Liv, I've been expecting your call." Hal's gruff voice rumbled through the phone.

"I just saw the headlines. I'm out of town right now. Aaron left a message."

"We expected this suit to come up sooner or later. You shouldn't worry, though."

We? Why wasn't this discussed with her part of the 'we'? "How can I not worry? I'm being sued by God only knows how many people."

"Twenty-six, at last count."

Liv dropped her forehead onto the steering wheel. "Oh, my God. What am I going to do?"

"Let me handle this. I've already talked with Aaron and Nathan. The only reason they didn't include Lauren in the suit was because she was a minor when Adam was arrested. She can't be held liable."

"I should hope not. And why are the boys named in the suit? What exactly are we being sued for?"

"The claims are that you and your sons had knowledge of Adam's business dealings and that you each reaped the benefits of his actions. These are angry people who want their money back. And if they can't get it, they at least want revenge."

"I don't have their money or I'd gladly give it back. I don't even have my own money."

"You can't get blood from a stone. That's my point. They want to raise a stink, make their voices heard.

They want justice."

"Who doesn't?" Liv sat back and took in a deep, shuddering breath. "They already got justice. Adam was convicted of his crimes. Everything we owned was sold to make restitution."

"Unfortunately the houses, the cars, the boat, the airplane—that didn't bring in enough to make a dent. When will you be back in New York? We should meet."

"Sunday evening. But I can leave now and meet with you first thing in the morning."

"No, no. Don't rush back. I'm working on gathering the proof that the rest of you had no part in Adam's business dealings. Call me when you're home and we'll set up a meeting—all four of us. In the meantime, just take care of yourself, Liv. Try not to worry. I'll talk to you soon. I've gotta run."

"Bye." But he was already gone. Liv dropped the phone onto the passenger's seat. Her body trembled as if an ice cube had rolled down her spine. She flung open the car door, leaned out, and vomited.

She wiped her mouth with a tissue, then sat back, closing her eyes. This was the moment she had been waiting for—when the other shoe would drop. And it had. The thing that surprised Liv the most was the absence of noise, of fanfare or a gaggle of news hounds. Of course, no one knew her whereabouts. It would be impossible for her to return to her apartment. If she wasn't already fired from her job, it was only a matter of time. The medical practice couldn't afford to have photographers and journalists lurking outside the doors.

What if she could just disappear?

"Liv? Are you okay?"

She turned to see Clare peering in at her.

"What are you doing out here?" Clare glanced down. "Were you sick?"

"I…" But no words would come. Liv stared through the bug-pocked windshield.

Clare rounded the car and got into the passenger's seat, setting Liv's cell phone in the center console. "You look awful. If you're sick, I have a doctor I can call."

"No." Liv shook her head. "I'm not sick."

"Well, you're not okay. You threw up. What's going on?"

"I'm being sued. It's a huge mess, and I don't know how to even begin to explain…." But explain she did, from the beginning to the end. The retelling of her story carried her through a myriad of emotions, from hurt at Adam's betrayal, to anger and, finally, to fear. "I don't know what to do."

Clare squeezed Liv's hand. "I'm so sorry. I'd be frantic, too, if it were me. What can I do to help?"

Liv shook her head. "I appreciate the offer, but there's nothing anyone can do." She gazed past Clare to the dark clouds that had begun to build over the ocean. "I've never been so scared. For myself and my sons. I can't believe Adam did this to us. I can't believe I was so stupid and naive." She forced a smile. "Well, at least I don't have much more to lose. This car is about the only thing I have left. I don't even have my good name to hold onto."

Clare put an arm around her. "You have friends—me and the others. We'll figure something out." Clare reached to open her door. "I have an idea. Come on."

Lightning streaked across the horizon and fat drops of rain pelted the car windows. Liv dashed behind Clare to the house. Clare strode through the living room and into the kitchen where Andi made coffee. "Have you seen Julia yet?"

"Nope. Her door was still closed when I came downstairs. I think she knows curious minds are waiting

Ladies In Waiting

to hear about the mystery man and her beach walk."

"You and Liv stay put. I'll be back."

Andi poured a second cup of coffee and offered it to Liv. "You don't look so good."

Liv sighed and accepted the mug. "I got some bad news this morning."

Clare returned, dragging a disheveled Julia. "Okay, sit down. Can I get you coffee?"

Julia blinked in the light and stared down at Clare. "What the hell is going on?"

"Sit. I'll explain." Clare filled a mug with coffee and set in front of Julia. "Okay, Liv's in trouble and needs our help. At least, she needs your help, Julia."

Liv leaned forward. "I don't think...."

But Clare was off and running. "She's being sued for what her husband did, even though they're now divorced." She glanced to Liv. "Maybe you should tell her."

Julia yawned and turned toward Liv. "What is she talking about?"

"I'm being sued by some of the people Adam bilked out of their investments. So are my sons."

"Don't you have an attorney?"

"Of course, Hal Siegler handled Adam's defense."

Julia's head jerked up. "Your ex-husband's defense lawyer? Excuse me for saying this, but his first obligation is to Adam. You need your own attorney, as do each of your sons."

Liv gasped. "I can't afford an attorney. I don't even know how I'd pay Hal."

"Can't you represent Liv?" Clare asked.

"I'm a prosecuting attorney and New York is out of my jurisdiction. But there is someone I can call."

Liv shook her head. "No, look, I'll be okay. As I said, I don't have the money to retain a new attorney."

"Oh, you won't have to worry about that. This guy owes me. A lot. I think I can convince him to at least meet with you at no charge. He lives in Westchester County." Julia stood and headed toward the living room. "I'll call him as soon as I get dressed."

"Who is he?" Liv asked.

"Ellis J. Graham."

Andi's eyes widened. "You know Ellis Graham? I've read about him. He's one of the best defense attorneys in the country."

"Know him? I was married to him."

Thunder cracked and each woman startled.

Chapter Twenty-Four

Something Wicked Comes—and Goes

The women, with the exception of Markie, were gathered in the living room listening to Clare's account of the emergency call from Ben and her rushed return home. "It turned out be a good thing. I had a chance to talk to Ben and told him I will be enrolling in nursing school."

"And he's on board with it?" Andi asked.

"Not exactly. But I know what will happen. He'll whine and complain to his mother. And she'll set him straight." Clare smiled. "Have I told you how much I love my mother-in-law? I didn't want to go to her about this, but once Ben does, the door will be open. She and I have talked before about my going back to school and she's really behind the idea. I know she'll take care of the kids while I'm in class."

"I'm glad you two had a chance to talk," Liv said. "I was worried for you. You're young and you have a lot of opportunities ahead of you."

Julia grimaced. "We all have opportunities ahead of us, if we just open our eyes and look at them."

Andi grinned. "Yeah, about that *opportunity* that showed up here last night. Who was that?"

Julia flushed. "Tom Wilder—my boss. He came to see if I was okay."

"Are you?" Liv asked.

Shrugging, Julia said, "I'm not sure."

"How thoroughly did he check?" Andi asked.

Julia's expression froze, but then she slowly smiled. "Very."

The phone rang and Andi, closest to it, stood. "Hold that thought." She picked up the phone. "Hello?" Pause. "Really? Can you stall him for a few minutes?" Pause. "Okay, thanks Nick."

The women watched and waited.

Andi ended the call and faced them. "Nick says a guy is on his way over here looking for you, Liv. He thinks the guy is trying to serve you with court papers. He's carrying an envelope and asking for Olivia Zacharias."

Liv's face lost all color. "Oh, here we go again."

Julia held up a hand. "Wait. You are no longer Olivia Zacharias. You don't have to accept anything from him. Just follow my lead."

"The rain stopped. Let's go out to the porch so we don't have to let him inside." Andi headed toward the front door.

"You should all stay in here. I'll talk to him and get him on his way," Liv said.

"You'll do nothing of the sort." Julia snatched Clare's huge sunglasses from her hand. "May I borrow these?" She placed them on Liv's face.

Markie came up the steps from the beach as the women emerged from the house. "Good morning. What's going on?" She cautiously climbed the steps and stood looking at them.

"Nick called to say some guy is on his way over here to serve Liv with a summons. We're going to make that very difficult." Julia straightened her shoulders like a soldier.

Markie grinned. "Oh, goodie. War against the establishment. Can I play, too?"

Removing Markie's floppy brimmed hat, Julia

Ladies In Waiting

plopped it onto Liv's head. "Sure. You can start by contributing this prop. Now, Liv, don't say anything. Just sit here and look anonymous. Do you think this guy will recognize you?"

"I doubt it. Right before I came down here I got my hair cut and colored. I used to be a blonde." Liv stared at Julia. "About your shade."

The women each assumed a spot on the porch and waited. A beaten up, older-model Mercedes—silver but with one black door on the driver's side—rumbled up the driveway and stopped. The brief storm had left stifling humidity in its wake.

"Methinks we have a dark visitor," Andi said in deepened voice.

A short, balding man resembling a bulldog in an ill-fitting brown suit climbed out. His necktie had been loosened and the top buttons of his grayish-white shirt were opened. He bent back into the car and straightened again with a brown envelope in his right hand. With his left hand, he shielded his eyes as he moved toward the porch. "I'm looking for Olivia Zacharias."

Julia stood at the top step. Even on level ground, she would tower over the man. Andi was impressed by Julia's formidable stance.

"Are you Olivia Zacharias?" he asked.

"No, I'm not. What is your business with her?" Julia demanded.

He held up the envelope. "I need to see that she gets this."

"What is it?"

"It's...uh...important papers. She's expecting them."

Sweat beaded on his bald spot and rivulets ran down his temples. He removed a handkerchief from his pants pocket and wiped away the moisture. "Well, is she here?"

Liv stepped forward before anyone could stop her. "I'm Olivia Zacharias."

Andi popped to her feet and, reminiscent of an old TV show her mother watched—*What's My Line?*—said, "No, I'm Olivia Zacharias."

Markie followed suit. It was almost laughable when Clare said, "I'm Olivia Zacharias, too."

The man frowned at them. "You're interfering with official court business."

Julia remained cool and descended the steps slowly, taking each step with purpose until she stood directly in front of him. "Oh, really? And you're an officer of the court?"

"That's right."

"Then you have proper identification, I presume."

"I…uh…well…."

"That's what I thought. Look, it's hot out here and I'm sure you'd like to get back into your air conditioned vehicle. That thing does have air conditioning, doesn't it?"

He followed her gaze to the Mercedes. "I can't leave here until I give Mrs. Zacharias these papers."

"Ah, well, you see, there is no Mrs. Zacaharias here."

"Then I'll have to wait." He leaned against the car and crossed his arms over his chest.

Julia shrugged. "Have it your way, but it's only going to get hotter out here." She turned back to the porch, then stopped and called over her shoulder. "I could see that she gets those papers for you, if she should turn up."

Andi watched the man twitch and knew Julia had him on the hook. She was good.

"I don't know. They're legal papers," he whined.

Julia smiled like a shark spying fresh meat and turned. "Today's your lucky day, then. I'm an assistant district attorney. So I can serve those papers for you when Mrs. Zacharias returns."

He regarded her with a narrowed gaze. "Maybe I should call my boss and...."

"And tell him what? That you drove all the way down here from New York on a wild goose chase and now you can't deliver the papers? He or she is not going to like that. Well, we need to get back to our meditation." Julia shielded her eyes and glanced up at the blazing sun. "You might want to get some bottled water if you're going to wait. It's easy to dehydrate in this heat." She turned on her heel and ascended the steps, still smiling.

"Wait. I...uh...you'll make sure she gets this and you won't open it?"

Julia paused, then turned. "Sir, I am Philadelphia ADA Julia Lane, an officer of the court. I have an ethical responsibility." She narrowed her gaze on him. "Unless you are, for some reason, suggesting I can't be trusted."

He seemed visibly shaken. "No. Why would I do that?"

"Fine. Then we're on the same page." Julia extended her hand. "I assure you I will show this to Mrs. Zacharias the moment I see her."

He reluctantly handed over the envelope. "Thanks. I gotta get back to the city." He returned to his vehicle and took one last look at the women before backing out of the drive.

"Idiot," Julia muttered.

Andi stood and applauded. "Bravo. You must be one terrifying bitch in a courtroom."

Julia grinned. "Thank you. I've had my moments."

Liv removed the sunglasses that covered half her

face and handed the hat back to Markie. "That doesn't solve everything, though. I still have to open that envelope."

But Julia switched the envelope to her other hand. "Ah, ah, ah. It's probably a summons and, once it's in your hands, you are liable to respond."

"Yes, but if you don't give it to me, you'll be in contempt…or something. Won't you?"

Julia laughed. "For what, failure to deliver the mail? I'm not an officer of the court in the State of New York or New Jersey. And a summons is only good if it's delivered directly into the hands of the recipient for whom it is intended. Besides, I only promised I'd *show* it to *Mrs. Zacharias*. Last time I checked, there was no *Mrs. Zacharias* here." Julia shook her head. "Some law clerk's head is going to roll for that mistake, missing the fact that you had divorced and changed your name."

Liv looked from Julia to the envelope. "How will I know what's in there?"

"You want to know?"

"Of course I want to know. I mean, I need to know."

"Okay, then." Julia ripped open the envelope and extracted a bundle of papers. She read them, nodding. "You're named in a civil suit. Not surprising. This is an order to appear in court on July second." She looked up. "We should fax these to Ellis who, by the way, is more than happy to represent you. Pro bono."

Andi whistled. "You, Jules, are a woman of many talents and hidden secrets."

"Of course I have hidden secrets. If they weren't hidden, they wouldn't be secrets. And, no, I can't tell you why Ellis was so agreeable when I asked for a favor. Let's just leave it that he and I parted less than amicably and he owes me." She stood. "Liv, are you okay with all of this? With my asking Ellis to help?"

"Okay? Are you kidding? He's one of the most respected defense attorneys around. Will he handle the case for Nathan and Aaron, also?"

Liv shook her head. "They should each have their own attorney. Perhaps Ellis can recommend a few others. Come on, there's a fax machine in the office. Let's get these papers to Ellis. I'm sure he'll call and want to discuss them with you later."

~ * ~

Before Liv and Julia could return to the front porch, Nick came ambling up the drive with Buster on a leash.

"Good Lord, it's raining men around here lately," Andi said.

Nick reached the bottom of the steps and ordered Buster to sit, which he did. Nick then nodded to the women. "Thought I'd make sure everything was okay over here. Did that guy leave already?"

"He's gone. Thanks for the heads-up call," Andi said.

"You're welcome. There was something sleazy about the guy." He glanced at the three women, then stretched his neck and stared at the door. "So, is Liv here?"

"She's inside with Julia faxing some paperwork. Sit down, I'll get you a glass of iced tea," Markie said. She stood and wobbled a bit before turning to open the door.

"That ankle still giving you trouble?" Nick asked.

"Only a little." Markie went inside and returned momentarily with a glass of tea for Nick and bowl of water for Buster.

"Thanks. So…oh, did Liv mention my offer?"

Andi lifted her eyebrows. "Your offer?"

"Guess she didn't. A friend of mine has a cabin cruiser. I offered to take you all out for a ride if you like. Well, if Liv didn't mention it, maybe she doesn't like boats. But the offer still stands. I know Bree hasn't gotten back, so that must leave you ladies schedule free." He drained the glass and handed it back to Markie. "Thanks. Buster and I will be on our way and let you get back to meditating about transition."

Clare screwed up her face. "Transition?"

Nick tugged on the leash and the dog stood, tail wagging. "Maybe Liv would give me a call later? Just to let me know everything's okay."

Andi suppressed a grin. This guy had it bad for Liv. "I'll be sure and ask her to do that. You take care, Nick."

After he and Buster cleared the end of the driveway, Andi picked up a magazine from the table and fanned her face. "What is it with this place and men? I think our friend Nick is smitten with Liv."

"Yeah, but I'm not sure Liv is looking for a relationship any time soon," Clare said. "She's pretty upset about what's happened with her ex-husband and, now, this lawsuit. She's literally sick about it."

"If anyone can get her clear of this, it's Ellis J. Graham. Don't you wonder what Julia has on him?" Andi turned to face Markie. "And that ankle is still giving you trouble walking. I've seen it. Maybe we should take you the hospital to get checked out."

Markie shook her head. "Absolutely not. No hospital. I'll be fine."

Andi wondered if the issue was no health insurance, money, or something more. She couldn't help but notice the darkness that shadowed Markie's face when the topic of conversation was her health. Then she thought about what Julia had said about hidden secrets.

Markie had originally seemed like an open book, but something lay beneath the surface. Had the marijuana been prescribed for medical purposes? Or was Markie an addict and afraid a visit to the E.R. would reveal the problem?

Andi mentally shrugged. She needed to mind her own business. And right now her business was about getting things out in the open with Michael. As much as the truth might hurt, she needed to know and then to make a decision.

"By the way, Markie. We never got to hear what it is you're waiting for," Andi said.

Markie gazed out at the ocean. "Inspiration." She turned and headed into the house.

Chapter Twenty-Five

Every Picture Tells a Story

Markie struggled down the steps to the beach with a sixteen by twenty inch blank canvas, a wooden tripod, a folding TV tray and her box of paints. It was time. Time to see what she could still do, despite the occasional numbness in her fingers. Time to capture this place and what this experience meant for her. Besides, her patience with all the men issues was beginning to wear thin.

Clare didn't say much, but it seemed she and Ben were at odds. Andi was still teetering on the fence over what to do about Michael—to confront or not to confront. That one seemed a no brainer to Markie. Get to the truth and then live with the consequences. Then there was Liv, the object of Nick's interest if not affection. He seemed like a nice man, and Liv deserved a nice man after all she had been through. The mystery man who showed up and whisked Julia down to the beach for hours, returning a kinder, stronger, more sympathetic Julia to their group was her personal favorite. She smiled at the thought.

Then her smile faded as her mind drifted back to Doylestown and to George Christopoulos. By now, George was probably wondering what had happened to Markie. For the past two years, she had dined at his restaurant almost every Friday night. Alone, until eight months ago when George invited himself to join her for dinner. It was the most consistent non-date she had ever had.

George owned Christos Greek restaurant. He was a widower, ten years her senior and with four grown sons. He liked Markie, she could tell. And his son, Nicholas, always pushed George in the direction of Markie's booth once he saw her seated. Then Nicholas would personally serve the two of them a bottle of Vatistas Malagousia that Markie knew from a trip to the liquor store sold for around thirty-five dollars a bottle. George would tell her stories of the Greek Isles and then say she should visit someday. She would love to paint the Aegean. He could show her the islands if she liked. And Markie would smile graciously and tell him it sounded beautiful there. And then she would change the subject. No point in making those kinds of plans or feeding George's hopes. Her course had been set and she had no power to change it.

Markie found a level spot to set up the tripod and secured her canvas. She placed her box of paints on the open TV tray and removed a brush from its slot. Often she would sketch out a painting first. But today she wanted to paint freestyle, to let her soul guide her brush across the canvas. Unable to carry one more thing, she elected not to bring a folding chair with her, but chose to stand before the canvas. She felt better today. Stronger.

She closed her eyes and drew in a deep breath, exhaling slowly. She held out her hand and observed no tremor. "Good." She opened tubes and squirted colors onto a wooden pallet. And then she began to paint, using broad strokes.

By the time she finished, the sun had moved to the west, behind her. There was virtually no breeze which was good in that the canvas didn't move and sand didn't swirl into her paint. But the heat of the sun, combined with the lack of a cool breeze and sufficient hydration, began to take its toll. She wavered and then eased herself down to sit in the sand beneath her painting in the shade afforded by the canvas. She pulled a bottle of water from her canvas bag and twisted the cap, gulping greedily.

The painting reminded Markie of her early efforts—raw and real, but with softer colors and more subtle shading. David had taught her to harness her strokes, hide the rough edges. He was good at that. He had hidden his own rough edges from her at first. She twisted around to glance up at the painting and smiled, satisfied with her work.

Markie stared past the tripod to the ocean where seagulls swooped and shrieked, diving for morsels abandoned by the receding waves. She thought that, in some ways, they depicted her life. She had never been particularly assertive. Probably the most assertive, self-possessed thing she had ever done was to leave David. And that had seemed a matter of life and death.

Life and death. At that time, the distance between the two had seemed so vast. Now the dividing line was barely visible. One misstep would be all it would take. She wanted to be angry. But at whom or what? At God? She didn't believe in *a* god. She believed in many gods and goddesses. Should she be mad at them all? She was angry for a while at the doctors—both the ones who failed to diagnose her condition and the ones who were finally able to do so. Knowing something was wrong and not having a name for it made her crazy. Then having that thing that stalked her and tormented her given a name, having it defined, terrified her.

Multiple Sclerosis. Multiple meaning many. A legion. She preferred M.S. Two little letters. How bad could that be? But the information the last doctor, a neurology specialist, had given her painted both the best and the worst scenarios. She gave a tiny laugh as she thought of her doctor as a painter. Painting her future in shades of black and gray.

    She stretched her legs out in front of her and a spasm grabbed her right foot and rolled up the calf. She bent double, reaching to work on the muscle. She imagined the deteriorating muscle twisting beneath her grasp.

    Eventually, she wouldn't be able to carry her paints and canvas on her own. Wouldn't be able to walk down the steps to get to the beach. Hell, she would require help getting to the bathroom across the hall from her bedroom. And if she faced the worst case scenario the video and brochure described, she would only see the sky from her east-facing bedroom window while humiliated as a hired attendant fed, cleaned and bathed her.

    A tremor rolled through. Not from her affliction but from pure terror. What was she going to do? She had no one. No one. Sure, George was interested in her, but she wasn't about to saddle him with her illness after the man had buried his wife following her three year battle with cancer.

    She could look for Carly. And…what? Walk, stumble back into her sister's life expecting to be taken care of when she had just walked away and left the four-year-old in the care of someone else?

    What did other people do? Well, she supposed, they checked themselves into a nursing home. She bit her bottom lip until she tasted blood. Her body shook as a sob erupted. She had lived a free life—free to love, free to move around, free to create her art. Being bound to a room, a bed, a wheelchair, dependence on someone else for basic needs felt much like being in prison.

    Then she stopped, sniffled and looked around. Options. The women had talked earlier about having options. And she still had one option that left the control in her hands. All she needed now was a plan.

Markie tucked her feet beneath her and pushed up. She got into a squat, but could not get onto her feet. Now what? She could drag herself to the steps and pull herself up, but what if someone saw her? Better to just sit there and wait until someone came along. She lay back, pulled the hat over her face to protect herself from the relentless sun, and dozed.

~ * ~

Julia wasn't used to being with people, not so constantly. She had let her guard down and found she liked these other women. Even Andi who had, at first meeting, seemed abrasive. But Julia was a creature of routine and solitude. After four days of immersion in this informal study of the female psyche, she needed space. She walked into town alone and browsed the shops. Then she made her way to the end of the beach where Clare had taken them on their bike ride. She was sitting in the shade away from the fray on the beach when she heard laughter from somewhere behind her.

She glanced back in the direction of the sounds. A woman raced across a yard chasing two little girls in matching outfits. A little boy ran after a soccer ball kicked by an older boy. Then Julia remembered Clare saying her in-laws lived behind this spot. *Those must be Clare's children.* Julia turned her body on the rock and watched. Something inside her clenched, but this time it was different lost children—the children she never had, the grandchildren she would never have.

Julia had convinced herself she was a career woman and that was the most important thing in her life. Of course, that had been her way of coping with the divorce after her all-too-brief marriage to Ellis. He didn't want children, so Julia didn't want children. But when Ellis came to her with divorce papers prepared for her signature just shy of their second anniversary and told her

Ladies In Waiting

about the other woman and the baby...the betrayal still cut like a knife.

She had actually begged. Julia, in tears, had begged Ellis not to leave her—right before she threw him out. The following morning when she woke with a pounding headache and an even more painful heartache, Julia stood up. She surveyed the empty half of the closet. She reviewed the papers Ellis had left on the kitchen table. With a flourish, Julia signed the divorce papers, wiped her eyes, sucked in a breath and squared her shoulders. That had been the extent of her grief. And the worst of it was that his betrayal had left her incapable of trusting another man.

She closed up the house and closed up her heart. Ellis passed the New York bar and moved to Westchester County where he and his new wife raised not one but three children. Julia moved to a new apartment and assumed the identity she had claimed to want—a career attorney with no other life to speak of outside the courtroom. And she was damned good at what she did. Then she thought of her last case. *Sometimes too good.*

She glanced once more at Clare's children with their grandmother. Not only would Julia never become a mother, odds were against her becoming a grandmother. Tom Wilder had a daughter and two grandchildren. *Where did that come from? Oh, hell no.* She was on her feet like a shot, brushing the sand from the seat of her slacks.

Julia walked to the end of the boardwalk and took the cut-off path that would lead her to the fence and their beach. As she danced with the rising tide, letting the cool water lap her ankles, she stopped and shielded her eyes to gaze down the beach. A tripod stood in the sand. When she approached, she saw the canvas and Markie's form lying beneath.

Trying not to disturb the sleeping woman, she peeked around the edge of the canvas. And then she gasped. The painting was breathtaking, so real it looked like an extension of the ocean and sky behind her. Then she squinted and looked more closely at the five figures dancing on the beach. Well, four were dancing. One remained off to the side, seated on a driftwood log. At closer inspection, Julia saw that the limbs on the seated figure looked thin, misshapen. Withered. Almost like a stick person. What was that all about? But she knew enough to know you never asked an artist to explain her work.

Markie stirred and lifted the hat covering her face. Peering up, she squinted and asked, "Julia, is that you?"

"Yes. This painting is spectacular."

"Thanks. I needed to dabble." She sat up and rubbed her palms along her legs.

"Dabble? This is not dabbling. What I could do with a sketchpad would be dabbling. This is exquisite."

"Again, thanks. Uh, seems my leg went to sleep. Can you give me a hand up?"

Julia extended her hand and Markie gripped her wrist and pulled up to her feet. "Thank you. I've been here in the heat too long. Are you heading up to the house?"

"Yes, do you need a hand with this stuff?"

"I'll take the painting. It's probably not completely dry yet. Can you bring the tripod and table? Both fold up."

"I've got it." She watched Markie once again rub her limbs. "Are you okay?"

"Fine. I must have been pressing on a nerve when I fell asleep." She lifted the painting carefully from the tripod and, with her other hand hiked her canvas bag onto her shoulder and picked up the paint box.

Julia folded up the tripod and the TV tray and followed her to the steps. "I can carry that box for you." She tucked the tripod under one arm and reached out. Markie didn't argue, but handed over the paint box. Then, with one hand free, she grasped the railing and pulled herself up the steps.

Her effort was not lost on Julia. Something was off, but Markie clearly didn't want to discuss it. At least not with her, and not now. When they reached the house, Julia set down the art supplies and proceeded to the kitchen.

Andi stood staring into the freezer.

"Are you in charge of dinner tonight?" Julia asked.

"No. Just trying to bring my body temperature down by about forty degrees. This is one time when I'm pretty sure God must be male. No woman would wish this on another woman." She tugged at her shirt as steam from the freezer wafted around her head.

"You're going to thaw the contents of that freezer if you stand there long enough."

Andi closed the freezer and turned. "I guess I'm going to have to bite the bullet and consider the HR therapy my doctor recommended. I can't stand this much longer. I think Markie's doing dinner tonight. Have you seen her?"

"She was on the beach, painting. She is one talented artist." Then remembering Markie's efforts to get up the steps to the house, Julia said, "I was thinking we'd go out tonight for dinner. My treat."

"Really?"

"You don't have to sound so skeptical. I'm not totally self-absorbed and rigid."

Andi nodded. "You're right. You've changed these last few days, Jules. And you still haven't finished the story about Tom Wilder."

Julia smirked. "And I won't. I'll let the others know we're going out. Hopefully Clare won't mind taking her van. What do you think, dinner in town at the family restaurant or back at that bar in Wildwood? You know—The Spot."

"*The G Spot*. Wasn't that the name of the place?"

Julia rolled her eyes. "Yes, that was the name of the place."

"Clever, don't you think?"

"And how is that clever?"

"Well, it's a spot every man wants to find and every woman wants to lead him to. Great marketing idea. I'd bet they're busy all the time."

Julia silently cursed the flush that spread up her body. She wasn't embarrassed by the conversation. But the suggestion reminded her of making love with Tom. He had found just about every sensitive spot on her body—including *that* one.

"What's the matter, Jules? Hot flash?" Andi grinned and winked.

Julia crossed the room, pulled open the freezer, and leaned forward.

Chapter Twenty-Six

We're Coming Out

"I can't believe I've lived around here all my life and I never came to this place before. Now I've been here twice in one week," Clare shouted over the bass rhythm that bounced off the walls of the bar.

Andi had hurried ahead and waved them over to an emptying table.

Liv, wearing sunglasses, glanced around surreptitiously. "I feel like everyone's staring at me and someone is going to figure out who I am."

"Look at this crowd. They're mostly under the age of thirty and unlikely to be up on the latest financial news. I'd bet you could introduce yourself to anyone in this room and they wouldn't recognize you," Julia said.

Liv shoved the sunglasses up on her nose. "I don't think I'll test your theory." She reached out a hand. "Just direct me to a table."

Julia hung back, waiting for Markie who brought up the rear. "You okay?"

"Just a little tired. Probably too much sun today." Markie pushed past Julia and took a seat at the table Andi had secured.

A waitress hurried by, dropping menus on the table and promising a prompt return to take their orders.

"Okay, ladies. Dinner and the first round of drinks are on me. After that, you're on your own," Julia said.

"I'll buy the second round," Andi said.

"We'll all take a turn," added Markie.

Julia glanced down to see Liv riffling into her wallet to count bills. It occurred to her that Liv was probably more cash-strapped than the rest of them. "You know what? On second thought, this evening's on me. It was my idea and I did say I would treat."

Clare began to protest, but Julia waved her off. "Look, this isn't exactly fine dining. And at least one of us has to stay sober to drive home."

Liv lifted her hand. "I volunteer."

"You, of all people, need a drink. I'll drive, if Clare doesn't mind," Andi said. "I don't need to unwind and I don't need a drink to have fun."

"How well we know," Markie said with a laugh.

The waitress returned with a pad in hand. "What can I get you ladies?" Then she smiled with recognition. "Oh, it's you girls."

"You remember us?" Clare asked.

"All we've talked about since you were in here the other night."

Liv shifted her confused gaze from Clare to Andi. "You were here before?"

"This is where we came when you went to dinner with Nick," Andi said.

They ordered drinks, Andi requesting a glass of white wine. "One drink to toast us, then I'm on Diet Coke for the rest of the night. So, what did everyone do today? Seemed like you all took off after lunch."

"I slipped home to check on the kids, but no one was there. I sat in my living room and listened to the quiet for about an hour. I haven't had quiet alone time in my own house in nine years. It was kind of weird," Clare said.

"Your kids were at your mother-in-law's house," Julia said. "I walked to the end of the boardwalk and down to the spot you showed us the other day. They were playing in the yard. They're beautiful children." Julia cleared her throat in an effort to disguise the thickness in her voice. "Your girls look a lot like you."

"Thanks. Markie, what did you do today?" Clare asked.

"I spent some time on the beach, painting."

Julia laughed. "She told me she was dabbling. You should see the result. It's fantastic."

The waitress balanced a round tray on one hand and set their drinks in front of them with the other. "You ready to order?"

Andi shook her head. "We still need a few minutes. Thanks." She lifted her wineglass. "I want to propose a toast to us." She gazed at each of them. "To us—five of the most unique, the strongest women I've ever known. And I include myself in that count."

"Here, here." Julia raised her glass and the others followed, clinking the glasses together over the center of the table.

"Liv, did you ever call Nick?" Andi asked.

Liv shook her head. "No, not yet. Why?"

"Because he's over at the bar watching us." Andi nodded toward the bar and the other women all turned.

Nick smiled and waved but didn't leave the bar stool.

"I feel bad that I didn't call and thank him for giving me a heads up about that guy showing up to serve me with papers."

"Nick's a big boy. He'll understand. Besides, we already agreed to no man talk tonight," Andi said.

"Amen to that," Julia said.

"Yes, you were more than eager to agree to that stipulation for tonight. But there's always tomorrow." Andi grinned.

After they had ordered their food and a second round of drinks, Julia felt herself begin to relax. She liked these women, enjoyed being in their company. And the fact that she was once again sitting at *The G Spot* and shouting over loud country music made her smile. There might be hope for Julia Lane yet.

"What are you grinning about?" Clare leaned close and asked.

"Just enjoying myself, that's all. I haven't done anything like this in a very long time. Probably since college."

Clare raised an eyebrow. "You haven't been to a bar since college?"

"Of course, but not with…with…friends." Julia bit her bottom lip to check the emotion that flooded her. She had no friends. When she went to a bar in the city, it was always with other attorneys from the DA's office. Colleagues, but not friends. When Julia closed her heart to love, she had closed it off from everyone. And, yet, these women had found their way in.

Clare reached down and clutched Julia's hand. "I've lost touch with many of my friends, too, since the twins came along. Just think, if Bree had been here this week, things might have gone so differently. She might have sent me home for being under-age."

Julia squeezed Clare's hand. "I'm glad you're here."

The waitress appeared with a second round of drinks. "These are from the guy at the bar."

They all looked over to see Nick smile and wave, then exit.

"Could I have Diet Coke, please?" Andi asked. "I'm the designated driver."

"Awe, and I was hoping you'd liven this place up again tonight," the waitress said with a grin.

"I'll leave the livening up tonight to my friends. What time does the band start?"

"No band. It's karaoke night. You ladies should check out the song menu. I'll bring one by. Starts at nine."

Clare clapped her hands together. "Karaoke sounds like so much fun."

"Oh, no. I'm not going anywhere near that stage." Liv readjusted her shades.

"Me, either," added Julia.

"Count me out, too," Markie said.

Clare stared across the table at Andi. "Guess that leaves you and me."

"Fine, but I get to pick the song."

"You're on. This is gonna be fun." Clare's eyes gleamed.

Their dinners were delivered in plastic baskets lined with waxed paper.

Julia stared at Liv. "Are you going to wear those dark glasses all night? I can barely see my food in front of me, it's so dark in here."

"I don't care. I'm not going to risk being recognized. I'm sure my face has been in the news now that I'm being sued." She felt in front of her until her fingers located a french fry. She leaned forward and steered it toward her mouth.

"Maybe you should try a different approach to your situation," Markie said.

Liv lowered her head and looked over the top of the glasses. "And what would that be?"

"Hold up your head with pride and refuse to take the blame for something you didn't do." Markie made it sound so simple, even Julia considered taking the advice.

Julia set the burger back in the basket. "You know, Markie might be right. Why are you hiding? Why am *I* hiding, for that matter? Each of us came here escaping something. And as long as we continue to run from our lives, we can't run toward something new."

Andi stared at her. "Have you been into Markie's stash?"

"Of course not. I'm serious. Look at us. We're all in hiding here." She pointed to Andi. "You're hiding from the judgment of your daughter and others who think you should only date a man your own age. And, Clare, you came here escaping the disillusionment of marriage. Liv, you're hiding from guilt over the actions of your husband and for which you are not responsible." She turned and faced Markie. "And you…well, you may be the only one here not running from something. We all know my story. Well, I'm not running and hiding anymore." She stood and lifted her drink. "Here's to coming out!"

Julia shouted her last words to compensate for the music. Unfortunately, the music had been silenced at the same moment she spoke while the karaoke machine was being set up.

Heads turned to stare. Andi spit Diet Coke onto her burger basket.

The bar erupted with applause and patrons lifted their glasses toward Julia.

"You tell 'em, sister." The encouragement came from a woman at the bar.

Heat flooded Julia's face. "It's not what you think."

"It never is, honey," said another woman with a buzz cut and wearing leather.

Julia sat, sliding down in her chair. "That was embarrassing."

Andi snorted as she laughed. "Just don't get drunk and crawl in my bedroom window tonight, Jules."

Someone turned on the karaoke machine to set the volume.

Julia announced, "I'm not gay. I'll have you know I had sex on the beach with Tom." The announcement escaped her mouth before she had a chance to think.

Again, the last of her words echoed through the bar as the music stopped.

And, again, applause and laughter erupted.

"Oh, God," Julia groaned. "I'll never live this down."

Liv started to laugh—a low, rumbling laugh that shook her body. "I guess I can take my shades off now. No one's going to pay a bit of attention to me." She dropped the sunglasses on the table.

"Please tell me you two didn't do the deed in the same spot where I was napping this afternoon," Markie said with a snicker.

"Of course not. We would have been seen there. And for the record, it is not wise to have sex in sand. Damn stuff gets stuck everywhere."

Clare giggled and the others laughed aloud.

"I'm glad you're all so amused by this."

The waitress delivered another round of drinks. "These are on the house. You ladies are the best entertainment we've had here in a long time." She set a tall glass in front of Julia. "Here you go. Sex on the Beach."

Julia removed the skewered orange slice and cherries and took a gulp. "Damn straight." Then realizing what she had said, she laughed.

Liv lifted her glass. "To coming out." Then she added, "Of hiding."

Most of the karaoke participants were women, with the exception of one guy with long, graying hair who was channeling Willie Nelson. Clare and Andi studied the song menu.

"Oh, this is perfect," Andi said. "You're probably too young to know this one, though."

"Are you kidding? It's a golden oldie. I love that song," Clare said. "Let's do it." Then she pointed to another title. "And let's do this one to close."

Andi chuckled. "Perfect. I'll tell the waitress to get us on the list."

Julia narrowed her eyes. "What are you two up to?"

"Karaoke. You want to join us?" Clare asked.

"No, I think I've made quite enough of a spectacle of myself for one evening. You two go right ahead." Julia pushed the empty basket toward the center of the table and sipped on a glass of water. "I've also had more than enough to drink."

The waitress announced, "And now we have a couple of duets by Clare and Andi. Come on up, ladies."

Clare and Andi took the stage to a rousing round of applause and whistles. The music started and they broke into an enthusiastic, albeit off-key, version of *Respect* that would surely have put Aretha under the table. When the song ended, the two women took a bow, but remained on stage.

"We're sending this next one out to Julia and our friends at the table over there." Then Andi and Clare proceeded to sing the Diana Ross hit *I'm Comin' Out*.

Julia buried her face in her hands as the patrons hooted and cheered.

When the song ended, Clare and Andi sauntered back to the table. "Well that was fun," Clare said.

Andi fanned herself. "Is it hot in here, or is it me?" Then she glanced at Julia. "Sorry, Jules. We couldn't resist."

Julia stared at her, then burst into laughter. "You

Ladies In Waiting

are both crazy. You're all crazy. And I haven't had this much fun in a long, long time."

"Well, hell, Jules. If we'd known, we'd have filled you with scotch and sung to ya' sooner," Andi said.

Julia wiped her eyes and sighed. "I don't want this retreat to end."

"Me, either," Liv said.

Clare drained her beer. "I have to go home to my kids when this week is over. Although my mother-in-law told me to stay the full eight days. And after my confrontation with Ben last night, that extra day is looking even better."

"Apparently, I have to go to court," Liv said.

Andi turned her half-empty glass in her hands. "I have to find out what the deal is with Michael and that redhead."

Julia turned to Markie. "What about you?"

"Me? I may never leave." She pushed to her feet. "Except to use the ladies' room. Then I think we should probably head home."

"You're right. It's getting late. I don't know about the rest of you, but I'm beat." Liv stood. "I'll go with you." She followed Markie across the bar to the restrooms.

"What about you, Jules? What's next on your agenda?" Andi asked.

"For the first time in my life, I don't have an agenda. I may call Bree and ask if I can stick around here for another week or so. I have a lot to think about."

Chapter Twenty-Seven

Liv

Liv felt as if she had taken hold of a live wire. Alcohol always had that effect on her. Rather than making her sleepy, she buzzed with energy. She slipped out of the house and walked to the stairs leading to beach, sitting down on the top step. Waves rolled onto the sand with a gentle whoosh and in the distance night birds shrieked. At least she hoped they were birds and not bats. She shuddered and wrapped her arms across her knees.

A warm breeze caressed her. She closed her eyes and drew in a breath of salty air, considering what Julia had said earlier about no longer hiding. Shame and unwarranted guilt had caused Liv to deny her own identity, to become a stranger looking back at her from the mirror. Lines of worry had aged her face by ten years. Her eyes had lost their sparkle. She touched her hair, remembering her honey blonde color that Adam had so loved when they first met.

"Damn you, Adam. Damn you to hell for what you've taken from me. From our family." She pounded her fists into the soft sand. "Well I'm finished paying for your sins."

A shadow moved along the beach at the edge of the surf. Liv froze until she saw the dog race along the water. It was Nick. If she remained very still, he'd never know she was there.

Buster, however, must have caught her scent and came racing up the steps.

"Buster, come back here." Nick trotted to the bottom of the steps and gazed up. "Oh, Liv."

"Hi. Late night stroll on the beach?"

"He needed to go out and I couldn't sleep. I've been writing and I can't shut my mind down."

"Yes. I know what you mean."

He climbed the steps and stopped in front of her, tugging on the dog's collar. "You ladies looked like you were having a good time tonight."

"We were. Thank you for the drinks. And I'm sorry I didn't call you back."

He shook his head. "No problem. I'm just glad you're okay. You are okay, aren't you?"

"I will be. Julia handled that server and then got Ellis Graham to represent me."

Nick whistled. "He's one of the best. How'd she manage that?"

"She called in a personal favor." Liv studied him for a moment. "Do you want to walk? I need to move a bit."

"Sure." He guided Buster past him and gave the dog a tap. "Go, boy." Then he offered Liv a hand which she accepted. "It's a perfect summer night on the shore. Not much of a moon, though. It's a little dark. You might want to hold on."

His hand felt warm and strong and reassuring around hers. "Thanks." She fell into step beside him when they reached the bottom of the stairs. "How is the writing going?"

"I'm at that critical point in the book where it could go either way, so it demands closer attention to detail and pacing. It could arc nicely, or begin to sag."

"Your books always keep my attention, so you must be doing something right."

"Thank you."

They continued along in silence for a few moments, then Liv said, "Nick, I didn't call you back because…." She stopped walking and released his hand. "There's so much going on in my life right now. I don't know what you're seeking, but I'm nowhere near ready for a…a relationship. Maybe I'm misreading you, but…."

He tilted his head slightly, gazing at her. "Could you use another friend?"

"Oh." Embarrassment warmed her cheeks. "I'm sorry. I guess I read too much into things."

"No, you didn't. I like you, Liv. But I know you have a lot to sort out. I won't complicate life any further for you. I won't make demands or have expectations. But dinner now and then would be nice, don't you think?"

She stared at him noticing the planes of his face, the strong jaw, kind eyes. "That would be nice."

Nick took hold of her hand again and began to walk. "Friends it is." Then he added, grinning down at her, "For now."

As they turned and strolled back down the beach toward the house, Liv stopped. "I'm going to be all over the newspapers soon. People are going to say that I knew what Adam was doing and looked the other way for my own convenience. It's not true, at least I don't think it is. But if we're going to be friends, you should know all the truth."

He nodded. "Okay. Tell me."

"I lost everything except that car parked in the driveway. My sons won't speak to me and my daughter lives in London and I miss her terribly. I'm fifty-two years old, and I have nothing. I live from paycheck to paycheck, and I work as a receptionist in a medical practice. That is, if I still have a job when I go back home. I rent a small apartment over a garage. I'm being sued for more money than I'll ever again see in this lifetime. And...." She paused.

"There's more?"

"I'm blonde."

Nick gasped. "Well, that's just the last straw."

Her eyes widened and her breath caught.

Nick grinned and drew her close. "I like blondes, too. Mostly, I like you, Liv McKenna. And I'll be here for you, no matter what."

She sank into his embrace. "Thank you."

"I'll be staying here for the next two months. I'd like to offer my apartment in New York, if you need a place where the reporters won't hound you. I can assure you the doorman is fierce when it comes to fending off unwanted visitors. It should have everything you'd need, and I can have my assistant go in and fill up the fridge."

"Thanks, but my job's on Long Island. Besides, I need to face things head on. Of course, if I return home to find out I've been fired, that could change everything."

Nick removed his wallet from his hip pocket and slid a business card from a slot. "Just call if you change your mind. Or if you need anything at all."

She accepted the card, pinching it hard between her fingers as if it were a lifeline. And it could be. Tears stung her eyes.

"Hey, don't get choked up. It's only a business card," Nick teased.

"No, it isn't." She gave him a wan smile. "Not very many people have been so kind to me lately." She stood on tiptoe and kissed his cheek. "Thank you, again."

"You're welcome. So, have you and your friends discussed my offer?"

Liv hesitated. "Your offer?"

"The boat ride. Your retreat is half over. Tomorrow is supposed to be perfect weather for sailing."

Heat crept up her cheeks. "I didn't tell them about

it. I was afraid…I thought you were pursuing me for…well, for something more than friendship. I didn't want to encourage you."

He grinned. "Now that we've got that settled, you want to invite them out for a ride and lunch tomorrow? I'll take care of everything."

"Walk back to the house with me and we'll see if the others are still up. But we can take care of lunch. I insist."

He slipped his hand around hers and began walking. "Deal."

Liv fell into step with Nick, enjoying the warmth of his hand over hers. She wasn't falling in love with him, but she was falling in like. Nick was a good man offering his friendship and making it clear he would be open to more than that when she was ready. Right now Liv needed all the friends she could find—trustworthy friends. Nick fell into that category, along with the women she had met this week. The thought of leaving the safety of the retreat and returning to face accusations, anger, even facing her sons, made her stomach do a backflip. As if sensing her anxiety, Nick gave her hand a squeeze.

"What's the story you're working on this summer?" she asked.

"I don't usually talk about a book before the first draft is finished, but I know I can trust you. I'm writing the story of that sad case in Philadelphia where the woman got acquitted, then killed herself and her two children. But I'm writing it from the police perspective."

Liv froze. "You can't."

Nick stopped and stared at her. "Why not?"

"You…it's…oh, no." She released his hand. "I don't think the boat ride is going to be such a good idea after all."

His eyebrows knit together in confusion. "How does my story change that? What's going on?"

Liv chewed on her lip. She lifted her gaze to meet his. "It's Julia."

"Julia?" He seemed to be rolling the name around in his head. "Holy hell. *That* Julia? She was the prosecutor in that case?"

Liv nodded. "What happened was not her fault."

"Yeah? Well, I've talked with the officers who responded to the call when that woman killed her husband and to the detectives who investigated. Even they said the woman seemed to be out of it, talking out of her head. But your Julia fought against an insanity plea and won. Now two little kids are dead. A prosecutor is supposed to work *with* the police, not against them."

Liv's jaw dropped. "So you're saying you blame Julia for the outcome?"

"Who else? That woman needed to be locked up and your Julia flubbed the trial and set her loose."

"Will you stop calling her *my* Julia?"

Nick studied her face. "You cannot tell her I'm writing the story. I told you that in confidence."

"I should just let her be blindsided? I know how that feels, Nick."

He threw his arms up in the air. "I trusted you, Liv."

"And I trusted that you were a decent human being. I guess I was wrong." Liv turned to stomp away as quickly as the sand beneath her feet would allow.

Nick strode to catch up. "I am a decent human being. I'm also an author who tells stories. This one happens to be based upon actual events."

"There are a lot of stories to tell. For all I know you could already be plotting your next book about the ex-wife of a jailed investor who had to know what was really going on and lived it up at the expense of other's losses." She stopped and whirled on him. "Is that why you're interested in me, Nick? So you can take notes?"

"Of course not."

She didn't wait for more of a response, but practically jogged to the steps leading to the retreat house.

"Liv, wait."

She jammed her toe on the top step. "Ouch, dammit." She danced across the rough surface of the drive and up the front steps, locking the door behind her. In her room, Liv dropped her shoes and slumped down on the bed, massaging her sore toe. What was she going to do? Rationally, she knew Nick wasn't evil and that someone was bound to write the story of what happened in Philadelphia. If she told Julia about it, she would betray Nick. If she didn't tell Julia, she felt as if she were colluding with Nick to ambush Julia. The weight of so many lies, deceptions, half-truths, and betrayals threatened to press all the oxygen out of her.

"Enough! Enough dancing around other people's secrets and my own." She grabbed her purse and fumbled for her cell phone. "Enough hiding from truth." She turned on the phone and located Nathan's number. She would start there, then call Aaron, and then figure out what to do about Nick and Julia. She glanced at the clock to see it was past midnight. "Tough," she muttered as she pressed her son's number.

When he answered gruffly, she said, "Nathan, this is your mother. Do not hang up on me or I will be on your doorstep first thing in the morning." Her hand shook as she pressed the phone tightly to her ear.

Liv heard him mumble something and then the rustling of sheets. "What is it, Mother?"

His formality forced a surge of anger from her.

"Oh, cut the crap. You never called me 'Mother'. I know you and Aaron don't like the ugly truth about what happened between me and your father, but you're old enough to deal with it. I'm tired of being treated like the villain here and I'm not going to stand for it one more day."

"Do you have any idea what time it is? Have you been drinking?"

"I have had a few drinks, but that's not what prompted me to call. And, yes, I know exactly what time it is. It's time this family of ours stood together instead of at odds with one another. I've gotten some sound legal advice from my new attorney, Ellis Graham. He says you and your brother should each have your own legal representation and that it's a conflict for Hal to represent any of us. He's your father's defense attorney and has to act in Adam's best interest."

"Now you're giving me legal advice? You're part of the reason we're in this mess."

Liv gasped. This was new. "What?"

"Oh, come on, Mom. Are you telling me you never had a clue what Dad was doing? Even you can't be that naïve."

Liv sighed. "Unfortunately, I was that naïve. I believed your father. Now, in retrospect, I admit I may have chosen to believe him rather than to doubt him. If that's a crime, then I'm guilty. But I'm finished with being the target of your contempt, as well as Aaron's. If you want to be angry with me for not protecting you, well, you have that right. Perhaps I should have been more aware of what was going on. I'm sorry. That's all I can say. I'm sorry if I failed you both. But I'm done being your whipping post in this."

Liv waited, but he offered no response. "Nathan?"

"I'm still here."

She dragged a hand through her hair and exhaled. "I love you. I've always loved you and Aaron and Lauren, more than anything. It kills me to see how this has hurt each of you and torn us apart. We're family. We don't always have to agree, but we need one another. Whether you realize it or not, you need me as much as I need you."

"Lauren said pretty much the same thing when she called a couple of days ago. But then Aaron said...."

"Aaron said what, honey?"

"He said we'd be better off if we distanced ourselves from both you and Dad. That way we could look more like the innocent children caught in the middle of a scheme."

"Oh."

"Mom...I think Aaron was involved."

The words hit Liv like a boulder sliding from a cliff.

"He worked more directly with investments and you know he did everything Dad told him to do. I think he's in this thing up to his ears and scared. He hasn't exactly admitted it to me, but he has talked about leaving the country."

"How can I reach him?" she asked. The last time she had tried, Aaron's phone number had been changed and unlisted.

"He won't talk with you."

"But maybe he'll listen. I can ask Ellis to represent Aaron. He's the best defense attorney around."

"You said he would be representing you."

"I can find another attorney. Nathan, please. Give me Aaron's phone number."

She opened the drawer of the nightstand and removed a pen and notepad, then jotted down the two numbers Nathan gave her. "That second number is his girlfriend's cell, just in case he doesn't answer the first one. Can I suggest you use a different phone so he can't see who's calling?"

"Thank you, honey. I'll be back home Monday evening. Can we get together for dinner?"

"And create a media circus? Are you crazy?"

"Crazy? Yes, I suppose I am. I'll call you when I get back and we'll set up a meeting somehow. I'm sorry I woke you so late."

He yawned into the phone. "It's okay, Mom. I was having a nightmare. Actually, the movie version of what we've just discussed."

"I'm so sorry this is happening to you. To us."

"I tried to visit Dad, but he won't see me. I know he's talked to Aaron."

"He won't talk to me, either," Liv said. "Maybe in his own way he's trying to protect us now."

Nathan snorted. "It's a little late for that, isn't it?"

"But it's not too late for us. I hope you can get back to sleep. And, Nathan, thanks for taking my call."

He hesitated, then said, "Mom, I'm sorry I've been such a jerk. Call me again if you need to talk before you get back home. And, Mom?"

"Yes?"

"I love you."

Tears spilled down her face. "I love you, too. Goodnight."

Liv pressed the phone against her breast and cried with relief. She couldn't manage a call to Aaron right now. She would try to catch him first thing in the morning.

Chapter Twenty-Eight

And On the Seventh Day

"I can't believe this is our last full day here. Has anyone talked to Bree?" Clare asked.

"I did. She's not coming back for another week. But Markie and I might stay for a few extra days," Julia said.

"I may be joining you if Ben is still in a mood when I get home. Or maybe I'll send him over here for a little attitude adjustment." Clare grinned. "I'm sure you could help him see the light, Julia."

"I'd be happy to." Julia poured a cup of coffee.

Liv and Markie came in from the front porch. "Looks like Julia *cooked* again," Liv said, eyeing the spread of food on the kitchen island.

"I'll have you know I slaved over several hot take-out boxes to provide this breakfast. Help yourself," Julia said. "Markie, there's some special tofu dish in that last container for you."

"Thanks. Mmmm, it smells delicious." Markie spooned the contents onto a plate. "What's on the agenda for today?"

"Andi popped in earlier and said she had an idea and that we shouldn't plan anything for this evening. She probably booked the Chippendales," Julia said.

Clare wrinkled her forehead. "Cartoon characters?"

Liv chuckled. "You've been around five-year-olds

too long. We're talking male strippers."

"Who's talking about male strippers?" Andi asked, entering the kitchen.

"We're guessing what your idea is," Julia said. "Grab a plate and have some breakfast. I *cooked*—in my own way."

Andi joined them at the table, munching on a strip of bacon. "My idea isn't nearly as exciting as male strippers. And I'm not telling you what it is. You just have to be on the beach at sunset, but not for the hour before. Dinner will be provided." She stared at Markie's plate. "Is that tofu? Do you mind if I try some?"

"Go right ahead." Markie lifted her plate and Andi took a forkful of what almost looked like scrambled eggs.

"I guess this won't kill me. I'm making some dietary changes to manage these damn hot flashes, so I'll need a list of foods and some recipes from you before I leave tomorrow," Andi said.

Markie grinned. "No problem."

Clare turned her juice glass between her hands. "I can't believe we're leaving here tomorrow. This time has been amazing for me."

"Yeah, me, too," Liv said. "I wish I could stay longer, but I have a court date coming up. And I have to go home and see if I still have a job."

"And if you don't, maybe it's an invitation to open that flower shop," Clare said.

"Or to at least try to find a job in one," Liv replied. "I was thinking of walking into town after breakfast and browsing the shops for a few souvenirs. Anyone want to join me?"

Julia began to respond, then noticed the cloud that shadowed Markie's face. "Why don't we drive in and save our energy for walking around? Then we won't have to carry packages back here."

"Great idea. Let's leave at eleven, shop a bit, then grab lunch at *The Widow's Walk*," Liv said. "You'll love the place."

Three hours later the women piled into Clare's van. "Okay, kiddies. Everyone buckle up and no fighting."

"Yes, Mom," Andi said. "Can we have ice cream if we're really good?"

The lightness of their laugher touched Julia. The transformation she had experienced in the past week seemed remarkable to her. And she had these women to thank. She determined she would try to slip away from the group and find some meaningful parting gift for each of them. Nothing could adequately repay them for their patience, acceptance, and friendship. Julia sat beside Markie in the furthest back seat of the van. She nudged Markie with her elbow. "I'm almost ashamed to ask, but do you still have that crystal you offered the first day we arrived?"

Markie smiled and shifted onto one hip to dig into the pocket of her long skirt. She withdrew a small silk bag closed with a drawstring. Removing the quartz, she handed it to Julia. "Here you go."

Julia rolled the gem around in her palm. "Thank you. I'm sorry I was such a bitch that day."

Markie squeezed her arm. "No problem. You've come a long way this week."

"I have, haven't I?" Julia's smile broadened. "I'm glad you're staying the extra days with me."

Markie nodded, but didn't reply, which struck Julia as odd. Was Markie upset that Julia was staying? After all, Markie had been the first to say she planned to ask Bree about staying longer. Mindful of the chatter of the other women, Julia let it drop. She and Markie could discuss this later.

Clare found a parking spot in a public lot and pulled in. "Okay, girls. Are we planning to stick together, or do you want to meet up in an hour or so?"

"Let's meet in front of the restaurant at one, okay?" Julia suggested.

Liv pointed them toward the location of *The Widow's Walk*. "See you all there."

~ * ~

Liv slipped away to the beach, locating the area where they had picnicked with Clare earlier in the week. She settled on the large boulder in the shade and opened her cell phone. She had programmed in the phone number for Aaron. Liv had no idea if her eldest son had found employment with another investing firm. Odds were good the scandal with his father would work against him. She punched the number and waited. She had considered Clare's advice to use a different phone, but in the end decided there had already been enough secrecy and deception in their lives.

"Hi, this is Aaron."

Liv's breath caught. Obviously he hadn't checked the screen before answering. "Aaron, don't hang up. It's Mom. We have to talk."

She waited and listened to the hiss of silence. Then he said, "The only person I have to talk to is my lawyer."

Liv decided to switch gears. "Do you remember when you were twelve years old and you wanted more than anything to go on that school trip to Quebec?"

Silence again before Aaron said, "I remember."

"You had just had an appendectomy three weeks earlier. And even though the doctor said you could travel, your father and I didn't want to let you go."

"I remember. You left Nathan and Lauren with

Grandmother Zacharias and volunteered to go as a chaperone. What's your point, Mother? That I should be eternally grateful?"

"No. My point is that you should remember that as family we make sacrifices for one another, that we put someone else's needs above our own. I didn't go on that trip because it was what I *should* have done as your mother. I went because I love you and I saw the disappointment in your face when your father said you couldn't go. It seemed such a simple thing to do."

No response.

"Aaron, I'm still your mother. I love you so much, and I'm here for you. No matter what happens. Do you think it was easy for me to divorce your father? You're an adult now, and I'm sure you have an understanding about relationships and hurt and betrayal."

"You didn't give him a chance."

"I did. I gave him almost thirty years of chances. You don't know everything, just as most children don't know everything about their parents' relationship. And you don't need to know. I loved your father. I still do love the man I married. But he changed and the changes led to his downfall and the destruction of our family."

"Everyone changes."

Liv nodded even though she knew he couldn't see her. "Yes, we do. But one thing will never change—that's how much I love you. I'm afraid for you, Aaron. Just how deeply are you involved in your father's business dealings?"

"Now you're calling me a thief?" he shouted.

"I didn't say that. But I know you worked very closely with him. If you're in trouble, I can help."

He exhaled into the phone as if he had been holding his breath. "It's not your concern, Mom. Stay out of it."

Mom? Seizing the chip in his armor, Liv said, "Aaron, I'll never be out of it, out of your life. Your joys are my joys, and your troubles are my troubles. Let me help you."

"I'm taking care of it. I…I might be going away for a while. Out of the country."

"Aaron, no. Running away is not a solution. I know this better than anyone. At least meet with me and an attorney before you do anything hasty. And you have to have someone other than Hal represent you. I have an appointment next week with Ellis Graham. I'll let you know when and where."

"How in the hell can you afford Ellis Graham?"

"He's a friend of a friend and is doing her a favor. Just don't do anything until I'm back at home. I'll be there tomorrow evening."

"Fine. Anything else?"

"Do you know what your name means? In Hebrew it translates to 'mountain of strength.' I know you can be strong, stubborn even." She chuckled. "Use that strength now to stand up for yourself." She paused. "Just one other thing—I love you Aaron. You're my first born and…." Her voice cracked. "It would break my heart if I could never see you again."

A sound, as if he were swallowing hard, came through before he said, "Call me once you're back in New York."

She snapped the phone shut, a sad smile tugging at her mouth. He couldn't say the words 'I love you, too', but he hadn't hung up and he had agreed to talk to her again. She was torn between wanting to slap him for being rude and wanting to hug him close and protect him from the hurt he must be feeling. When she saw him, she would no doubt choose the latter.

~ * ~

Markie was already sitting on a bench outside the restaurant when Julia arrived and joined her. "How much shopping could the rest of them be doing in this town?" Julia asked as she sat and dropped two shopping bags at her feet.

"So, what day are you planning to leave?" Markie asked.

Julia shot her a sideways glance. "Are you trying to get rid of me already?"

"No, I was just wondering."

"I'll probably leave early Friday, try to beat traffic back into the city. You?"

"I'll be gone on Saturday." Markie stared off at the ocean. "Bree won't be home until Sunday. I'm sorry I won't get to meet her."

"Me, too," Julia said. "But she did offer us another retreat at no charge. I may take her up on it. Maybe we can all meet here again next year."

Markie shook her head. "I won't be able to make it."

Before Julia could question further, Andi, Liv and Clare approached.

"I'm famished. Let's go inside," Andi said.

Upstairs, a hostess greeted them and led them to a table by the expansive window overlooking the beach.

"Ben and I came here once for our anniversary dinner. The only thing as good as this view is the food." Clare opened her menu.

The waitress delivered glasses of water and recited the lunch specials. "I think we need a few minutes," Julia said.

Liv excused herself. "I need to wash my hands."

As Liv returned, Markie glanced up and said, "Nick's here."

Turning in her chair, Andi waved. "Nick, want to

join us?"

From behind Andi, Liv said, "No, he does not."

He stopped by their table. "Ladies…uh…thanks, but I'll leave you to your lunch." He glanced from Liv to Julia before crossing the room to take a table in the back.

Julia watched him go, then turned to Liv. "What was that about?"

"Nothing. I just thought we should spend this day together, just us." She sat and unfolded the napkin into her lap. "What's everyone having?"

The tremor in Liv's voice didn't get past Julia. Something had definitely happened between Liv and Nick to bring on this sudden cold front. Julia leaned forward, "Liv, you can talk to us if something happened."

Liv's eyes flashed toward Nick, then back at Julia. "I'd prefer you just drop it."

Julia backed off. "Sorry. I didn't mean to pry."

"Ooo-kay," Clare said. "Let's change the subject." She closed her menu and folded her hands on the table in front of her. "I want to thank you all again for accepting me at this retreat. You have no idea how much your wisdom has helped me. I would never have found the courage on my own to confront Ben about nursing school."

"Hey, hey, hey. Don't start reminiscing about this week. You'll spoil my plans for this evening." Andi motioned to the waitress to come and take their lunch orders.

Julia was in a key position to observe both Nick and Liv. He cast furtive glances toward their table and Liv cast them back, a scowl on her face. Julia thought only she had the power to emasculate a man with a stare. She had underestimated Liv.

Chapter Twenty-Nine

The Wisdom of Age
-or-
What I Learned the Hard Way

"Don't come down to the beach until I call you." Andi waved her cell phone at Clare.

"Okay, but the suspense is killing me."

Andi ignored her and headed toward the wooden steps. The sun had begun its descent behind her and the water lapped lazily onto the sand. She spied her accomplice, Nick, already on the beach and stacking wood in the fire ring. "Thanks for your help."

"No problem. I set up the grill back there for you. The steaks are on ice in that blue cooler and the drinks are in the red one. I took the liberty of providing a bottle of Dom Perignon—my treat."

"Wow, you sure know how to treat a lady—ladies. By the way, Nick—and you don't have to answer this—but, what happened between you and Liv?"

He continued to check the placement of the wood in the stone ring. "What do you mean?"

"I could almost hear glaciers calving earlier today at the restaurant. I thought I'd have frostbite. I'm sure you did."

Nick stood and slapped his hands together, clearing them of debris. "We seem to have a difference of opinion on something that's important to Liv. And I have to say I respect her for her position on the subject, but I wish she could understand mine."

"And the subject would be...?"

"You'd have to ask Liv about that. It's not my place to say." He glanced around. "Well, it looks like you're all set. It's been a pleasure meeting all of you. Have a nice evening."

"Thank you. For everything."

He smiled and turned to head back down the beach.

Andi checked the coals on the small grill, then returned to the house to fetch the rest of the food—potato salad, a fresh veggie platter with Ranch dip, and freshly-baked cheesecake that she spent the afternoon preparing. This would be her parting gift to the others.

"Can I give you a hand or are national secrets at stake?" Liv asked as Andi came out of the kitchen.

"You can give me hand. May as well call the others, too. Let the festivities begin."

Liv called up the stairs for Markie and Julia. Clare came through the back door and picked up the bowl of potato salad. "This is a feast."

The women trouped single file down the steps to the spot where Andi had set up a folding table. "The potato salad can go into the blue cooler with the steaks."

"Oooh, steak," Clare said.

Andi grinned. "Only the best. I'll put them on the grill and we should be ready to eat in ten or fifteen minutes. Unless anyone wants their steak well-done." Then it occurred to her she hadn't thought of a substitute for the meat for Markie. "Oh, gosh. Markie, I have a salad and veggies for you, but I didn't think of a substitute for the steak. Maybe I can run and pick up something?"

Markie stared at the filets. "You know, I think I'll have one of these tonight. It won't kill me and it's been so long since I've eaten a good steak. And make mine rare."

Julia squatted in front of the fire ring and struck a match, setting the kindling ablaze. Liv and Clare spread the beach blankets in a circle around the fire.

When the steaks were grilled, the women each filled their plates and sat cross-legged in a circle. "Oh, I almost forgot. We should begin with a toast." Andi jumped up and hurried to the cooler, returning with the bottle of Dom and five plastic cups. "This is a gift from Nick." She handed the cups to Clare, then worked at the cork until it popped. Clare caught the spout of golden liquid in a cup while the other women applauded. Everyone except Liv, that is.

Andi passed the cups, then lifted hers. "I should have had enough class to bring down the actual champagne flutes in the dining room, but these will have to do. So, here's to us—old strangers and new friends, women of wisdom and courage and hope."

"Women who are no longer waiting," Julia added.

"Women who are not afraid to change and reinvent themselves," Liv said.

"Women who won't be defined." Clare lifted her glass higher.

Markie stared back at the eyes locked on her. Then she stretched her arm and said, "Women who know when to hold on and when to let go."

Andi repeated, "To us."

As each woman drank, a cloud that had covered the moon slid away sending a silver beam of light over their faces. That combined with the firelight made them look, Andi thought, lit from the inside. And perhaps they were.

She set down her glass and settled the plate back in her lap. "I kind of hate to see this week come to an end."

"Me, too," Liv said.

Julia set down her fork and looked around the circle. "We could have a reunion here next year. Bree offered us each another retreat free of charge."

"Yes!" Clare clapped her hands. "Oh, let's do it. Let's come back a year from now and touch base with one another, see how we're all doing. I can check in with Bree as soon as she gets back and book a week for us."

Liv lifted her fork and stopped midway to her mouth. "I'll be here if I'm not in jail."

Julia smacked Liv's knee. "You won't be in jail. Trust me on that."

Markie shook her head. "I'm not sure where I'll be. I doubt I'll be able to make it."

"But you have to be here," Andi insisted. "We all have to be here."

~ * ~

Markie heard Andi's words, but knew they were talking about two separate realities. The one that was here—on a physical plane, and the one that was invisible, unbordered, other-wordly. She couldn't possibly explain this to Andi or any of these women. They would just think she had been smoking her special blend. The fact was her mind was clearer in the past day or two than it had been for a long time. She was focused and had a plan that she could execute. She knew exactly where she was and pretty much where she was going.

"Earth to Markie," Clare said.

Markie looked up. "Pardon?"

"I asked where you planned to be this time next year," Clare said.

"I'm not certain just yet. I…." Markie detested lies more than anything, but in this case, the truth would be harsher. "I may return to California."

"Do you have family back there?" Clare was being relentless and Markie wanted to shift the subject.

"No." She wanted to get up and get more salad, but didn't trust her legs after sitting cross-legged for so long. When Liv stood, Markie seized the moment. "Liv, would you mind putting more veggies on my plate. I'm afraid after being off meat for so long, I've lost my taste for steak."

"I'll be happy to." Liv accepted Markie's plate. "Anyone else need anything?"

Andi leaned forward and poked at the fire, sending up a stream of bright orange sparks. "I was thinking we could take some time tonight to talk about what this week has meant for us. After all, the retreat was supposed to be about 'Embracing the New You.' I don't know about the rest of you, but I don't feel all that new. I have, however, thought about a lot of things that have happened in the past few years and where I want to go from here."

Liv handed Markie her plate and then sat again, passing around the bottle of wine she had also retrieved. "I know what you mean. Maybe the reinvention takes time once you live into the things you learn about yourself."

"I like that idea," Julia said. "I certainly learned a few things about myself that I need to live with for a while, see who I can be."

Andi stared at her. "Okay, who are you and what have you done with Julia Lane?"

Julia grinned and blushed. "I know, I know. I came in here like a bitch on wheels, angry with the world. I was really angry with myself, you know. And I'm sorry I took it out on all of you at first."

"It's amazing what hot sex on the beach can do," Andi said.

Julia laughed. "It is amazing. But that wasn't when things changed for me. They changed the morning I was in charge of breakfast. I did things the only way I knew how—to pay for what I needed. But none of you chided me about my lack of cooking skills and more than one of you said you would have helped, if I had asked. I realized my self-sufficiency is really a front for my fear of not being accepted."

Markie rested a hand on Julia's bent knee but didn't say a word.

Julia continued, her eyes glistening in the firelight. "I don't have friends. Not really. I have acquaintances or colleagues. But there isn't anyone I could call in the middle of the night if I had a crisis." She lifted her face and looked at each of them. "I leave here believing I could call on any of you and you would be there. And that realization both amazes and humbles me. If it weren't for all of you and this week, I'd probably have sent Tom packing when he showed up here." She smiled. "I'm glad I didn't, though, and I have all of you to thank. The new and improved Julia actually has something to look forward to."

Liv and Clare both wiped at their eyes. Andi fought down the lump in her throat.

Markie patted Julia's knee. "Thank you for trusting us enough to say those things. The old Julia wouldn't have, you know. But, like I said at the beginning, my money was on you."

Julia emptied her wineglass in one gulp. "Okay, who's next?"

"Wait, you can't stop there." Clare leaned forward. "What's going to happen with you and Tom?"

Julia lifted an eyebrow. "That remains to be seen. I guess you'll have to come back for our reunion to find out."

Clare sat up straight and smiled. "I can't tell you all how grateful I am that you allowed me to stay this week. Now, don't take this the wrong way but…I used to be able to talk to my mom about anything and everything. As she's been drawn deeper into that horrible disease, I've had to find ways to cope on my own. My mother-in-law is a gem, don't get me wrong. But I never wanted to put her in the middle between me and Ben, so there were things I couldn't talk about with her."

She shifted and stared down at her hands in her lap. "You've all given me something this week that my mom would have given me." She looked up at Liv. "Liv, you stepped past your own troubles to listen to me and you never once judged me or tried to sway me in making a decision. And Markie, you reminded me that I need to be creative, in my own way. It was such fun playing on the beach in the sand. When I do that with my kids, I still have to be the adult and watch over them."

Markie smiled. "You're a great builder of sand castles. The practice shows."

"And I get lots of practice." Clare shifted her gaze to Andi. "My mom loves a good laugh and to have fun. Singing karaoke with you…it was something she would likely do, or would have done before…." She pulled a wad of tissues from the pocket of her shorts and blew her nose. "And Julia—honestly, you scared the daylights out of me at first."

"I'm so sorry," Julia said.

"It was a good thing, though. Because you pushed me to see the anger in myself over what's happening to my mom and how I was feeling in my marriage. I knew I had to do something about it now or…." She stopped and bit her lower lip.

"Or you might find yourself a lonely, bitter old woman?" Julia asked.

"That wasn't exactly what I was going to say," Clare replied.

Julia nodded. "But it's true. And I'm glad I didn't scare you off completely. I've learned from you this week, as well. But you go on, I've had my turn."

Clare grinned at Julia. "We're coming back to that, you know. Anyway, I got a glimpse through each of you women who have weathered storms in life and who still stand tall. My mom has always been that kind of woman. And I want to be like that, too. I want my kids to see me as a woman who faces life head on, not as one who puts her desires aside and walks around with her head down, harboring regrets. I want to trust the love between Ben and me enough to push it a little, poke at the edges so it has to stretch. In the end, I think it will grow."

Andi nodded. "I know what you mean. I....oh, I'm sorry. Were you finished?"

"Am I finished? I'm probably a work in progress, but I'm finished talking." Clare stretched her arms out behind her and leaned back.

"When I arrived here, I came fighting for my life, or so I thought. I hated my body for the way it was betraying me with those damned hot flashes and other changes. I hated having to face menopause, being a woman in my fifties. I hated that the love of my life was snatched away from me far too soon. I hated what that loss had done to both me and Katrina. I hated that the age difference between me and Michael overshadowed the joy I found in our relationship. And I was fighting against all that hate in myself."

She poured the dregs from the wine bottle into her cup and continued. "I like to be in control and I really don't like not having a choice. I discovered that those things I hate have been controlling me and that the only way to regain control is to let go and accept reality. I'm fifty-three years old." Lifting her chin, she said, "A damned good looking fifty-three, if you ask me, but that's my age. I don't have a choice about menopause, but I have a choice about how I go through it. I don't have a choice about losing Paul, but I have a choice about loving again, even if it's not the same kind of love. And I have a choice about repairing my relationship with my daughter. It's funny how we sometimes push away the very people we need the most. I don't think I pushed Kat away so much as allowed her to become distant. She's where I need to start. I can't reinvent myself without her being a part of whatever new thing is to come."

Andi's eyes settled on Markie and she waited.

The fire danced in Markie's eyes as she looked up at Andi, and then swept across each of the other women. "I would never have guessed on that first day we arrived that we'd be having this kind of conversation tonight. Well, without Bree insisting we do it."

The others snickered.

Markie stared into the fire again. "I've had a truly interesting and adventurous life. I've literally dined with royalty and slept beside paupers. I've been given the privilege of having a talent for art, for creativity and I've worked alongside some of the finest artists around. But I have never been in the company of women the likes of the four of you."

Julia snorted. "I can only imagine."

Markie's gaze fell on Julia. "No, I don't think you can. See, it's one thing for an artist to take clay and sculpt it into a form that pleases the eye. Or for one to take scraps of metal and piece them together into a work that demands admiration. But true creation lies within—with the ability to take what is whole and what is broken in us and remake it into something powerful and unique. And then to claim it." She shifted position, slowly stretching out one leg and wiggling her foot. "Do you have any idea how amazing you all are? How courageous you are for opening yourselves to the questions you've held?"

"So have you, though," Liv said. "I remember that first day on the porch when you talked about Gaia and gave us these crystals." She pulled the crystal from her pocket. "I remember thinking 'here is a woman who has a secret, something I need to know.'"

Shaking her head, Markie said, "You honestly didn't take one look at me and judge me as an aging hippie out of her time?"

Liv reached over and took Markie's hand. "I judged you as being a kind, soft-spoken woman who knew who she was and what she wanted. You didn't have to pretend to be anyone else."

A wan smile tugged at Markie's mouth. "Oh, we all pretend. Even me. I've lived the role of the free-spirited artist for so many years. Maybe that's truly who I am, I don't know. But like you, Julia, I convinced myself I didn't need other people." She frowned. "It's funny because I have hundreds of people in my life—in my email address book and my cell phone directory. But there isn't one person I'd call upon to help me make a decision."

"Who would have thought you and I would be kindred spirits?" Julia said.

"Who would have thought?" Markie stared hard at Julia before shifting her gaze back to the fire. "So, I just want to thank each of you for this time, for your challenges and your support and encouragement. I wish we had another bottle of champagne for a second toast."

Julia pushed to her feet. "Will cheesecake do? We haven't had dessert yet."

"Perfect. I'll give you a hand." Clare clambered to her feet and followed Julia to the cooler.

Andi continued to study Markie. There was something in her expression that worried Andi. She was almost too calm, as if resigned to something. And she was closed about what the future would hold. Well, it wasn't up to her to push. She shared what she chose to with the others and she had to respect Markie's right to do the same. Still, she asked, "Markie, do you have something else with you that you might want to *share* one last time?"

Markie frowned at first, then grinned. "Oh. Of course. The icing on the cake." She produced a large joint and a lighter.

Chapter Thirty

Liv wiped tears of laughter from her cheeks. "I haven't laughed like this in years." She exhaled heavily. "I'm going to miss all of you."

"Just remember—when you're in that courtroom, we're all standing there right behind you," Clare said. She gazed up at an indigo sky sprinkled with stars. "I don't want to go to bed. Let's build another fire and sleep here on the beach."

Julia held her wrist near the dying embers of the fire and checked her watch. "Do you all realize it's nearly four a.m.? The sun will be coming up soon."

"Let's stay and watch the sunrise," Clare said.

"I'll make coffee. I saw a couple of thermoses in the pantry. Somebody grab up some more wood for a fire." Andi headed toward the house.

Markie reached up to Clare. "Help an old lady to her feet. I think the left one fell asleep an hour ago. And I don't know about the rest of you, but I need a bathroom break."

"Good idea. Here, hang onto me until your leg's awake." Clare supported Markie until they reached the steps where she could grasp the handrail.

Julia and Liv were the first to return to the beach. They shook out the beach blankets and resettled them in a semi-circle facing the black horizon where the sun would soon emerge. Julia took on the task of rebuilding the fire before she settled onto the blanket beside Liv.

"Are you all set with Elllis?" Julia asked.

"I have a meeting with him on Tuesday. Thank

you very much."

Julia hesitated, then asked, "Do you want to tell me what's going on with Nick?"

Liv gave her a quick sideways glance. "Nothing. I just…I'm not looking for a relationship right now. That's all."

"Uh-huh. What's it got to do with me?"

When Liv faced her with an expression of surprise, Julia said, "I'm not a winning prosecutor for nothing. I know how to read body language and facial expressions. I noticed at the restaurant that you looked at me before scowling at Nick, and he did the same before trying to catch your eye."

Liv sighed. "I promised I wouldn't say anything."

Julia sat in silence for a few moments, then asked, "He's writing about the Lansdale case, isn't he?"

"I tried to talk him out of it. He's committed to telling the story from the perspective of the police. I think it's a low blow."

Julia shook her head. "Someone was bound to write the story. Hell, I'm surprised it hasn't already become a made-for-TV movie." She turned to face Liv. "Is he a good writer?"

"He is. Very good."

"Well, then, at least the story will be well-told. I can only imagine how it will be portrayed from his perspective."

"I'm truly sorry."

Julia uncharacteristically looped an arm across Liv's shoulders and gave her a squeeze. "Not your fault, but I appreciate your concern. This is the price for putting oneself in the public eye. Well, I don't have to tell you that."

"It's not fair. He doesn't even know you," Liv said.

"You shouldn't let this get in the way if the two of you might have something," Julia said.

"We agreed to friendship. I'm not in the market for anything more. Besides, friends deserve loyalty."

"Friends?" Julia's eyes filled as she faced Liv. "You chose me over Nick? I...I don't know what to say."

"We women have to stick together. Life can be rough at times."

"Yes, but you know what they say—what doesn't kill us makes us stronger. I should be a flippin' Amazon by the time this is over. Able to bench press a city bus. I've already got the height."

Both women were laughing when Andi returned, followed by Clare and Markie who were laden with bags of snacks. "Munchie time," Markie said.

Liv was relieved to see Markie smiling and joking. She had been far too quiet all evening, like she had retreated into herself. "It's all your fault I've gained five pounds this week, you know," she said.

Markie grinned. "Don't thank me, thank Mary Jane."

Clare once again showed her youth when she asked, "Who's Mary Jane?"

"Mary Jane. Marijuana?" Markie said.

"Oh, now I get it. I've sure gotten a history lesson this week," Clare said.

"Thanks. I think." Andi opened the thermos and poured coffee into the ceramic mugs she had carried with her.

After sipping the hot brew, Julia yawned and lay back on the blanket. "I just have to close my eyes for a few minutes. Don't let me miss the sunrise."

One by one, the women gave in to exhaustion and settled on the blankets.

Liv blinked and turned her head to see whose

body backed against hers. The auburn curls belonged to Clare who was huddled close to Liv's back. A few feet away, Andi and Julia—the strangest of bedfellows—shared a blanket. Markie sat with her back to them, face raised to the sun. A narrow line of orange defined the horizon.

"Markie, what time is it?" Liv whispered.

Markie shrugged. "I'm not sure, but the sun's just about to come up."

Liv edged away from Clare and stretched, every muscle complaining. She rolled onto her knees, stood, then bent and tossed her half of the blanket over Clare. "Are you meditating? I don't want to interrupt," she said as she moved next to Markie.

"Just appreciating another day. We should waken everyone."

Liv gently nudged Clare's shoulder. "Sun's coming up." She then roused Andi and Julia.

The women edged forward in line with Markie, each putting an arm around those next to her. They sat in silence as the orange dome of the sun crested the far horizon and sent a warm glow across the water.

Liv breathed in the morning air and let the sun's rays warm her face. "It's beautiful here. But I suppose it can be beautiful in a lot of places if you know how to look."

Markie nodded and then struggled to her feet, stretched and began sweeping Tai Chi movements. "That's a very profound statement."

Liv chuckled. "The new and improved Olivia McKenna—after fifty." She considered the purpose of the retreat, then said, "We never did get down to naming exactly how we'll reinvent ourselves."

Stretching out a leg and wobbling slightly, Markie said, "Haven't we?" She glanced at the other women.

"Julia and Andi shared a blanket. That first day, I thought we'd be pulling you two apart to prevent blows. And this young one," she nodded toward Clare, "has gone from Cee Cee to Clare, a woman with clarity of purpose. Strange that your name is Clare, huh?" She stretched and then faced Liv. "How about you?"

"Me? I don't feel all that different. Maybe a little less anxious than when I arrived. Why? What do you see?"

Markie studied her for a moment. "I see a woman who has shed her past, who can hold her head up and take pride in herself. You barely made eye contact with anyone those first few days. I think your dinner with Nick helped loosen you up a bit."

Liv nodded. "Probably because I told him my secret about Adam and that whole mess and he didn't run away screaming or accusing. And then I was able to tell all of you. I'm not so sure about having shed the past and claiming pride in myself. I still feel partially responsible for what Adam did. If only by my omission of not having demanded answers from him." She sighed. "But I can't change that now. Still, I feel like there's something I'm waiting for, something that might never happen."

"None of us can change the past. We can only take hold of the present and wait."

Clare yawned and stretched. "We almost missed sunrise." Then she rubbed her eyes and glanced at her watch. "And breakfast."

Julia got onto her knees and pushed up to her feet, groaning. "I'm too old for this."

"You weren't too old to roll around in the sand when Tom was here," Andi wisecracked.

Julia slid a glance sideways toward her. "Yeah, well, you're not Tom."

One by one, the women got to their feet and fell

silently into Tai Chi movements with Markie.

Liv was struck by the fluidity of their dance together. She had arrived here broken and frightened. Now, as she glided barefoot along the sand in concert with these women, she smiled. She may not be able to name exactly how she had changed, what reinvention had occurred, but she was not that same woman. She vowed she would never be that woman again. She would go back to her life and she would carry with her Julia's strength, Andi's fearlessness, Markie's gentleness, and Clare's youthful optimism. These were the gifts that would make her into someone new.

Chapter Thirty-One

Back to Reality

Liv shoved her suitcase into the trunk and returned to the house where the other women prepared for departure. "This week went by so quickly."

Andi tugged at the top of her blouse and blew down into her chest. "I know. I hate to leave, but the AC in the car is calling me."

"So, you think we'll all stay in touch? We exchanged addresses and phone numbers, but you know how that goes," Liv said.

"I'd better hear from you, or I'm going to come calling. Toms River isn't that far from Long Island." Andi drew Liv into a hug. "Thanks for all your good advice this week. About Michael."

Liv leaned into the warm embrace. "You'll know the right thing to do once you see him and the two of you talk again. Trust yourself and forget what everyone else has to say."

"Sounds like sage advice." Julia descended the stairs. "I may follow it myself."

"And would that have anything to do with Tom, dark and handsome?" Andi teased.

Julia's face flushed, but she smiled. "It might." She turned to Liv. "You know where to find me if you need anything. And if Ellis behaves at any time like a little prick, let me know."

Liv gasped and Andi gave a fist pump. "Go, Jules.

I didn't know you had that language in you."

"Oh, you forget. I was married to Ellis. He's basically a good man but, once upon a time, he was a little shit." She put an arm across Liv's shoulders. "Seriously, he is one of the best in a courtroom. You're going to come through all of this just fine."

Liv patted Julia's hand. "Thank you for everything."

Clare and Markie came through the front door.

"I'm going to miss each of you," Clare said. "You're each like a surrogate mo…I mean, like old friends."

"*Old* friends?" Andi asked, arching an eyebrow.

But Liv wrapped her arms around Clare. "I'm going to miss you, too, sweetie."

"Hey!" Clare pulled back from Liv. "Same time next year?"

"I'll be here," Liv said.

Julia nodded. "Me, too."

"Ditto," Andi said. "Markie, you in?"

They all faced Markie. She hesitated, then said, "It would be great to see you all again, but I have no idea where I'll be in a year."

Julia narrowed her eyes. "I thought you were going back to Doylestown? We're meeting up for dinner soon."

"I am, but I…I don't know if I'll be staying there."

"Well, wherever you are, get yourself back here next year." Liv picked up her purse. "I'd better hit the road. I need to prepare for my meeting with Ellis day after tomorrow."

"I have to head out, too," Andi said. "I want to have dinner with my daughter tonight, if she's free. We have a lot to talk about. And then I need to see Michael."

Clare hitched her over-sized purse onto her shoulder. "As much as I've loved being here with you ladies, I can't wait to be with my kids. I'll talk to Bree when she gets back about our reunion and send you all some possible dates."

Liv slowed as she headed down the driveway and glanced back to see Julia and Markie standing side by side on the porch, waving.

~ * ~

Clare

"Mommy's home!" Benji raced out the front door and threw himself against Clare. She bent to kiss the top of his head, breathing in the scent of sweaty little boy and smiling.

Margie herded the twins out onto the porch, holding each one by a hand. "Mama." Beth tugged on her grandmother's hand until she was loose and ran for Clare.

Clare cuddled and kissed each of her children before picking up her purse and suitcase and heading to the house. "Where's Sean?"

"He's at work with Ben today. Ben had a special landscaping job to do and today was the only day to do it. Here, let me take something." Margie reached for Clare's oversized purse. "He told me about your…discussion."

Clare nodded. "I'd like to know what you think."

Margie held the front door open for the kids to enter and then for Clare to drag her suitcase inside. "I just made a fresh pitcher of iced tea. Let's sit for a few minutes."

Once Clare had presented each of the kids with the little gifts she picked up for them in town and they were occupied, she sat at the small kitchen table across from her mother-in-law. "Did Ben make it sound like I wanted to desert him and the kids for a new life?"

Margie smiled. "Something like that. I don't understand how my son grew up to be such a chauvinist."

"He's not really. Just when he feels threatened, like he might lose something important. I guess it's a compliment, in a way." She sipped the tea. "I have to do this, Margie. I really have to do this. But…if it means losing Ben…" Her eyes filled. "I don't know what I'll do if he forces me to make a choice. I mean, I would choose Ben, but how would I ever get past him forcing that choice?"

Margie leaned forward, her hands folded in front of her on the table. "He won't make you choose."

"I don't know. He was pretty angry the other night when I told him."

Margie shook her head. "He won't make you choose. He might be a chauvinist at times, but my son's not stupid. You go right ahead and do what you have to do to get registered for nursing school. I don't want to interfere, but if Ben comes to me, I will tell him a smart husband would support his wife with a career she wants to pursue, and I did not raise a stupid son. And I meant what I said when I offered to care for the kids while you were at class. They keep me young."

Clare snatched a paper napkin from the wooden holder on the table and dabbed her eyes. "Thanks. So you don't think I'm putting my family second by doing this?"

"Of course not. Your kids will benefit from you going to school, and so will Ben. He just doesn't know it yet. He hasn't even considered what two incomes can do to build college funds for four kids. If nothing else, he'll understand that."

Clare laughed. "You're right. Ben is always practical."

Margie stood. "And on that note, I'm taking these three home with me. Ben is dropping Sean off after work.

You two will have the entire evening to talk things out. I'll bring the kids home tomorrow after lunch. That should give you and Ben plenty of time to...work things out."

Clare flushed at the wink her mother-in-law gave her.

~ * ~
Andi

"Kat, I'm on my way home. Can you come for dinner this evening? I want to talk."

"Tonight? But won't you be with Michael? I don't want to have dinner with him," Kat said.

"Just you and me. We need to...*I* need to talk with you. Please?"

"Sure. Okay. What time?"

"Six? That'll give me time to stop at the grocery and cook."

"Can't we just go out somewhere? I could meet you."

Andi shook her head. "I'd like to cook, and it's a conversation best had in private. Please?"

"Fine. See you then."

She ended the call and then dialed Michael.

"Hey, how's my girl? On your way home?"

"I am. I need to spend some time with my daughter this evening, but can you and I meet tomorrow for lunch?"

"I'll be on a job tomorrow. Why don't I come by late, after Kat leaves? We have a lot of catching up to do."

The huskiness in his voice sent a tremor through her. "And we'll do that tomorrow. I promise."

"I've missed you. I can leave for lunch, I suppose."

He sounded so sincere, but the doubt planted in her mind made her shake her head. "I missed you, too. I'll meet you tomorrow at noon at Alexander's."

"But...."

She ended the call before he finished. After a quick stop at the grocery, she headed home and prepared Kat's favorite meal—grilled salmon with wild rice and a spinach salad. She picked up a bottle of White Zinfandel.

Kat arrived just before six. "Mom?"

"In the kitchen." Andi turned and walked to her daughter with open arms. "Thanks for coming. I wasn't sure if you had plans tonight."

Kat stiffened in her embrace and Andi's heart clenched. She remembered when Katrina was a child and would snuggle into her arms and say, "I love you, Mommy." But she didn't push her away, and that was a new start.

~ * ~

Liv

Liv felt a loneliness deeper than any she had ever experienced as she drove away from *Síocháin*. The house was true to its name. She had found peace there, but not without a fair amount of chaos. She smiled as she recalled the women who had met on that porch just eight days earlier. Had it really only been eight days? Could so much change in just a week? She had, though. She was going back to her job in the medical office. Back to ongoing court battles. Back to her tiny apartment alone. But she was not going back to being a woman clothed in shame because of her husband's actions. She was going home with her head high and a promise to herself to stop waiting for life to get better.

Three and a half hours later, Liv dragged her suitcase up to her second floor apartment, opened the door and stepped inside. She glanced around at what was now home. The entire apartment would have fit inside the master suite of the apartment she and Adam had shared in the city. But this place provided a peace and serenity she was just now realizing.

    She emptied her suitcase and started a load of wash. Then she turned on her computer. When she scanned the list of emails, her breath caught. One message received two days earlier from A_Zacharias. Her hand trembled as she steadied the cursor over the message, wondering if it was from Aaron or from Adam.

Chapter Thirty-Two

Time to Go

Markie

Waves broke and rolled their white froth onto the sand, almost up to Markie's heels. She tried to find an argument against what she intended to do next, but instead found nothing—no cautioning voice, no damning god or goddess to insist she turn back. Only a sense of peace. A wave crashed and sent sea foam and seaweed up around her calves.

She was almost certain of what she wanted, and very certain of what she did not want. The past twelve days had given her clarity. Julia had arrived as 'that woman who set a murderer free to kill again,' and had transformed before Markie's eyes into a woman who could accept her flaws and failings and move forward. Liv was 'that woman whose husband stole millions from innocent people.' But Liv had left the retreat prepared to do battle and hold her head high. Andi labeled herself as 'a foolish woman trying to cling to her youth with a younger man,' but headed back to Toms River with the resolve to know the truth and to make the best of whatever that truth offered. Markie thought there was no label for Cee Cee. Not yet. She had taken one step forward by claiming herself as Clare. The girl still had time on her side and the opportunity for redemption. And she had love that, in the end, would guide her.

Markie knew one thing—she did not want to be pitied as 'that woman, a once-talented artist, now crippled by multiple sclerosis.' She did not want to be remembered as that once potentially great artist who now drooled on herself in the dark corner of some nursing home activity room while she glued popsicle sticks together to make a snowflake. She would rather be dead. There was no way she could leave this place transformed. Well, there was one way.

The sun sank lower behind her. She thought Julia would never leave. So much for her "early start to beat the weekend traffic." But, finally, Julia called out her goodbye and waved, then Markie heard a car crunch down the driveway.

Markie watched as the rising tides swallowed her shadow and released it again in the dark stain left on the beach. The breeze whipped at her hair, freed from its usual restraint. She tensed, then relaxed her muscles, then closed her eyes and drew in a deep breath of ocean air, filling her lungs to capacity. She held it in as long as she could, perhaps hoping the scent would infiltrate her tissue and she would carry it with her. Lifting her face, she let the sun kiss her cheeks, her eyelids, her lips. She let its warmth infiltrate every pore.

She opened her eyes and studied the hands that she had always considered her best feature. They had worked together with her brain, her imagination—that inner vision—to create art in several mediums. She shook them to dispel the pins and needles that prickled beneath the surface of her skin, but to no avail.

Her fingers dug into the sand, the crystals oozing between each digit. Her senses seemed heightened— waves slapping the shore and gulls screeching overhead, the breeze offering a warm caress, the remnants of the afternoon sun kissing the back of her neck. She closed her eyes and again breathed in the heavy scents of ocean—fishy and salty and natural. She opened her eyes and gazed at the far horizon. Everything came into sharp focus, with brilliant hues and defined edges. She wanted to remember this, all of it. If you could carry a moment, a memory into a future life, she wanted to take this moment with her. It was funny, she thought, how alive she felt right then.

Struggling to her feet, she stretched and tested her body once more in a sweeping Tai Chi movement. Maybe her bones and muscles had decided to work together after all. Her ankle turned and she stumbled sideways. The sand didn't exactly provide a solid surface. She sighed. It was time to go.

Markie took one step toward the incoming waves, settling her feet deliberately into the moist sand. Then another step, and then another. The frothy water splashed up around her knees and a chill shook her, despite the bright sunlight. The sand gave way beneath the soles of her feet as the water receded. But she kept walking, envisioning the arms of Mother Earth opening to welcome her home.

~ * ~

Julia

Julia returned and paced the house from front to back. Where the hell had she left her cell phone? She had driven into town before realizing she didn't have it with her. Perhaps subconsciously she didn't want to return to the city. When she arrived here, she had been broken, fractured by guilt and accusations. The uncertainty of what awaited her back in Philly made her wonder if she could curl up in a corner and remain here, unnoticed. Probably not. Julia had always been noticed, if not because of her height, certainly because of her abrupt manner. These worked to her favor in the courtroom, but not so much in the rest of her life. And, then, there was Tom.

"Ha! There you are." Pocketing the phone that lay on the kitchen counter, she stepped out onto the porch wondering now where Markie could be. Her old, faded Volvo still sat in the driveway. The rolling waves on the beach below seemed to call to her. Julia felt herself being drawn by the sound and descended to the beach for one last dance with the ocean. At the bottom of the steps, she removed her shoes and buried her toes in the still-warm sand. As she gazed out over the water, she saw—something. Was it Nick's dog out there in the surf?

"Oh, Christ." Julia dropped her shoes and keys, breaking into a run. "Markie!"

Julia wasn't a strong swimmer, and the incoming tide terrified her. But Julia plunged ahead into the grayish green water, her eyes fixed on the figure floating just yards away. When the crest reached her chin, she kicked off and reached out with long strokes. The tide seemed to be carrying Markie farther away from her. Julia's eyes stung, either from tears or salt. She wasn't certain which. Adrenaline pumped through her and, just when she thought she would have to turn back, a wave rolled up and pushed Markie toward the beach and within Julia's grasp.

Julia had never learned life-saving. It was all she could do to keep herself alive in six feet of water. But either instinct or the memory of what she had seen on old Baywatch reruns kicked in. She turned Markie face up and looped an arm around her neck. Kicking for all she was worth, Julia dragged Markie's lifeless body onto the beach and dropped into the sand beside her.

After placing her cheek near Markie's nose and

feeling nothing, she knelt over the body and began compressions. A few moments later, her efforts were rewarded when a gush of sea water spurted from Markie's mouth and the woman coughed and gagged.

Julia dropped back onto the sand, laughing and crying at the same time.

Markie coughed again and moaned. "What have you done?"

Julia stared down at the long brown hair splayed on the sand like a woven halo around a ghostly pale face. "I got you out just in time. Are you okay?"

Markie gazed up at the sky, then at Julia. "I'm not dead."

"No." Recognition illuminated Julia's brain. She expelled a breath, as if she had been punched. "Oh, my God. You were trying to commit suicide?"

Rolling onto her side, Markie curled into a fetal position and shivered. "I don't know if I can do this again."

Julia wasn't sure if Markie meant live or try to kill herself. "What are you talking about? Look at me," she commanded.

Markie's body shook and it took a moment for Julia to realize the woman was sobbing. She pressed a hand lightly on Markie's arm. "Whatever is wrong, I'm sure we can figure out a solution. Let's get back to the house and out of these wet clothes." She stood and walked around the woman who looked a bit like a seal washed ashore. Julia bent over her. "Can you get up?"

With a hand covering her face, Markie began to laugh.

The cold fear that had gripped Julia now took on the deep, hot tones of anger. "We both could have drowned out there, and you find this amusing?"

Markie rolled onto her butt and struggled to sit up.

"I'm sorry. Can I get up? That seems to be the question."
Julia stood, folding her arms across her chest. "Okay, you're alive and you're breathing on your own. I'm going to get dry clothing from my suitcase and get changed. If you decide to walk back into the ocean I...I'm not coming after you again."

Growing quiet, Markie let her forehead drop onto her raised knees. When she looked up, tears spilled down her cheeks. "I'm very sorry, Julia. I can only imagine what this is like for you, I mean after...I waited until you had gone."

Julia shivered. "Want to tell me what you were thinking?"

Markie patted the damp sand beside her and Julia plopped down. Markie wrapped her arms across her soaking body. "I have M.S."

"M.S.?"

"Multiple sclerosis. I decided I would rather choose when and how I die than to wait for the disease to cripple me completely. If...when I can no longer use my hands to make art, I'll be dead inside anyway."

Julia swallowed hard, staring out at the darkening water. She hesitated, then slipped an arm around Markie. "Maybe it won't be that debilitating for you. Lots of people live productive lives with M.S."

"And some don't. What if I'm one of those people, the ones that can't walk, can't lift a spoon to feed myself, can't even control my bodily functions. It terrifies me to think of living like that. Where would I go?" Panic tinged her voice.

Julia recognized the moment for what it was—an opportunity for change. She could squeeze Markie's arm and reassure her she would be fine and tell her there were facilities to care for people with those needs. And then stand and return to the house. Or she could step up and be a friend. How hard could that be? Probably not as difficult as cooking breakfast. She tightened her hold around Markie's shaking shoulders. "You're not alone. You have me."

Julia stood and offered a hand to Markie, who accepted the help. At the top of the steps, Julia stopped to catch her breath. Her heart still pounded. "I'll get my suitcase. It's too late to drive back to Philadelphia now. And we need to talk."

She hauled her suitcase from the trunk and lugged it up the front steps. Inside, Markie paused on the stairs. "I'm sorry, Julia. I didn't mean for you to find me like that. Why did you come back?"

"I forgot my cell phone. Which reminds me…" She dug into the pocket of her puckered linen slacks and extracted the phone. "I won't be using this phone again."

"I…I'll replace it. It's my fault."

Julia shook her head. "No, it isn't." She dropped the waterlogged phone into her purse and picked up her suitcase, heading for the stairs. "I'm going to take a shower and change clothes. Can I trust you not to do anything crazy until I'm finished?"

Markie reached the top of the stairs and paused. "Don't worry. You sufficiently broke the mood. I'll see you downstairs soon."

Julia headed past her toward the Rose Room, then stopped and turned. "Markie, I meant what I said. You're not alone. I'll do whatever I can to be of help to you."

As she stood in the warm shower and shampooed the salt water from her hair, Julia began to shake. She had never been so scared. Life and death had lay just a few feet beyond her grasp and, with the help of the ocean's swell, had lifted Markie into her arms much like a gift. She had put her own personal safety aside for the sake of another. Maybe she wasn't as lost as she had thought.

Perhaps there was hope for her yet.

When she had fought so strenuously against an insanity plea for Amanda Lansdale, Julia was driven by what she believed to be justice. In truth, it had been her reputation that she fought to preserve. Take no prisoners. She gambled with lives that were not, *should not have been,* in her hands. And she lost.

Markie's disease was unpredictable. The woman could live for years with minimal symptoms, or she could be confined, overnight, to a wheelchair. Julia had saved Markie's life. Or had she? Who was she to decide the sentence for someone like Markie? In saving her, Julia may have just condemned her to hell.

She wondered now, did saving a life redeem her for the lives her self-righteous actions had cost? No. Each life held its own value and worth and place in the world. She remembered the time when she was seven years old and dragged a sick kitten home. When she asked if her mother could make the bedraggled kitten better, her mother had said, "Are you prepared to take care of it if I do? Because, you know, when you save a life, you are then responsible for that life."

Julia had been unable to sustain a marriage for more than a few months, much less produce and raise children. She had no friends and only a few acquaintances she trusted. Hell, she didn't even have a gold fish. Not because she never wanted those things in her life, but because she never trusted she could nurture them. Just like the kitten she and her mother nursed back to health, only to find it smashed along the curb one day. Julia was toxic. Now, how was she going to explain this to Markie, the woman whose life she had saved and who had Julia's promise to be there for her?

Linda Rettstatt

~ * ~
REUNION
~ * ~

Chapter Thirty-Three

Clare hurried up the steps of *Síocháin* and tapped on the front door.

"Clare, you're right on time."

"Quite by accident, I can assure you, Bree. Thanks so much for giving us the house for a few days."

Bree hooked her purse over her shoulder and picked up a duffle bag. "It's all yours. I'm glad to have a long weekend away. Tell the other women I'm sorry I couldn't stay long enough to meet them. But I want to get to Baltimore before dinner."

Clare followed her to the driveway. "I'll tell them. You have a safe trip." Once Bree's car was out of sight, Clare opened her van and carried in bags of groceries. She filled the fridge and freezer and was emptying the last bag of snacks when a car pulled into the drive.

Julia stood by the driver's side door, stretched, and then rounded the car. She bent and when she straightened, Markie emerged from the car, holding onto Julia for support. Both women smiled and waved to Clare.

"Let me give you a hand with your bags." Clare hustled toward the car. She stopped abruptly when she saw what was taking them so long. Julia reached into the car and handed Markie a metal tri-pod cane.

When Clare called to confirm the dates for the reunion, Julia had asked about a downstairs bedroom and bath for Markie, saying she was having difficulty with stairs because of MS. Still, it was a shock to see the once-vibrant woman struggle to take a few steps. "Bree prepared her rooms for you, behind the office off the kitchen. She said you should make yourself at home there."

"Thanks for arranging that," Markie said. "These few steps are about all I can handle." Markie steadied herself with the cane on the first step, then grasped the hand rail to pull herself up the front steps. Clare stayed close behind to catch her should she stumble.

Markie headed for the first chair on the porch and settled into it. "Aaah. Ocean air." She smiled at Clare. "You look good in those scrubs."

"I didn't have time to change. I came straight from class. I'm not sure what time to expect Liv or Andi. I think they're driving down together. I can't wait to hear what everyone's been up to."

"Well, I haven't been up to much," Markie said.

Clare noted the slight slur in Markie's speech. The disease had certainly progressed in one year's time. Then she thought about her mother and how quickly Alzheimer's had stolen her ability to communicate, to understand, or even to recognize her own daughter.

Julia ascended the steps carrying two soft-side suitcases. "I'll put these inside and get something to drink."

"There's lemonade in the fridge," Clare said.

Julia returned shortly with a tray bearing refreshment. The three women sat, enjoying the afternoon breeze and awaiting the arrival of the last two.

~ * ~

Andi smiled as she parked the Toyota beside Clare's van. "We made good time, considering."

Liv stared at her. "Considering you drive like a ninety-year-old?"

Ladies In Waiting

"I got us here alive, didn't I?" Andi softened her tone. "You can't be too careful, especially when the traffic's heavy with tourists."

Releasing her seat belt, Liv said, "If I'd been driving, we'd have arrived half an hour ago."

Andi shoved her door open. She hadn't told the other women about the accident she survived thirty-two years earlier that claimed the lives of her best friends. It wasn't something she liked to remember, much less talk about. But each time she drove down the shore during tourist season, she tensed. She rolled her neck and shoulders to loosen the tightness.

Clare raced down the steps and met Liv with a warm hug, then moved to Andi. "It's so good to see both of you again."

"Likewise." Andi held Clare at arm's length. "Look at you, Nurse Clare."

"Not quite yet. I do find the scrubs to be comfortable and practical, though." Clare leaned close and whispered. "Try not to look shocked when you see Markie. She's changed."

Andi glanced over Clare's shoulder to the porch where Markie sat in one of the wicker chairs chatting with Liv and laughing. "She looks okay from here."

Clare shook her head. "She's not. She has MS and she has to use a cane. That's what was going on with her last year—the stumbling, the falls, her legs always falling asleep. I'm sure she'll explain to all of us later. Come on, let's get this party started. I chilled the champagne."

"That's my girl." Pulling her bag from the back seat, Andi followed Clare.

Once everyone was settled on the porch, Clare went inside and emerged shortly with a bottle of champagne and five flutes. "I thought we should have a toast to us to welcome one another back. We can catch up over dinner and dessert with what we've all been up to for the past year."

She poured the bubbly amber liquid into each of the five glasses and passed them around. "Who wants to do the honors?"

Andi stood. "I will." She cleared her throat and lifted her glass. "Here's to the most unique, often irritating, always fun-loving, sometimes insightful women who I'm proud to call friends."

"Here, here," Liv said. "And to Bree for giving us use of *Síocháin*."

"May I add something to the list?" Markie glanced at each of them, her eyes settling on Julia. "I want to add that you are all the kindest, most caring women I've ever known."

Andi watched Julia's mouth tighten as if the woman fought back tears. She was eager to hear the story of how Julia and Markie had ended up such good friends. "I agree."

Clare cleared her throat. "Now, you all sit and relax. Julia's offered to help me with dinner."

"Jules is cooking?" Andi asked, incredulous.

Julia stood and nodded. "I've discovered that if one can read recipes and is willing to take directions, one can prepare a decent meal. Healthy, even. So, if you'll excuse us...."

"We can all help," Markie said.

"Yes, you could. But the rest of you will be in charge of meals tomorrow and the next day. Don't worry, Clare promises a menu tonight that even I can't screw up."

"That's right. Come on, Jules. Let's strap on the aprons and get to work."

Andi lifted her glass. "We'll be right here, waiting patiently."

~ * ~

Liv stood in the doorway and admired the dining room. Flowers graced the table and white taper candles glowed softly in the dimmed lighting. The elegant table setting briefly reminded her of the dinner parties she used to host. Julia entered from the kitchen carrying a pitcher of water.

"Here, let me do that," Liv said. "By the way, this is lovely and dinner smells wonderful."

Julia beamed at the compliments. "Thank you. I'm learning."

"Aren't we all?" Liv asked as she took the pitcher to fill the water glasses.

As the others gathered, Clare and Julia delivered steaming plates and bowls to the table. The women sat and stared at the feast. "Wow, you two really delivered."

Clare grinned. "The menu was all Julia's doing. Eggplant parmesan, steamed asparagus, and a spinach salad with strawberries and toasted almonds in a light raspberry vinaigrette. Oh, and garlic bread for those who wish."

When they were nearly finished, Julia asked, "Are you enjoying the dinner?"

Liv nodded and forked the last bite of eggplant into her mouth.

"Good. Some of you may have just eaten your first vegan meal."

Andi stopped chewing and stared at her plate. "Vegan?"

Markie snickered.

After a pause, Andi forked up another mouthful. "Just tell me there's *real* chocolate something for dessert."

Liv sat back in her chair and sipped her wine. She took a moment to look, really look, at each of the other women and to appreciate them. She found it hard to believe that not quite one year earlier they had all landed in this place, each for her own reason, and with differences and tension she never thought they would move past. And, yet, here they were, some more whole, others perhaps more broken. But here, together. And she marveled at that small miracle.

Chapter Thirty-Four

Everything Old-er Is New Again

A light breeze carried the salty scent of the ocean. Julia closed her eyes and rested her head against the back of the Adirondack chair. Liv and Andi set up dessert and coffee on the small wicker table. The sound of the surf lapping along the beach below propelled Julia back to her previous time here. A strangled feeling caught in her throat as she remember that day, seeing someone in the water and then realizing it was Markie. And she was not swimming.

"Julia?"

She blinked and turned toward the voice.

"Are you okay?" Markie asked.

"I'm fine. Just taking in the peace of this place. I guess I zoned out for a minute."

"I started telling the others about our house, then I realized it's really *your* house and maybe you'd like to tell them about it."

"Well, it's our house in the sense that we both live there. You pay rent that goes toward the mortgage, so…." She looked at the other three expectant faces. "Okay, so after you all left last year and Markie and I stayed. Markie…um…confided in me about her physical condition. She was worried about managing alone in her second floor apartment. I'm tired of living in the city. It's too easy to never stop and breathe. And I'm tired of living alone. So I bought a restored two-hundred-year old farmhouse about forty minutes outside of Philly. And then I invited Markie to move in."

"Invited?" Markie asked. She shook her head. "Insisted is more like it." Markie steadied her gaze on Julia for a moment, then said, "Julia isn't telling you the whole story." She wove her fingers together in her lap and looked down. "The MS was getting so much worse and I was terrified. Terrified I wouldn't be able to function on my own. Terrified of losing the ability to create art. Terrified of ending up in a facility where I'd have to ask someone to come and open the curtains just so I could see the sun."

She paused. "I decided to handle things on my terms. So I…walked into the ocean."

Clare gasped. Liv wiped tears from her eyes. Andi sat frozen on the edge of her chair, her face ashen.

"This was a beautiful place to end the pain and the fear. Except Julia came back to fetch her cell phone."

"And a good thing I did. Though you scared the liver out of me. Besides, I'm an officer of the court. I was bound to stop you."

"Don't go throwing your legal weight around. I happen to know that suicide, obviously, and attempted suicide are not illegal. Foolish, perhaps." Markie grinned at Julia. "So Jules saved me and now she feels responsible for me."

"How are you doing, though? Really?" Andi asked.

"I have good days and bad. I hired a nice woman to come in during the week while Julia's at work. She helps me get bathed and dressed if I can't manage on my own. The thing about this disease is the unpredictability. I mostly need the cane or a wheelchair, but might suddenly have a day when I can navigate okay on my own. I've learned to paint differently. Sculpture is more of a challenge now, and I don't do much of that. But I'm alive, and I have Julia to thank."

Julia bit her bottom lip. She hated to cry, especially in front of anyone. Unable to speak, she just reached for Markie's hand and squeezed. When she'd swallowed the golf ball in her throat, she said, "This is a two-way street, you know. Who do you all think taught me to cook?"

Andi took a drink from her coffee mug. "Let me introduce you to beef before we leave here."

Julia grinned. "Yes, I'm sure you can teach me all about *beef*."

Liv leaned forward then. "Markie, I'm so sorry for what you're going through. I wish you could have felt comfortable telling us about it. But I understand. We were virtual strangers to one another."

"I couldn't risk letting anyone talk me out of what I thought I needed to do. But I'm so glad Julia interrupted me because...." Her eyes filled as she glanced around the circle of women. "I found my sister. I haven't seen her since she was four years old."

"That's wonderful," Clare said. "Have you seen her again yet? Was she excited to see you?"

"We've only talked on the phone. She's coming to spend Christmas with me. I have two nieces and a nephew I've never seen. I have a family."

It wasn't the first time Julia had heard Markie speak those words, but every time she heard them, it reminded her of what she had missed. She stared out at the darkened ocean. But she was happy for Markie.

"I can hardly wait to see Carly. She's coming alone for this first visit. She lives in Montana on a ranch. My baby sister turned out to be a cowgirl. I have some pictures in my bag. She's so beautiful. I'll show you those tomorrow." She sat forward. "I need a bathroom break. Someone give me a hand up, please."

Clare jumped to her feet and offered Markie a hand, helping her get the cane in place and then opening the door.

"Julia, how bad is it? Really?" Liv asked once the door closed behind Markie.

"Like she said, unpredictable. She's having more trouble this evening because of the time in the car. Some days she gets around quite well and then there are days when she can't get out of bed without help."

"It's good of you to take her in," Andi said.

"I don't think of it that way. It's funny, you know. When I came here last year, I had no friends and I didn't even know it. Markie has been a true blessing in my life." She smiled. "As have each of you."

"If we're going to keep this conversation going, I'll need wine." Andi stood and collected their empty coffee cups and dessert plates. "Don't start without me."

Andi returned a few minutes later following behind Markie. "Who wants some?" she asked, holding up a bottle of merlot.

Everyone but Markie accepted a glass.

"I don't think Markie was quite finished with her story," Julia said.

Markie's brow furrowed in confusion. "Oh, yes. I'm teaching an art class at the VA Hospital once a week. It's part of the rehabilitation program for veterans."

"That's wonderful, Markie. I'm sure you're a great inspiration for them," Clare said.

"Well, I've got this damned debilitating disease. I may as well make it work for me in some way. I'm the perfect one to argue with them when they say, 'I can't do it.' And it's rewarding to see those men and women light up when they create a painting. It gives me hope, too." She paused. "Okay, that's enough about me."

Ladies In Waiting

"Oh, you haven't finished yet," Julia said.

"And what did I leave out?"

"George."

"George?" Andi asked, swiveling her head around.

Julia watched as color flooded Markie's face.

"Markie's not-so-secret admirer."

"Come on, Markie. Spill. We want all the juicy details." Clare grinned and sat forward in her chair.

"George is a very good friend. There's not that much to tell. I used to go to his Greek restaurant in Doylestown a few times a week for dinner. Now he brings dinner to me twice a week. We've been friends for years. That's all there is to it."

"That's all there is to it because you are one stubborn woman. And believe me, I know stubborn." Julia emphasized her words with a finger pointed at Markie. "George would sweep you away to Greece in a heartbeat."

"And have a heart attack pushing me around in a wheelchair to see the Acropolis? No, thank you. Now, Tom and Julia—there's a story." She winked at Julia before picking up her glass of water to take a sip.

"Touché. But I don't want to start there." She took in a breath and exhaled. "When I returned to Philadelphia, I didn't know what to expect. Some of the hysteria about the trial had died down. I didn't go back to work right away. I spent a week looking for a house, once I realized I needed to make some changes. And that's when I thought of Markie. I drove up to Doylestown to spend a few days with her and convince her to move into my new house with me."

Julia shifted in her chair. She wasn't as comfortable as she would like to be with sharing her own story. But if she could learn to cook, she could learn to talk to these women about her life. "When we came here last year, the focus of the retreat was supposed to be reinventing ourselves. And we all realized that we were waiting for something to happen for us that we needed to make happen for ourselves. Right?"

Liv and Andi both nodded.

"I would never have considered that I needed to reinvent Julia Lane. I thought she was perfectly fine as she was—intelligent, strong, confident, reliable, and able to cut you off at the knees with one word. What I didn't have was heart. Not the kind of heart that makes you likable and needed and wanted." She strangled on the last word and stopped to clear her throat and regain composure. "I don't know how the rest of you put up with me."

Andi lifted a glass to her. "Wasn't easy, Jules."

"Andi!" Clare smacked Andi's arm. "That's not nice to say."

"The truth hurts sometimes."

"Yes," Julia said. "And the truth eventually brings freedom. All my life, I've felt I had to prove myself in order to be accepted. I had to make the dean's list at Penn to prove to my father that I could literally make the grade. I convinced myself that my failed marriage was all Ellis's fault because he cheated. But if I'm honest, it wasn't much of a marriage from the start. I put work over the marriage." She sighed. "I've spent my life proving myself for what or whom? I don't even know anymore. I came to realize that I was waiting for something to change so I wouldn't feel this way any longer."

"Don't most of us feel that way, though? Like we have to prove ourselves, work harder to be taken seriously as women?" Andi asked.

"Maybe we do, but I was so isolated from other women, I thought it was just me. And when that murder trial blew up in my face and I failed so publicly and with such tragic results, I lost all confidence in myself."

"Don't be too hard on yourself, Julia. You said before that you existed in a male-dominated world. You had to be one of the guys," Liv said.

Julia nodded. "You know what they call a woman who tries to be one of the guys? A bitch. It's not fair, but it's the truth. And I lived up to the title. And, then, I met all of you."

She drained her glass and held it out to Andi for a refill of wine. "I thought about how hard I worked at being Julia Lane and how little I had to show for all that work. No husband. No children. No real friends. And then you all teased me about being such a tight ass and calling me Jules and, well, it was like an invitation. I could be anyone I wanted to be. And I didn't know who that was yet, but I knew it wasn't the Julia I'd known all my life."

Markie rolled her head to the side and grinned over at Julia. "I knew there was hope for you from the start. And I was right."

"I'm a work in progress. Let's not march out the brass band just yet." She smiled. "Which brings us to Tom. I had to admit that I've been in love with Tom Wilder for years, even before he was divorced. But no one was more surprised than I when he showed up here."

Andi chuckled. "You do a very good deer-in-the-headlights imitation. If you could've seen your face."

Julia laughed with her. "I can imagine. But, you know, I found myself at a crossroads. I could be Julia Lane, the super woman who needed no one. Or I could lean into the new, improved Jules. Markie taught me that concept, by the way. So, I bought a farmhouse, cut back on my work hours, and pleaded with Markie to move in with me. And, yes, I've been seeing Tom. I've met his daughters and his grandchildren. Tom and I are going on a cruise over the Christmas holidays."

"Is it a problem with the two of you working together in the DA's office?" Liv asked.

"It won't be. I've resigned and accepted a teaching position at Penn. I'm looking forward to being out of the courtroom and in the classroom."

"Good for you," Clare said.

"Yes. It is good for me, on both counts. And I've promised myself I'm not going to screw this up." She yawned. "Oh, excuse me. I'm exhausted. The other thing that's good for me is a night's sleep. I think we need to pick this up again tomorrow. We only have a few days this time, and I want to hear everyone else's story."

They carried in the glasses and before each one headed to her room, Julia announced, "I'm taking care of breakfast. And I don't mean take-out. Is 8:00 a.m. good for everyone?"

"But you cooked dinner," Liv said.

Julia grinned. "I've learned to cook breakfast, and I guess I want to show off my new talents. Indulge me, please?"

"I wouldn't miss it," Andi said.

Julia was the last to leave the kitchen. She turned off the lights and checked on Markie.

"Do you need anything?"

Markie shook her head. "Not a thing. I can manage the bathroom by myself." She paused. "Julia?"

"Yes?"

"I'm proud of you."

A smile broke and stinging tears simultaneously erupted. "No one's said that to me for a very long time. Thank you."

Markie reached for her hand. "It's a shame you've been surrounded by so many short-sighted people. Just think, if I hadn't tried to drown myself, we might have never seen this side of you."

"I wish you wouldn't joke about that. But it's true. You pushed me past some wall I'd constructed for protection."

"I didn't push you. The universe provided you with an opportunity for change, and you seized it. More's the better for me. I missed out on a lot of years with my sister, Carly. But when I needed a sister the most, I got you. And now I have Carly, too."

Julia could barely speak, emotion clogging her throat. "We both better get some sleep." She held up her cell phone. "Ring if you need me. Shall I leave the door open?"

Markie nodded, still smiling. Still looking right through her.

If anyone had asked Julia a year ago what it felt like to be part of a family, she would have dismissed the question as silly. Now, with tears stinging her eyes, she knew the answer. This. This was what it felt like to be part of a family, to have sisters. And she wouldn't trade it for anything.

Chapter Thirty-Five

Morning brought with it bright sunshine and the hint of a pleasant day at the shore. Andi watched in awe while Julia whipped up scrambled eggs, adding veggies and cheese to the mix, tended to bacon strips in one pan and to sausage in another. She didn't ask if these were *real* or some fabrication of meat. Julia then opened a package of tofu, added onions and peppers and tossed that in a separate skillet.

"I'm amazed, Jules. You've come a very long way." Andi sipped her coffee.

"Thanks. I guess you can teach an old dog new tricks."

"Oh, you're not a dog, Jules."

Julia turned around, grinning. "But I'm old?"

"No more than the rest of us, except for Clare."

"Would you hand me that platter on the counter, please?" As Julia scooped the eggs onto the plate, she said, "And speaking of age, I want to hear how things are going for you and Michael."

Andi felt the tension stiffen her face and she fought it. "I'll fill you all in after breakfast. Not a story I want to tell more than once, and not while I'm eating." She slid down from the stool she occupied at the center island. "I'll call the others."

She found Markie and Liv on the front porch and Clare pacing the driveway while talking on her phone. "Breakfast is served." On her return to the kitchen, she paused. If anyone would understand her decision about Michael, it would be these women.

Once they were seated at the table, Andi said, "I have a suggestion. Let's pick up where we left off last night *after* we've eaten, maybe down at the beach?"

Liv nodded. "Probably a good idea. I'll clear the dishes when we're finished and meet you all down there."

Breakfast conversation centered around surface talk—changes in hairstyles, colors, stories of Clare's kids.

Julia and Markie stood on the porch staring down at the beach. Recalling what Markie had shared the previous night, Andi closed her eyes. "I'm such an idiot. I should never have suggested we all go down to the beach."

Markie shook her head. "No, it's fine. I almost died down there, but I didn't and it's proven to be a good thing." She turned her face to Julia. "Are you okay with this?"

Julia exhaled. "I'm fine if you are." But the pallor of Julia's face betrayed her words. Still, she donned her sunglasses and offered Markie an arm.

Andi and Julia helped Markie down the wooden steps and across the sand where Clare unfolded a canvas chair for her. Markie kicked off her shoes and dug her toes in the warm sand, lifting her smiling face to the sun. "Oh, this is so good. Thank you."

The other women sat on beach blankets and, once Liv joined them, all waited. Andi scanned their faces. "Okay, so here goes. I broke up with Michael about a month after I returned home from the retreat."

"Oh, honey," Liv said.

Andi waved a dismissive hand. "That's not what I need to tell you first, though. There's something else." She paused. "Thirty-two years ago, I was in a car accident. My two best friends were killed."

"That's awful," Clare said. "You were lucky."

Andi gave a sarcastic laugh. "I was lucky. Do you know what it was like to walk down the street in our neighborhood and have people point and whisper? Can you imagine going shopping and bumping into the mother of one of my friends?"

"Andi, I'm so sorry for criticizing your driving yesterday. I was teasing, of course, but if I had any idea..." Liv said.

"You didn't know. I wasn't driving in the accident. I was in the back seat. I almost always sat in the front, but Kath beat me to it. Jen was driving her new Camaro. She loved that car." Andi told them the rest of the story.

"When I married Paul, I didn't think of it as a new chapter. I closed the book and started a new one. Of course, not realizing you can't do that. Your past stays with you. I did a good job of shoving that past behind me until I found this." She produced a wrinkled and yellowing envelope. "I'd forgotten all about this letter."

"What is it?" Clare asked.

"I don't know. Kath's mother pressed it into my hand at Katrina's christening. She's named for Kath. She said, 'Kath would want you to know this.'"

"And you never opened it?" Clare asked.

"At first, I couldn't. I was afraid of what it might say. Then I put it away and forgot about it. Until last week when I was cleaning and found it again." Andi edged a fingernail under the flap of the envelope. The dried glue easily gave way. "I want to open it here, with all of you."

She lifted the flap and removed a single folded sheet of lined note paper. She stared and the writing—not in Kath's hand. "Oh, my God."

"What?" Clare edged closer to glance at the paper.

"It's from Kath's mother." Andi smoothed the letter and then read: *Dear Andi, I was angry at first every time I saw you and remembered what I had lost. My precious daughter, Katherine. You and Katherine were friends from grade school, inseparable, like sisters. I couldn't look at you much less speak to you at my daughter's funeral. I regretted that later. I had no right to punish you. I wanted to blame someone. I tried to blame Jennifer, but witnesses said the accident was not her fault. So I directed my anger toward you for living when my daughter had died. How awful is that? I want you to know that I don't blame you. Kathy would not want me to be angry with you. She would want me to hold you close and share our grief together. I didn't do that and I'm sorry. I only hope you can forgive me. It means so much that you named your daughter after my Katherine. Thank you for honoring her memory. With love, Anne McMichael*

Tears filled Andi's eyes and streamed down her cheeks. "Oh, my."

"That's a beautiful letter. Did she really blame you for her daughter's death?" Julia asked.

"If she did, I didn't know it. I was too busy with my own guilt. That's why, after I married Paul, I closed the book on that part of my life. But it's stayed with me when I drive, when my daughter started driving. Oh, how I made her crazy with my worry. I barely spoke to Mrs. McMichael after the accident. She was in church the day of Katrina's baptism, but I hadn't specifically invited her. I was surprised to see her. I had kept my distance from her and from Jen's parents." She ran her fingers over the page. "Kath wasn't one to hold a grudge or become angry. She loved life. If she'd only have gotten out of the front seat...." Andi dropped the paper and covered her face with her hands, her shoulders shaking.

Liv slid closer and wrapped an arm around Andi. "Just let it go. You've held onto this for over thirty years. Maybe you weren't ready to read that letter earlier." Liv held out a hand. "Anyone have tissues?"

Markie dug into her pockets and produced a small Kleenex package, tossing it to Liv who stuffed a wad into Andi's palm.

Andi wiped her eyes, blew her nose, and sniffled. "I'm sorry. This just took me back thirty-two years to that day of the accident. It was thirty two years ago today."

"Why didn't you tell us? We'd have scheduled this reunion for a different weekend." Clare said.

"Because I needed it to be this weekend. I needed to know that I've moved forward. I have a lot of friends, but not one single *best* friend, not since Kath and Jen. Not until I met all of you. I began to feel that loss, what it was I'd been deprived by my guilt. And that's not what Kath or Jen would want for me." She smiled. "We were quite a trio back then. We had good times and laughed. We enjoyed life and were there for one another. I thought I'd lost that forever when my best friends were killed." She glanced around at the other women. "But it seems we're given second chances." Andi reached over and clutched Liv's hand.

"And when you realized this, you broke up with Michael?" Clare asked.

"Oh, no. Michael has nothing to do with this. Fifteen years is just too much of an age difference and I'm tired of working so hard to look at least ten years younger than I am. I want to relax, enjoy being Andi. I don't think Michael was cheating on me a year ago, but I'll always feel it's just a matter of time. I loved him in a way, but not in that deep, lasting way that makes a lifelong relationship. Right now, I need to learn to live with Andi, let myself become the woman I'm becoming.

I think I might be growing up."

"You grew up the hard way a long time ago." Liv gave her shoulders another squeeze. "You deserve a break."

"And I'm taking one. I'm going on a ski vacation this winter with my daughter. Just the two of us." She twisted the cap to open a bottle of water and took a long drink. "So, Clare. What's new with you?"

Clare grinned from ear to ear. "As you all know, I started nursing school last fall. Got in just under the wire for registration."

The women applauded.

"You already know the drama with Ben and my uncertainty about my marriage. Well, we spent some time alone and talked a lot. And we had a second honeymoon of sorts."

"Of sorts?" Andi asked.

"Our first honeymoon was a long weekend in Atlantic City. Which was kind of crazy because neither of us gamble. My in-laws kept the kids for a week and Ben and I drove up to Maine before school started to visit my folks. And then we took our time driving home, stopping at a few places along the way. Once we'd talked everything out, spent time alone, it was like when we were first married. Ben is such a romantic."

"How did you get him to come around about nursing school?" Andi asked.

"I told him to think about what two incomes could do for four college funds. He may be unreasonable at times, but he's not stupid." She laughed. "It's not just about going to nursing school, you know. It's about feeling like a true equal in my marriage. If it wasn't school, it would have been something else that would have triggered my discontent. But Ben's been very supportive and encouraging."

"How is your mom?" Liv asked.

Pain shadowed Clare's face as she shook her head. "Not good. She didn't know me most of the time I was there and had no clue who Ben was. It's been taking a toll on my dad. I think we finally convinced him to look for a facility for her where she'll be safe. He can't leave her alone for a minute. And she's become combative with him." Her eyes glittered with tears. "It's like my mom isn't there anymore, but I know she is, behind that veil of confusion. And he knows that, too." She sighed. "Anyway, I think we convinced him she would be better off in a care facility."

"I'm so sorry," Markie said. "You're doing the right thing for her. If…when I reach a point where I need constant care, I'll do the same thing, find a place."

They sat in silence for a moment.

"It's getting warm and I think I need to get out of the sun," Markie said. "Damned steroids."

Julia stood and helped Markie up from the chair. "We should have brought an umbrella for you. Might be good to take a nap."

"Yes, Mother," Markie replied with a grin. "You ladies continue but, Liv, don't tell your story yet. I don't want to miss it."

"It'll keep for later. We still have two days," Liv said.

"Hey, I have an idea," Clare said. "How about we go out to dinner tonight? *The G Spot?*"

"That sounds like fun," Liv said. "Markie? Jules?"

"We're in," Markie called back over her shoulder.

"Andi? I hope you didn't give up karaoke and dancing on table tops," Clare said.

Andi grinned. "I'll warm up my vocal chords and put on my dancin' shoes." She bent to gather up the

Ladies In Waiting

blankets while Clare and Julia helped Markie up the steps. Liv folded up the canvas chair.

"Can I ask you something, Andi?" Liv asked

"Sure."

"Are you sure letting Michael go was the right thing to do?"

Andi stood and stared at her. "Honestly? I don't know. It seemed right at the time. But, since he's already moved on, it's a moot point."

"Oh."

Andi narrowed her eyes. "Why are you asking? Oh, my God, Liv. Are you involved with a younger man?"

"Younger? No. And not involved. I was just wondering how you would know if someone was the right person, despite the differences."

"So who is the mystery man?"

Liv tucked the folded chair under her arm and picked up the extra water bottles. "Oh, no one. Only in my head."

Andi watched Liv slog through the sand to the steps. She turned and faced the ocean, the sun bathing her face in warmth. Closing her eyes, she looked up as she clutched the letter in her hand. "Thank you, Katherine McMichael. Thank you for this gift. I'm sure you had something to do with your mom writing it. I hope you and Jen have been together all this time. I wish you were both here. You'd like these women and I know they'd like you." She swiped at a tear and sniffled. "I love you guys. Even now. And, you know what, I think I love Markie, Liv, Clare and Jules, too. What was it you said once, Jen? 'Boyfriends are fun for a while, but girlfriends are forever.'"

Chapter Thirty-Six

Motorcycles lined the parking lot when Clare pulled the van in at the *G Spot*.

"There's our place, next to the Dumpster," Andi said.

"Great. Last time I parked there, I left the window open a crack and the van smelled like garbage for two days." Clare swung the vehicle into the tight space with ease. "Can everyone get out?"

One by one, the women emerged from the van, each smoothing clothing and hair.

Most of the patrons were lined at the bar or gathered around the pool table in the side room. Clare and Andi reorganized two tables with chairs near the stage to accommodate the five of them.

The waitress approached and smiled at them. "Hey, I remember you ladies from last summer. Now I won't mind working overtime tonight. This is sure to be fun. What can I get'cha?"

They ordered drinks and the *G Spot* version of appetizers—fried pickles, fried zucchini, fried cheese sticks, and chicken wings.

"They'll be able to slide us out of here with all that grease," Julia muttered.

"Look who's become a healthy eating advocate," Markie said. She grinned at Julia. "You're welcome. And you all could have ordered a salad like I did."

The waitress returned with their drinks. "I hate to tell you, but there's no karaoke tonight. We have a band coming in. Shame, though. I would have enjoyed your performance."

"A live band will be fun," Clare said. The others nodded with a little less enthusiasm.

Andi scanned the leather jackets lined up at the bar. "Is it my imagination or has the crowd here aged in a year?"

Clare and the others all turned their heads. Men sporting silver ponytails and beards stood beside women whose lined faces put them in the senior age group.

"Wonder what's going on." Liv squinted. "Can you read what's on their jackets?"

"Second Time Around Motorcycle Club," Andi said.

Just then, one of men smiled and waved. He looked to be about sixty. Andi smiled and waved back. The man pushed off from the bar, beer in hand, and sauntered toward their table.

"Oh, no," Andi groaned.

He flashed a blinding smile and nodded. "Ladies. I've not seen you here before." His eyes fixed on Andi. "And I would have remembered."

"Oh, please," Andi said. "That's a terrible line."

He chuckled. "Have mercy. I'm not as young as I used to be. I'm Gabe."

Andi introduced herself and each of the others. "Aren't you all a little old to be wearing leather?"

Gabe patted the vest that covered what appeared to be a muscular chest. "Age is all in the mind. You know what they say, if you don't mind, it doesn't matter." He sipped the beer. "Well, I don't want to intrude on your evening. Just thought I'd introduce myself. Maybe one of you ladies would dance with me later when the band starts." He turned to leave.

"Wait. I'm sorry," Andi said. "I've been rude. Tell us about your club."

Gabe pulled up a chair, sat backwards on it, and told them about the seniors only motorcycle club he and his former wife had started. "She always said our later years were really just a second time around." His eyes clouded when he said, "Tessa died a little over a year ago. Ovarian cancer. We do a ride every year in her honor. We finish up here. It was one of her favorite places. We came here almost every Saturday night."

"I'm sorry for your loss," Markie said.

"Thank you." Gabe stood and shoved the chair back to its rightful table. A band began to set up on the stage. He fixed his gaze on Andi. "I'll be back to see about that dance."

"He's kind of cute in a sixty-ish way," Clare said once he'd left. "Reminds me a little of my father."

"I think it's great that they have a bike club," Markie said. "If I thought I could hold on, I'd ask to go for a ride. I used to love riding motorcycles, feeling the wind against my face, blowing my hair."

When Markie said she needed to use the restroom, Julia was on her feet and helping her friend. Andi stood, too. "I'll be right back."

Clare and Liv watched as Andi walked to the bar and spoke with Gabe. He nodded a few times, called over another couple. The four of them talked and then Andi smiled and returned to the table.

"What was that all about?" Liv asked.

"A surprise for Markie. That other couple has a motorcycle with a side-car. They're coming to the house with Gabe tomorrow and taking Markie for a ride."

"Are you sure that's a good idea?" Clare asked. "What if she has trouble getting into and out of the side car?"

"Steve's wife…" Andi pointed to the woman at the bar. "…has a bum knee. She gets in and out of the side-car fine. Hell, if we have to we'll rub her down with vegetable oil and she'll slide into the car. But she's going for that ride."

"Here's come Markie and Julia," Clare said. "Don't say anything."

The two women arrived at the table at the same time their food was delivered. Clare observed how frail Markie seemed and the way she picked through her salad before declaring she was full and didn't want anything else to eat. Clare wondered how long it would be before Markie was bound to a bed.

Markie met her gaze. "What?"

"Nothing." Clare shook off the sadness that must have shown in her eyes. "Hey, did I tell you all I plan to specialize in pediatric nursing? I figured I might as well go with what I know, and I know babies."

"That's great." Andi lifted her glass. "To pursuing dreams."

The band started up and several couples took the dance floor. The women finished their dinner since conversation became impossible with music.

"It's hard to believe I used to enjoy music at this decibel level," Andi shouted.

"It's going to be like this the rest of the night. Maybe we should go," Julia shouted back.

But Gabe wound his way through the dancers and stood before Andi. "Well, have you thought about it?"

"It?" Andi asked.

"A dance." He extended his hand.

To Clare's surprise, Andi smiled and accepted. "Why not? I haven't been dancing in a long time."

Just as they reached the dance floor, the band switched into a slow, bluesy number. The other women laughed at the look on Andi's face as Gabe pulled her close and grinned down at her.

"That man can dance," Liv said.

"I'll bet that isn't all he can do," Julia said.

"Jules!" Clare said, grinning.

"What? Even I can see from here that age hasn't impaired his flexibility." She lifted her drink. "To flexibility."

"Here, here," Liv said, laughing.

Andi returned to the table when the song ended. "What are you all laughing about?"

"That was some dance," Julia said.

"It sure was. The man knows how to move." Andi fanned her face and picked up her glass of water. "There may be something to be said for a more mature man after all."

In between repeat dances with Andi, Gabe invited each of the other women to dance. Only Clare accepted when the band broke into a western line dance. It was a little past one when Julia suggested it might be time to head for home.

~ * ~

"I was thinking of going down to the beach for a while if someone will give me a hand," Markie said as they cleared away breakfast dishes.

"You can't," Andi replied. "I mean, wait a bit and we'll all go." She needed to stall until Gabe and Steve got there with their bikes.

Markie regarded her for a moment. "I was going to spend some time alone in meditation. But if you're too busy…."

The roar of a bike engine and the crunch of gravel drew Andi's attention. "Who could that be at this early hour? I'll be right back." She hurried through the living room to the front door.

Gabe dismounted his Harley and removed his helmet. "Morning."

"Good morning."

Steve removed his helmet and reached into the side-car, lifting a leather jacket and a second helmet. "These are for your friend. Is she ready to roll?"

"Uh...not exactly. I didn't tell her yet that you were coming. I wanted to surprise her. I'll be right back." Andi reached the door and then turned. "Do you guys want coffee or anything?"

"No, thanks. We had breakfast at the diner before we rode out here," Gabe said.

"Okay. Be right back." She hustled to the kitchen again. "Where's Markie?"

Julia nodded toward the back bedroom. "Good luck."

Markie had just made her way to sit on the edge of the bed when Andi burst into the room. "Come on. You're going for a ride."

"I'm what?"

"Last night you said how much you'd like to take a bike ride. On a motorcycle. So, your chariot awaits."

"I can't ride a motorcycle. I don't have the balance or the strength to stay on."

"You don't have to. Steve...that's one of Gabe's riding partners...has a side-car on his bike for his wife. He offered to take you."

Markie frowned. "He offered?"

"Okay, so I asked him. Don't worry. I didn't tell him about the MS. I just said you had some trouble with your legs but you'd love to go for a ride. And then he offered. So come on. They're waiting."

Markie grumbled, but Andi could see the anticipation in her eyes as she stood and set her cane in place.

Outside, Andi and Julia helped Markie down the steps. Steve held his wife's leather jacket for her to slip into and then handed her the helmet.

Gabe removed a spare helmet from his bike and another jacket, offering them to Andi. "Here you go."

"Oh, no. I'm not getting on that thing."

"You don't look like the kind of woman who's afraid of a little ol' bike."

Markie grinned at her. "This *was* your idea."

From the porch, the other three women clapped their hands and chanted, "An-di. An-di. An-di."

"I'm not getting on that bike," Andi insisted.

"Then I'm not riding, either," Markie said, unzipping her jacket.

"Oh, alright." Andi snapped the jacket out of Gabe's hand and shrugged into it.

He set the helmet on her head and tapped it once. "Don't forget to hold on tight." Gabe swung his long leg over the bike and motioned with a nod for her to climb on behind him. Steve had managed to ease Markie into the side-car of his bike and handed the cane off to Clare. Seconds later, engines roared and Gabe led the way down the drive.

At first, Andi clung to Gabe, her face lowered and pressed against his back, praying for her life. When they slowed for a stop sign, she heard Markie's shout of delight. As the bike pulled out again and picked up speed, Andi looked up and watched the ocean off to their right. She felt the warm wind lashing through her hair, the sun kissing her face through the visor. And she smiled.

By the time they returned to the house, clouds had begun to roll in over the water. "Just in time," Gabe said. "Looks like it might storm this afternoon."

Andi dragged her fingers through her hair, not caring how wild it looked. "That was fun!"

"See, and you weren't going to go," he teased.

Gabe and Steve both helped Markie from the side-car and Clare ran down the steps to greet them, carrying Markie's cane.

Markie's smile stretched ear to ear. "I can't thank you enough," she said to Steve. "Thank your wife for the loan of her jacket, helmet and husband."

Steve laughed. "She'll be glad you had a good time. I am, too."

Gabe folded the spare jacket and stuffed it into his saddlebag and then reattached the extra helmet to his bike. "Andi, it was a pleasure. Do you think you'd like to go again, sometime? Or dancing?"

The invitation took her off guard. "I...uh...."

"That's okay. I don't want to pressure you. I had fun."

"Wait. It's just that I don't live here. I live up in Toms River."

He smiled. "I live in Long Branch." He dug into his saddlebag again, retrieving a small notepad and pen. "Here's my number. If you ever feel like joining me for a ride along the shore, give me a call."

She accepted the paper. "Or dancing?"

His blue eyes twinkled as he smiled. "Dancing." He climbed on the bike, donned his helmet, and gave a thumbs up as he followed Steve down the driveway.

Andi ran a hand through her tousled hair and turned back toward the house.

Clare grinned at her. "I thought you swore off men."

"That's the beauty of being a woman. We're expected to change our minds."

She had enjoyed Gabe's flirtation the night before and dancing with him. The bike ride, though it began as a terrifying prospect, turned out to be exhilarating. But it was Gabe. Something about being with a man nearer her age. A twinge of sadness hit as she considered Gabe was probably close to Paul's age, had Paul lived. Maybe she was ready for a new relationship with a man her own age. Maybe she would give Gabe a call once she got back home. She grinned as she practically skipped up the steps and past the other women.

Inside, Markie abandoned her cane and threw her arms around Andi. "Thank you so much for arranging that ride."

Andi returned the hug. "You're welcome. Though I was not planning to accompany you."

"Admit it, you had fun."

"I did. I'm glad you did, too."

Markie released her and dropped onto the sofa. "One more thing I can mark off my bucket list—a last motorcycle ride."

Julia flinched. "Will you stop talking like that?"

Markie shrugged. "It's true. There are fewer things I'll be able to do or to re-do. Don't worry, I still have a long list to complete. Sky diving is next."

"Don't count me in on that one," Andi said.

"Me, neither," Julia added.

Lightning flashed beyond the windows and thunder rumbled. "Looks like the storm is about here. I guess we're inside for the day now. I saw some board games on the bookshelves. Anyone want to play?" Liv crossed the room and pulled the boxes of games from the shelf.

They played for the next three hours, stopping only briefly for a light lunch courtesy of Clare.

Stretching, Liv said, "This weather makes me sleepy. I'm going upstairs and take a nap."

"We haven't heard your reunion story yet," Andi said.

"Oh, you will. I have a lot of good news to share." With that, Liv climbed the stairs.

Chapter Thirty-Seven

Darkness blanketed her room, save for the occasional flash of lightning beyond her window. Liv sat up and reached for the bedside lamp. Nothing. She rubbed her arms against the damp chill. The storm still raged outside, heavy clouds blackening the sky.

With one bright flash, she located her shoes and slipped them on. Fumbling her way to the door, she opened it and stepped out into the darkened hallway. No lights anywhere. Suddenly a narrow beam appeared on the wall in the stairway.

"Hello?" Liv said.

"Hey. We lost power. I found a couple of flashlights and some candles." Clare appeared at the top of the stairs. "I came up to see if you were awake and give you some light to come downstairs."

"Thanks. It's really pitch dark up here. Come up and let me find a sweatshirt." She then followed Clare and the beam of light down the stairs. "Are the others still napping?"

"Andi is. Julia and Markie are in the living room. We got a fire going in the fireplace." Clare stopped on the stairs and placed the flashlight under chin. "Good night for telling ghost stories. Bwaahaahaa."

"Not unless someone else plans to share my room tonight," Liv replied.

In the living room, a soft orange glow emanated from the fireplace. Julia walked around the room, lighting candles. Markie was settled in one of the recliners, covered with an afghan.

"Can you believe how chilly it got in here with this storm?" Markie asked.

"I know." Liv pulled her sweatshirt over her head. "Feels more like October than May."

Thunder boomed and shook the house.

"Hello-o?" Andi called from the top of the stairs.

"Hey, Andi. Stay put. I'm coming for you." Clare picked up the flashlight and headed to the stairs. Moments later she returned with Andi in tow.

"Can you believe this storm?" Andi asked. "That last clap of thunder practically bounced me out of bed." She moved to the fireplace and rubbed her hands together. "What time is it, anyone know?"

Julia held her wrist near a glowing candle. "Half past five."

"Anyone else hungry? I'm going to rummage in the kitchen and find us something to munch on." Clare's flashlight swept across the wall.

"I'll give you a hand," Andi said, following behind.

Julia added wood to the fire.

Andi and Clare returned with plates of cheese, crackers, and fresh vegetables and with a bottle of wine in hand. Clare glanced out the window. "I wonder if Nick's at the cottage again this year."

"He's not. If this is the sixteenth, he's in Chicago." Liv continued to fill her plate.

"How do you know this?" Andi asked.

Liv shrugged. "Because I made the flight arrangements. Oh, I haven't told you all. I'm Nick's assistant."

"Really? What all do you *assist* him with?" Andi padded the sofa beside her. "Do tell us more."

Liv sat and placed her plate on the coffee table in front of her. "I assist him with his schedule, his

Ladies In Waiting

correspondence, and even with his manuscripts. I get to read them before everyone else." She took a sip of wine. "Last year, after the hurricane hit the coast, I lost my job and my apartment. If I hadn't headed out of town when they announced evacuations, I'd have lost the car, too. I just drove west and holed up in a motel. Nick called me to see if I was okay. When I told him what had happened, he offered me a job. His former assistant's husband had recently transferred to Maryland."

"Oh, my God. You lost everything?" Clare asked.

Liv smiled. "Oh, honey, I'd lost everything once before. I was just grateful to get out with my life. The biggest loss for me was the job. I wasn't sure what I would do."

"It must be fascinating working for an author," Clare said.

"I really enjoy the work. Honestly, I didn't think I could do anything more than filing and answering the phone. It had been so long since I went to college and then I only had a bachelor's degree in English. Once I married Adam, my life pretty much revolved around him and the kids. Making life easier for him and entertaining."

"I was glad to see the court found in your favor," Julia said. "I told you Ellis was one of the best. As a lawyer, that is."

"He was wonderful. So were the two attorneys he recommended for Nathan and Aaron. Things have gotten much better between me and my sons. I arrived home last year to an email from Adam. Nothing would have surprised me more. But he wrote to apologize, to say he would set things straight with our sons, and that he hoped I would have the life I deserved."

"That was big of him," Andi muttered.

"At least it helped with the suit and I got my sons

back. That's all that mattered to me." Liv dabbed at her eyes. "Anyway, I've been working for Nick since November. And..." Liv sat forward, smiling broadly, "I'm going to be a grandmother."

"That's wonderful," Markie said.

The others all congratulated her.

"My daughter is expecting in December. I'll be taking time off and flying to London for Thanksgiving. I'll stay until after the baby's born, through Christmas. I can't wait."

Julia studied Liv for a moment. "It's nice to see you happy and so confident."

Liv sat back on the sofa. "I'd lost my sons, most of my friends, my future, my trust. But the greatest loss was losing Liv McKenna. Being here with all of you last year made me realize that fact. I had to get back to myself before I could repair any of the other damage that had been done to my life because of Adam." She looked around at each of the women. "You gave me that gift and I am so very grateful."

Andi frowned. "So are you telling us there is nothing more going on with you and Nick?"

Liv shook her head. "Nothing more. We're friends and I work for him. And it's good."

"What about your flower shop?" Clare asked.

Liv shrugged. "Who knows? It could still happen one day. But, for now, I'm happy."

Clare bit her lower lip. "I can't tell you what it's meant for me to get to know each of you. I don't know what I would have done if you all had sent me home for being too young."

Andi drained her wineglass. "We couldn't send you home. You had the van and were our designated driver."

Laughter rippled around the room.

"We need to do this every year," Clare said.

"I agree." Andi refilled her glass and offered the bottle to Liv.

"Hey, you all can come to our house next time," Julia said. "We have lots of room and it's not that much farther from here." She glanced at Clare. "It'll be more like a vacation for you. We don't have the ocean, but we have the country."

"Do you hear that?" Markie asked. "The storm's ended."

Liv walked to the window. "Wow, it sure has. The clouds have broken up and the sky is gorgeous. There's a nearly-full moon rising."

Andi jumped to her feet. "Come on, ladies. Porch time. Everyone grab a blanket or jacket."

Outside, a cool breeze carried the fresh aroma of earth after a hard rain. Andi and Clare wiped down the chairs and each of the women took a seat.

Liv drew in a deep breath. "I arrived here last year waiting for the other shoe to drop, waiting for one of you to realize who I was and what my husband had done. Julia, when you told me about your brother, I almost stopped breathing. I could only pray he wasn't one of Adam's clients. I went home waiting for the court case to be resolved. Waiting to feel normal again. Waiting for Liv McKenna to come back to life."

"We were all waiting for something weren't we?" Markie asked. "Of course, I was waiting for the opportunity to end my own life." She glanced at Julia. "Would you stop looking at me like that. I tried. I failed. Life goes on."

"I was waiting for Ben to force me to make a choice between my family and my dream of becoming a nurse," Clare said.

Julia stared into the fire. "I'm not sure what I was

waiting for—the madness to end over that botched case so I could go back to business as usual? I think I was waiting for some insight. I hadn't been truly happy for a long time. I told myself that was the nature of my work. It wasn't about being happy. It was about being good at what I did. And that last case shook me, shook my foundation." She turned her face toward the others and smiled. "I think I was really waiting for a friend, someone to lean on. And I got all of you—the superfecta of girlfriends."

"We were ladies in waiting," Markie said.

"We need to celebrate...us." Andi stood and picked up the flashlight. "I'm breaking out another bottle of wine." She paused at the door and glanced back. "Unless you have something else to share with us, Markie?"

Markie shook her head. "Gave it up. I live with an *officer of the court.* And I already walk sideways most of the time. I don't need anything else to throw me off balance."

When Andi returned and as the women lifted their filled glasses, the lights of the house flickered on behind them. Liv thought the lighted windows looked like smiling eyes. Night birds sang and, on the beach below, waves broke onto the sand.

Clare pulled a sheet of folded paper from the hip pocket of her jeans. "Hey, you know that agenda we all decided to ignore last year? I saved the last page. This was supposed to be our sharing the last morning before we all left here. I thought it would be appropriate to do this now."

She unfolded the paper and smoothed it on her lap, aiming the flashlight. "We were supposed to share what it was that we most wanted in our next stage of life—what we were each waiting for." She paused, then

said, "I would have said fulfillment."
    She looked to Markie. After a thoughtful moment, Markie said, "Hope."
    Julia gazed around the circle of faces. "I think I would have said friendship."
    "I wanted true love again," Andi said.
    Liv gazed up at the inky sky littered with stars. Moisture pooled in the corners of her eyes. "Peace, that's what I most wanted. *Síocháin.* Here's to peace." Liv raised her glass.
    "*Síocháin.*" The other women shouted.

The End

Linda Rettstatt

Author's Note

Ladies In Waiting is my twentieth book. That alone makes it special to me, a milestone marker of sorts. Every author will tell you that each book is special and the characters take up their own space in our hearts and minds. This book found a very special place in my heart as I wrote the stories of Julia, Markie, Andi, Liv and Cee Cee. Early in the writing, I found myself immersed in the lives of these women, feeling a bit like a sixth in their party as they waded through their own life questions and secrets that placed them at a turning point. I found myself drawn back to the year I turned fifty. (Yes, I'm over fifty and I'm not saying how far! It doesn't matter.)

When I was facing my fiftieth birthday, I felt the shifting in myself as concretely as one feels the earth moving in an earthquake, though possibly in a more subtle way. Everything changed—the way I viewed life, the way I made decisions, what I considered to be important and what I then realized was insignificant in the larger scheme. It was a wonderfully freeing experience, though frightening at times when I wasn't sure I recognized myself anymore. We women go through so many transformations in our lifetime. I like to think of it as a refining process to becoming our best self.

I like the woman I've become. I know I'm not finished yet and I still have flaws—er—rough edges (plenty of them). *Ladies In Waiting* is a celebration of that process of transformation—of reaching an age and a point in life where we stop, look back, re-evaluate, then shake off what no longer fits for us and face forward. And what we can't shake off, we find a way to carry without being burdened down or held back. When I worked as a psychotherapist several years ago, my favorite clients were women in or approaching middle age who were shaken or confused by the changes they saw happening inside themselves. I loved accompanying them on this journey, just as I loved accompanying Julia, Markie, Andi, Liv and Cee Cee.

I hope you've enjoyed their journey, too. Now go and enjoy yours!

~ *Linda Rettstatt*

* If you have a book club or reading group and would like to have the author participate in a discussion of *Ladies In Waiting*, you can contact me at **lindarettstatt@yahoo.com**

I am also available for short workshops and retreats on Navigating the Waters of Mid-life and a new retreat/workshop on Creativity & Spirituality.

ACKNOWLEDGEMENTS

I want to acknowledge those spectacular women's fiction authors who have inspired me over the years and who have influenced my writing. Special thanks to Kris Radish, Claire Cook and Elizabeth Berg whose masterful storytelling makes me want to be a better writer. Thanks, also, to editor Amie Denman. It was such a pleasure working with you on this book.

About the Author

Linda Rettstatt is an award-winning and best selling author of Women's Fiction and Contemporary Romance. She likes to know what makes people tick and she loves a good story. This combination fuels her passion for creating stories that capture your mind and touch your heart. Linda grew up in Southwest Pennsylvania and suffers a bout of homesickness every October when she thinks of the fall leaves and trails at her beloved Ohiopyle State Park. She now lives in Northwest Mississippi with her cat, Binky, who only allows her to share the apartment because she cleans the litter box.

~ * ~

If you enjoyed **LADIES IN WAITING,** visit Linda's website
http://www.lindarettstatt.com
where you can find links to more of her books
or visit
Linda's author page on Amazon.com

this belongs to

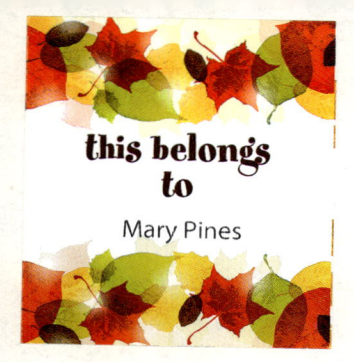

Mary Pines

Made in the USA
Charleston, SC
20 October 2016